Killer Collusion

Killer Collusion

S.M. Kahan

CAPTIVATE PRESS

This is a work of fiction. All of the characters, organizations, and events portrayed in this novel are either of the author's imagination or are used fictitiously.

No part of this publication may be reproduced, stored in a retrieval system, or transmitted in any form or by any means, electronic, mechanical, photocopying, recording, or otherwise, without written permission of the publisher. For information regarding permission, email Captivate Press at
Captivatepress@gmail.com

ISBN 979-8-8692-2408-8

Copyright © 2024 S.M.Kahan. All Rights Reserved. Publishing by Captivate Press, by arrangement with Ingram Content Group One Ingram Blvd., La Vergne, Tennessee 37086, US. Distributions by arrangement with Ingram Content Group One Ingram Blvd., La Vergne, Tennessee 37086, US.

The publisher does not have any control over and does not assume any responsibility for author or third-party websites or their content.

Printed in the U.S.A

First Captivate Press Printing, April 2024

KILLER Collusion

S.M. Kahan

Will you dare turn the page?

Read the entire Hunter Harden Series

By SM Kahan

Killer Dreams

Killer Greed

Killer Collusion

Killer Novel

Prologue
Compromised Convictions

"We are not going to compromise on that point. If we do, we're on a slippery slope to disaster," Charlotte Grace insisted. Pressing her cell phone to her ear, her purse looped over her arm and swinging from her elbow, she climbed out of the car. She rushed to the trunk and pulled out three shopping bags. Then she tried to get all of their handles over her other arm without dropping her phone, all the while making sure not to miss a word of her assistant's reply.

A gust of wind blew a lock of her fine chestnut hair into her face, stinging her eyes, and with no free hands, she shook her head to dislodge it. On this chilly day in late October, it looked like one of LA's first winter rainstorms was on the way.

"No. If we agree to that, then we've lost, and they've won. Don't you see that? They'll be able to use our words against us. Trust me, it's happened before."

Managing to slam the Toyota's trunk closed with her elbow, she leaned the bags on it briefly, because getting her point across in this discussion was more important than getting her groceries into the house. She was sure the storm would hold off a few more minutes.

She glanced at the quiet road and then across the messy front yard to the darkened windows of her small, lonely home. She didn't see anyone around. After the creepy experience yesterday, that was just as well. Things are tough right now. With what she was working on at the moment, a sense of threat simmered constantly inside her. The situation had all the potential to explode. It was huge, and she knew it could be dangerous. She should make some changes, and put better security in place, but with her work so busy, there had not been time.

With her quick security checkup complete, she refocused on the conversation.

"We can't take a soft stance on any one of those arguments. They're all equally important. There are lives at stake here! Innocent lives." The familiar fires of her conviction blazed inside her as she pressed the point home.

She frowned, as the assistant replied.

"What? You're saying they're going to think of us as extremists?" Now anger surged. Her own suffering, her own past experience, was still as raw and painful in her mind as if it had happened yesterday. "No. I totally disagree with you there. People look to us as a bastion of protection. It's up to others to be more 'reasonable'. I'm not in it to be reasonable. I'm not in it to compromise. They're not compromising! So why must we?"

She paused, listening.

"Yes, that's correct. We keep our press release exactly as it is, going all the way down to the toys themselves. That's where evil starts. And if it causes controversy and it gets people thinking and arguing, so much the better. That's our stance, it always has been, and it will be. And we'll get a new wave of support from it. It always ends up that way."

She took a deep breath. Frowning, she listened to the voice on the other end.

"No. That's where you're wrong. It's not just a toy. It's *not*. And this is not just a discussion we're entering into. It's war."

She hung up as the first raindrops spattered down and heaved the bags off the lid of her trunk. Mike, her ex, had always been amused by her determination to make only one trip from the car to the house, even if it was only a minute's walk. Now, with the onset of the chilly rain, her actions at least made sense.

Those were the days she remembered sadly. Family. Laughter. Togetherness. A feeling that nothing could ever go wrong or destroy the precious, love-filled life she'd had.

In one explosive instant, it had all changed. Tragedy, grief, and then the start of the conflict, the never-ending struggle she'd embarked on.

"This is war," she said aloud to herself, ducking her head to avoid the cold, blowing raindrops as she hurried along the pathway. It was darker than usual, and she realized the outside light wasn't working. That'd be another chore to do, adding to a lengthening list that she never seemed to have the time to tackle. In her situation, feeling constantly driven to her limits, it was difficult not to feel bitter and overwhelmed. But she couldn't step back.

In the dark, she almost missed one of the paving stones that led across the grass. Her shoe skidded on its edge, her ankle twisted, and the weight of the shopping bags tipped her off balance, so she almost fell. She righted herself with an effort, her ankle burning, glancing down to make sure nothing had tipped out of the bags.

And when she glanced up, he was there, darting from behind the cover of the overgrown jasmine bush.

Tall and strong looking, a black ski mask pulled over his head, the man was possessed of frantic energy as he rushed toward her, gripping a dark object in his hand.

He'd been hiding in her garden. Hiding! Waiting. That fact shocked her, as her astonished gaze took him in. A moment later, her brain caught up, and she realized the danger she was in. The worst had happened already. Deep down, she'd been in denial and had never thought that the threat would become real, and now it was too late.

Only one weapon to use, her bags. In a fierce, though ineffectual gesture, she flung them in his direction, screaming, "Get away! Get the hell away!" The bags scattered in front of her, doing no damage, not even reaching him.

She was the one who needed to get away! Her shocked mind finally latched onto what she must do to save herself.

She swung around, ready to run for the road, but it was too late. He was there, grabbing her. She could hear his breathing, fast and harsh. A gloved hand dug into her shoulder. He swung her around to face him and she staggered, slipping on a wet paving stone, her ankle flaring again. She cried out in fear as she saw what he was holding.

It was a gun, with a weird-looking barrel, a strangely long barrel. Maybe it wasn't real, her panicked mind begged her as he dragged her close. Maybe this was all a hoax, and she could still somehow fight her way out of his powerful, steely grasp?

She began to scream, but the gun was jammed against her head now, and in that frantic moment, as she struggled and clawed against him, she knew what that extension to the barrel was.

It was a silencer.

As she had the thought, something slammed into her head and the world went dark.

1

Undercurrents of Corruption

"Are you disputing that this issue is critical to the LAPD's survival?"

Exasperated, LAPD detective Hunter Harden tried his best to keep a controlled and rational tone of voice as he faced the assistant chief of police across the desk.

Perhaps he should have said "Sir" at the end of the question, he wondered briefly. He was trying hard to overcome the reputation he had earned as a renegade investigator and a rule breaker. But then again he reasoned since they'd been debating this issue for the past ten minutes, the word seemed superfluous. He couldn't keep saying it, and it wasn't helping.

"Harden, I'm not disputing it at all."

Sounding effortlessly calm, the chief leaned back in his leather director's chair, staring Hunter down.

In terms of physical appearance and demeanor, they were opposites. The assistant police chief, Gibson, was stocky and fleshy faced, with deep brown eyes and closely cropped graying hair, while Hunter was tall and rangy, with ice blue eyes and unruly dark red hair that he wore a little too long.

And while the police chief couldn't have seemed more relaxed, Hunter was the one on the edge of his seat as he pleaded his cause.

"There's corruption within the LAPD ranks. I know this for certain. It's the reason that there isn't a station commander in my precinct right now."

"I'm aware that you were caught up in that situation, and that handling it put you in personal danger."

Hunter tried to stop his mind from veering back to the final confrontation he'd had with Samuels. He never wanted to think about those moments again. The fact he'd been in personal danger wasn't the point. The point was that Samuels' violent actions and the threats he'd uttered before his death, as well as the anonymous message that Hunter had later received, proved that the corruption went higher. Samuels had to answer the people above him, but Hunter didn't know who they were or how widespread this was.

What he knew was that it needed to be rooted out.

The warning message he'd received a couple of weeks ago, sent from a burner phone, had threatened him that if he dug deeper into this corruption, he would suffer the consequences.

Hunter didn't care.

Whoever had sent that message should have known that trying to warn him off wouldn't work, and would have the opposite effect. It had made him more determined than ever. If they were threatening him, they were threatening others. No police officer could do their job under such circumstances, and he was willing to be the one to stick his neck out.

It was disturbing, though, that he was coming up against this level of obstruction.

Perhaps it was just that Gibson didn't fully understand the urgency, Hunter thought, trying again.

"It's not just that I was in personal danger. It came close to jeopardizing a case. A massive, high-profile case could have failed completely and gone cold. The evidence could have ended up being destroyed. We can't risk this happening again, and for all we know, it is happening right now. People within this organization, within our police departments, could be getting threatened, or silenced, or worse still, turned."

A brief thought flashed through his mind: could he really trust the assistant chief of police?

Was Gibson also part of this chain?

Hunter hadn't thought so at first, especially because everyone knew Gibson as a workaholic, but now he was rethinking, because these delaying tactics were decidedly strange.

"Hunter." Using his first name now, Gibson leaned forward. "Listen to me, please. I'm not saying it's not going to happen. I take this as seriously as you do."

"Then let me go ahead with the internal investigation. Please?"

But again, to his exasperation, Gibson shook his head.

"Harden, if and when this goes ahead, you won't be involved. You've been too personally affected by it. We'll put a task force in place to address it. That'll most likely happen after the shake-up."

"The shake-up?"

"High level," Gibson told him. "Very high. I'm talking Department of Defense level. The Secretary of Defense is collaborating with the board of police commissioners. At the state and county levels, there are going to be massive changes coming. I believe it'll involve a major realignment and reorganization of all police departments, all Army sectors."

Hunter raised his eyebrows. High-level politics at work in both sectors? He wondered what the outcome would be.

"Is that going to be beneficial for us?" he asked, wondering if Gibson would be able, and willing, to answer the question. To his surprise, he was.

"Yes. I think so. The guy's a mover and shaker who seems passionate about law enforcement at all levels – he only took the position three years ago, and already, he's tipped to be the next President."

"The next President?" Hunter asked, surprised. That was an unusual route for a rise to the top.

"I've heard rumors of massively increased budgets, major recruitment drives, expansion, and support. It sounds positive, and hopefully, he'll be tough on corruption. But right now, you need to be patient. Let the shake-up happen. And then, when we're all reorganized, we'll hopefully have a stronger team to go in and address it."

"I'll do that. Sir," he replied. "I'll be patient. But this thing needs cutting out, fast. Otherwise, it'll only spread."

That was how he thought of it, as a cancer. A rot within the LAPD. It was already affecting the way he perceived his fellow officers. It felt to him as if a layer of doubt and distrust that had never existed in the past was now present in every interaction. He only trusted a handful and beyond that, he'd learned from bitter experience, he couldn't trust at all. If he'd been in charge, he'd have insisted that the corruption was addressed before the shake-up, and not after.

"Understood." Gibson turned to his phone, indicating the meeting was over.

Hunter stood up, checking the time as he walked out and frowning as he saw the meeting had run later than he'd thought.

Those extra minutes, spent in fruitless argument with a superior, now meant a shorter time for him to get to his son. He'd better hope traffic was cooperating. At six p.m. on a weekday in Los Angeles, Hunter knew he'd have to be very lucky.

He raced out of the building, headed for the parking lot, and jumped in his car.

It was already getting dark, and a rainstorm was looming. He couldn't let Matthew wait outside in the rain.

Hunter wove through the backstreets, taking the routes he knew from experience were likely to be quieter. He pulled up outside the school building with seconds to spare. The drive had allowed him to put some mental and physical distance between himself and his work concerns. Now, he felt as if he could focus fully on Matthew and enjoy every moment of the journey that would take him from the school to his ex-wife Amy's house.

"Hey, Dad!"

The slim, redheaded boy who'd been standing alone, separate from the main group of boys, turned when he saw Hunter and ran over to the car.

"Hey, superhero!" He exchanged a fist bump with the boy before he scrambled into the back seat. At seven years old, Matthew had abruptly grown out of his hugging phase, and now it was all fist bumps and high fives. Hunter hoped the hugging phase would return. He made sure Matthew was belted into his booster seat and then pulled off.

Immediately, he sensed that there was something wrong.

Matthew was far quieter than usual. Put it this way, instead of having talked Hunter's ears off by the time they reached the street corner, he hadn't said a thing.

"What's up?" he asked, frowning. He knew he worried far too much about his son. Having inherited his own rebellious nature, as well as Hunter's love for literature and poetry that brought with it an innate sensitivity and empathy, Hunter had always worried that Matthew might be a target for bullies.

If he'd also inherited the tough-mindedness that both he and Amy possessed, then Hunter was sure the bullying wouldn't last long, but even so, it was a threat he was keenly aware of.

"Nothing," Matthew said.

That meant something, but his son wasn't saying more. Time to probe.

"How was school?" he asked, taking a gap in the traffic to turn onto the main road.

"Okay."

Another one-word answer? Hell, he'd thought this would happen when the boy was fourteen, not half that age. Something was very wrong.

"What were you staying late for?" He knew already but was asking anyway.

"School pantomime rehearsal," Matthew said.

From his tone of voice, Hunter surmised the play rehearsal hadn't been the problem.

"What do you hope Mom's making for dinner?" Amy had asked Hunter to stay for a quick meal. Maybe she'd know what was up with their son.

Matthew all but rolled his eyes as Hunter glanced at him in the rearview mirror.

"Mom doesn't cook," he said, stating the obvious.

"Yeah, okay. Poor choice of words," Hunter said. "What do you think Mom will be heating up for us to be eating up?"

That, at least, prompted a giggle from Matthew.

"Um, well, I don't think we'll get cake. Because Mom doesn't like to bake," he said, replying in turn and causing Hunter to grin widely. Silly conversations in rhyme with his son was a game they'd started a while ago, and as Matthew got older, he was enjoying them more. They were instant mood lifters for both of them, although he couldn't help noticing from the tone of his voice that Matthew seemed to have some resentment right now toward his mother. Maybe that was the issue. Perhaps Amy had been laying down the law and he was sore about it.

With the ice now broken, Matthew began to return to his chatty self.

"I was thinking, Dad, that you should get a pet," he said.

"Really? What kind of a pet?"

"I don't know. I think you need company, though, for when I'm not there, because you're spending so much time on your own now," Matthew said.

Ouch, Hunter thought, removing the metaphorical blade from in between his ribs as rain sluiced down onto the windshield.

"Well, I'm at work for a lot of the time. And when I'm home, you're with me a few days a week," he said.

"That means we could both enjoy the pet."

Hunter sighed. He was sure Matthew would set his heart on a puppy, and Hunter's working hours wouldn't allow for its care.

"We can definitely think about it," he said. "You make a shortlist of pets. I want to see a few different ideas, hey? Not just one species."

"And there's something else I need you to talk to Mom about," Matthew said quietly, as they turned into the road where Amy lived.

Aha, Hunter thought. Finally, he was getting to the reason why the earlier part of the trip had been strained.

"What's that?"

"I'll tell you later," Matthew muttered, seeing that they were already pulling into Amy's driveway.

"You want to give me a hint? So I can sow the seeds? Do some groundwork?" he asked conspiratorially, but Matthew shook his head, and again, Hunter felt that flicker of unease, because whatever this was, it sure meant a lot to his son. It wasn't like him to hold back words.

Amy was home earlier than expected, Hunter saw. He'd picked Matthew up because she'd been attending a client meeting out of town and hadn't known when it would wrap up. But now, hearing Hunter's car, she was opening the front door in welcome.

He heard Matthew give a soft, but audible sigh.

Yup, without a doubt, mother-son relations are strained right now. Hoping he could smooth things over, Hunter climbed out, buffeted by a gust of rain.

"Come in, quickly," Amy called.

Matthew slung his school bag over his shoulder and raced ahead of Hunter, who noted he didn't stop to give her a high five or a fist bump, or even one of his increasingly scarce hugs.

Hunter, however, hugged Amy warmly as soon as he was in the shelter of the hallway.

"Good day?" he asked.

"Long day, but fun," she said.

"This meeting was for the studio hire business, correct?" Amy had a pressured, unglamorous, but well-paying job on the admin side of a film and TV production company in Studio City. With her blond hair back in a French braid, wearing a black business suit and a lavender blouse, she looked every inch the well-groomed exec.

"Yes. The client loved it that we came out to meet with them, so hopefully they're going to be doing a lot of business with us," she said.

"Glad it was a great outcome," Hunter smiled, as they all hustled inside.

During and after the divorce, their relationship had reached a low point, a state of conflict that the strong-minded Amy had found difficult to back down from. One of her main sticking points had been Hunter's police work – his erratic, long hours, and the violence inherent in his job.

It was all the more ironic that her stance had changed this way because they'd originally met while flattened on the floor during a convenience store robbery.

Both students at the time, it was the helplessness of that situation that made Hunter turn away from using his master's degree to become a teacher or professor of English literature. Instead, he'd joined the police.

For a while, Amy had been supportive of his career choice. But over the years, and especially since having Matthew, her attitude had changed. It didn't help that as a more senior detective, Hunter had been handling ever more violent and dangerous cases.

Remembering how bad it had gotten between them, and how close he'd come to losing joint custody of Matthew, he was now immeasurably relieved that they were on a more even keel.

"You look like you only just got in yourself," he said.

"Ten minutes ago. I've been replying to some messages, and I haven't even made a start on dinner," Amy admitted.

"Let me help. What can I microwave?" Hunter asked. He knew how things worked in Amy's home.

"Well, I'll take a look in the freezer and ask Matthew what he feels like," she said, checking her phone. "I've just got a few urgent mails to handle."

"Let's start with a glass of wine for you, then?" he suggested, getting a grateful grin in response.

He'd hoped to have a moment to speak to her about Matthew, but with Amy tapping frantically away on her phone, it didn't look like that was going to happen.

For a moment, he wondered if this was work-related – or otherwise. Perhaps she'd gotten involved in helping with something he didn't yet know about, and that was why she was so much busier than usual, so late.

He poured a glass of Chardonnay from the bottle in the refrigerator and placed it beside her. With a sigh, she looked up from her phone and he got ready to broach the subject. But before he could speak, his phone started ringing.

Quickly, he picked up the call.

"Hunter?" It was the office calling, one of the LAPD duty officers.

"Hey, Boone. What's up?" He already knew something was. Now it was just a case of assessing the urgency.

"We've just had a murder case called in. A woman's been killed outside her home in Norwalk. We need to move fast on it because there are indications that it could be a hit."

2
Neighborhood Shockwaves Spread

Siren blaring, Hunter raced through the rainstorm to the murder scene. A suspected hit? In Norwalk, a relatively peaceful college town? What was this about, and who was the victim?

As he turned into Baytree Street, wipers working at full speed, he saw the flashing lights ahead, cutting through the rainy darkness. An ambulance and two police cars were parked outside the home, and a few neighbors and bystanders were watching at a distance, huddled under their umbrellas. Hunter guessed the downpour had kept most people away.

He parked by the side of the road and grabbed his umbrella from the trunk. With the rain spattering onto its canopy, he stopped by the police car to put on foot covers and a head cover before walking up the grassy lawn. This was a small house, probably a two-bedroom, in a modest neighborhood. The yard showed some signs of neglect, the grass was overgrown, the shrubs bushy and untrimmed.

The two paramedics had gotten a temporary waterproof shelter in place over the body, and under it, the coroner was already at work.

"Evening," he greeted the paramedics and police. "What's the background here?"

"Detective Harden." The nearest police officer turned to him. "We've IDed the woman as Ms. Charlotte Grace, and she has probably been dead half an hour. A neighbor from across the road noticed her lying on the grass when he arrived home. He called us immediately."

Hunter moved forward, staring down at the body, and frowning in puzzlement at the detritus surrounding it. Shopping bags with groceries spilling out of them. A cell phone, discarded on the grass and now wet with rain. A purse that looked to be unopened. Money and possessions hadn't been the motive for this attack.

And the woman herself?

Two bullet wounds in her head. One in the temple, one squarely in the forehead.

Totally different angles.

Although Hunter didn't know how it had happened and it would take the pathologist to prove it, he imagined a scenario where this woman had been grabbed, held, the gun forced against her head and the trigger pulled. She'd fallen, and then the killer had stood over her to deliver that second shot.

Chilling though it was, Hunter agreed with the theory of a hit. This was up close and personal; brutally violent.

He guessed the gun had been silenced. Two non-silenced shots would have been heard at a distance, even in a rainstorm. In this neighborhood, people would have come out to look.

Eyes sharpened in focus, he looked for further clues that might tell him how this had played out.

Looking to be in her forties, he guessed this woman must have come from work. She had make-up on and was wearing a gray jacket and black pants - a smart, corporate uniform. She'd fallen face up, her hazel eyes wide and unseeing, and her shoulder-length hair straggling onto the grass in wet rats' tails.

A woman on her own, killed after arriving home from work and – he guessed – getting out of the midrange Toyota sedan that was parked close to the garden path.

She must have been walking up to her house when she was attacked. And those shopping bags? Had she thrown them at her attacker as her only means of self-defense? Ineffectual as the attempt would have been, Hunter knew that panic would easily prompt a reaction like this.

In that case, seeing the groceries spread out in the direction of the house meant the attacker had approached from the front. He'd sprung out from somewhere – perhaps from the cover of one of these overgrown garden shrubs. Perhaps from behind that jasmine, whose blossoms were emitting a sweet fragrance in the light rain.

The man had been waiting, and this reinforced to Hunter that the attack was not random.

With his feet squelching on the grass, Hunter headed up to the home.

Were there any security cameras in place? His heart sped up as he saw he might just be lucky this time.

There was a camera positioned over the front door. He didn't know how wide the angle was but there was surely a possibility it might have captured some movement. Anything would help them.

Forensics would need to enter the house, disable any alarms in place, and locate the camera feed. That was a specialized job. Hunter couldn't go barging inside himself, even though the discarded bunch of keys he saw on the grass would have made that job easy.

He'd have to wait to see if the footage revealed anything.

For now, he needed to make the most of the golden hour following this crime.

The neighbors might not think they'd seen anything, but sometimes, people picked up on details without realizing it.

Hunter left the scene and went back down to the road, crossing to the house opposite, where the witness who'd seen Charlotte's body when he had arrived home lived.

This house was bigger than the victim´s and the yard looked neater, too. Hunter knocked on the white-painted front door and a few moments later, it was opened by a man in a gray tracksuit. He was plump with dark hair that looked damp and a concerned expression in his dark brown eyes. Behind him, Hunter saw a brunette woman in cycling gear hastening to the door.

"Detective Hunter Harden," he introduced himself. "Sir, I understand you were the one who reported this scene?"

"Yes. Yes, that's me." Seemingly in a daze, he moved aside to let Hunter in. The woman ushered him to the living room, which was tidy. Two bottles of beer stood on the coffee table. From the kitchen, his nose picked up the smell of roast chicken.

The couple sat down on the couch, where Hunter guessed they'd been having a beer together to soothe their nerves after the earlier shock.

"Your name, sir?" he asked.

"I'm Paul Healy," he said. "This is my wife, Marion."

"Tell me what happened, Paul."

"I got home about a half-hour ago. It was raining like crazy. I could barely see in front of me. But something – I don't know what – made me look up that way. I guess I saw her out of the corner of my eye. I thought at first she'd had a fall or maybe suffered some kind of seizure. Then when I got closer, I saw she had been shot. It was so unreal. I could see, from the bullet wounds, she had to be dead."

He swallowed, taking a deep breath. His wife held his hand.

"I checked her pulse anyway and then called the police immediately. I waited by the road until they arrived. Got myself soaked, but barely noticed it."

"I've never known anything like this to happen here," Marion emphasized. "This is such a safe neighborhood. Normally," she added doubtfully.

"Did you know Ms. Grace well?" Hunter asked. "Did she live alone?"

Paul glanced at Marion. "She lived alone, yes," he said.

"I spoke to her a few times, shortly after she moved in," Maria said. "That was over a year ago now. I think there was a reason – a divorce if I remember. Yes, that's right. She rented that place after a divorce. I asked where she worked, and she said she was a legal secretary for one of the tax law firms in town."

"And what was your impression of her?" Hunter was eager to know what kind of person she'd been.

"She was – well, I guess, a forceful person?" Paul glanced at his wife again and she nodded.

"Forceful," she agreed.

"We were never good friends with her, but we'd greet each other in passing, you know?" he added.

"Did you ever see any trouble, any fights? Hear anything from the house?"

"No." Both the husband and wife spoke in unison and shook their heads.

Hunter was puzzled. A legal secretary for a tax firm? If any payback was coming anyone's way, it would have been to the lawyer, surely? He wondered what had been happening in her personal life.

He needed more information. Perhaps the other neighbors could provide it.

Hunter thanked the couple and left the house. He then went to the home to the right of the murder scene. But it was locked up tight with nobody there.

How about the one on the left?

He headed there, checking the time as he walked. Passing Charlotte's house, he saw that her body had been removed, and forensic officers in white suits were combing the scene.

He got to the house and rang the bell.

There was a pause, a long one. Then footsteps pounded on the door and a woman's voice called out nervously, "Who's there?"

"Detective Hunter Harden," he said. He produced his badge, ready for inspection by the nervous-sounding occupant.

The door cracked open, and she peered out. Then, once she'd seen his badge, she opened it wider. He was face to face with a tall blond woman with a mass of flyaway hair, wearing black leggings and a frayed pink sweater.

"What's going on there? I know there must be trouble, but what's happening?" she asked.

"Your neighbor, Ms. Grace, was found murdered," Hunter said.

"Her?" Her eyes flew even wider. "Dead?"

"Did you know her?" he asked.

She wrinkled her nose, now looking sorrowful and conflicted. "Sort of. I didn't have much to do with her. We had a couple of issues, soon after she moved in, about my friends' parking outside her house. I tried to keep out of her way after that."

The victim hadn't been an easy person, Hunter deduced. He guessed that if her neighbors were anything to go by, she might have had more enemies than friends. But even though this neighbor didn't have much to do with her, she might have seen or heard something that could help.

"The murder took place about an hour ago. Were you here at the time?" Hunter asked.

She frowned, pushing back her rebellious hair from a furrowed forehead.

"I was here. I don't know if I heard or saw anything though. I've been working, and on the phone nonstop," she said. She glanced to the left, making Hunter wonder if her study window overlooked that area.

"Did you notice anything unusual?"

Hunter thought she was going to say no, but then she frowned.

"You know, I might have heard something now that I think about it. Like a banging noise. I thought it was a car backfiring or something like that. The sound of the rain made it difficult to tell. And then, I noticed a man rush past my window. But it was storming. Everyone was in a hurry. It was a guy, wearing a dark jacket. I wish I could tell you more, but that's all I saw."

"It's helpful," Hunter said.

If she'd heard the silenced shots being fired, and then seen the killer running, that meant he'd preplanned this well enough to have parked on a different street, in another place.

Hunter needed to know why someone had gone to so much trouble to target Charlotte Grace. So far he knew that she was a legal secretary, that she wasn't close to her neighbors, and that she was an argumentative, forceful person.

"Anything else?" he asked. "Any other impressions of her?"

"There was something about her," the blond neighbor blurted out. "Something weird. I'm not sure I should tell you." She hesitated, looking unsure.

"Please, tell me." Hunter encouraged.

"It's like I'm speaking badly of her. Like I'm talking about her behind her back."

Hunter stared into the blond woman's dark blue eyes. "If it helps catch her killer, I'm sure she'd be grateful to you," he said. "And whatever you say, I'll keep confidential."

"Well…" The woman frowned, then continued. "It was just that.. she'd sometimes have shouted conversations in her upstairs room, so loud I could hear her voice, if not her words. I guess she was on the phone because I never heard anyone else, only her. Sometimes she'd get up very early or very late and go out. Outside of working hours, but dressed for work. You know, it was maybe my imagination going wild, but I sometimes wondered if she had two different lives. That was the question I asked myself more than once."

Hunter thought that to be a very perceptive comment.
Thanking her, he left, going back to his car.
A secret second life?
He was going to try to track down the person he hoped would know more about this.

3

Murder Unveils Activists Secrets

Having a police officer arrive at your front door late at night was always going to be a shock to the senses. When Hunter reached the double-story home where Charlotte's ex-husband lived, in a quiet suburb a few miles from where the murder had occurred, there was silence for a minute after he rang the doorbell.

Just as he was about to try again, he saw an upstairs light go on.

Mike Grace must have been asleep, he thought.

While he waited for the ex-husband to make his way downstairs, Hunter looked around. This yard was in a better state than Charlotte's had been. The only thing that looked out of place was a rusty kids' swing on the well-mown grass. Its red and yellow paint was peeling, and it seemed as if it hadn't been used in a long while.

"Who's there?" A voice sounding hoarse with sleep called out from behind the door at the same time that the hallway light went on.

"Police," Hunter replied. "Detective Hunter Harden."

"Police?" the voice said incredulously.

The door swung open, and he was face to face with Charlotte Grace's ex-husband.

Mike Grace was tall – Hunter's height, and probably in his early fifties, with a mop of graying hair and a face that looked set in lines of permanent worry. He was wearing a pair of jeans and a tracksuit top over his pajama top. His feet were in slippers.

He stared at Hunter standing in the rain, which was still misting.

"What's this about?" he asked. "Is something wrong? Why are you here?"

"It's because of your ex-wife, Charlotte. I looked up your details earlier and drove straight here," Hunter explained. "I'm afraid Charlotte was murdered this evening."

Mike's face tautened in shock.

"What?" he exclaimed. "Murdered?" For a few long, horrified moments, he stared at Hunter. Then, as if gathering his thoughts, he said, "You'd better come in."

Hunter followed him into the home and closed the front door behind them. Mike led the way into a living room which bore the signs of a dinner for one, in front of the TV. An empty plate and fork were still on the coffee table and a pair of shoes was set under it. Mike grimaced in embarrassment, clearing the plate, and moving the shoes before offering Hunter a seat on the brown leather couch. He sat opposite, after taking a chair from the small dining room table at the far end of the room.

"What happened?" he asked, his hazel eyes concerned, clasping his hands together. "What on earth happened to Charlotte?"

"She was murdered outside her house. It looks like it happened when she arrived home, and it looked intentional. She was targeted." Hunter gave the ex-husband a moment for this shock to sink in. Then he continued. "I'm looking for reasons. I need to know more about who Charlotte was and what she did. I understand she was a legal secretary?"

Mike nodded. "Yes, that's right."

"May I also ask where you were earlier this evening?" Hunter felt he needed to ask that question even though Mike Grace's shocked look almost made him ashamed of asking.

"I was in a meeting which ran a little late, till around six-thirty. Two of my colleagues were going to The Red Bear for drinks and asked that I come along but I went to the gym instead and worked out for about an hour. Then I came home for dinner," he replied, pointing at the table where he cleared the detritus of his TV dinner a few minutes before.

Hunter nodded but pushed on. "What about firearms, do you own any?"

Mike Grace shuddered. "No, I do not own any firearm neither have I ever touched any all my life."

Hunter believed him. He had asked the heavy questions just to clear any doubt that might want to spring up. He made a mental note to check out the gym in a couple of days if he needed to but already ruled out the possibility of Grace killing his ex-wife. Now to other questions.

"I was wondering – outside of work, did you know of anything going on in her life?"

Immediately, Hunter could see that there was something. Mike's eyes narrowed and he gave a small, decisive nod.

"She did have something else that she was involved in. It was pretty much all-consuming," he admitted.

"And what was that?" Hunter waited expectantly.

"Charlotte started an organization a few years ago, called Guardian Moms."

"Guardian Moms?" The name rang a bell for Hunter. He'd heard of it before.

Mike stared at the beige carpet, his hands gripping each other tighter than ever.

"I should probably give you the background," he said.

"Go on." Hunter waited. Whatever the background was, he could tell it was painful for Mike to talk about.

"We had a son, Kyle. He was – he was killed in a shopping mall shooting a few years ago." Now, Mike's voice was tense and tight. His gaze was fixed on the carpet.

"I'm so sorry," Hunter said sympathetically. Now he felt like a heel for that firearm question.

"He was eight at the time."

Just a year older than Matthew, Hunter thought with a lurch of his stomach. He could empathize with the parents' grief. Now, that abandoned swing in the front yard made sense. Perhaps it was kept there as a memory or because nobody could bring themselves to remove it.

"It was just so shocking. So wrong. The guy fled the scene, police gave chase, and he ended up in a fatal crash. He was some twenty-two-year-old with an assault rifle and mental health issues." Mike swallowed hard. "It was devastating for us both. We'd tried so hard – Charlotte had trouble conceiving. Kyle was our miracle baby. That's what we called him. Our miracle baby."

Hunter nodded silently. He was finding this difficult to listen to. The pain in the man's voice was off the charts.

"Charlotte started Guardian Moms a year later. It was her way of trying to make sure it never happened again. Guardian Moms is a watchdog organization that's passionately anti-guns, anti-violence, and anti-anything that romanticizes guns and shootings. She did it in her spare time, but the organization has gained a big following. It's gotten teeth over the years."

"It must have gained some critics, too?" Hunter asked.

"Oh, yeah." Finally, Mike raised his head and made a wry face of acknowledgment. "There are many people who think she's an extremist. She decided, when she started Guardian Moms, that she wasn't in it to compromise. So she's always taken a more radical view. It made her some enemies along the way. When she set her sights on someone she considered an offender, it was like she'd declared war on them."

"Anyone in particular?"

Mike shrugged. "There have always been detractors. People who've vehemently opposed her stance. But we've fallen out of touch – our marriage didn't survive what happened to our son. It was an amicable divorce, but I haven't spoken to her for months," he explained.

"Understood," Hunter said. "What about when you last spoke to her? Was there anything she was particularly focused on?"

Mike frowned. "There was something she mentioned that stuck in my head. She said she was working on something potentially explosive, and that it was going to represent a massive breakthrough when it happened. But she was keeping it very close to her chest and I think she was having difficulty getting the information she needed. I remember she was angry and stressed about that." He sighed. "I wish I'd asked her more about it, but you know, I doubt she would have told me, and in the past, I think some of her massive breakthroughs had never happened, and just fizzled out. Often, things she thought would make waves didn't come to anything. Her sources of information weren't always reliable. Some of them were legitimate – the parents of the affected kids and her media connections. But others – the conspiracy theorists – were downright flaky."

Hunter took that in. He wished he knew more. Someone had dealt this woman a violent death, and suppressing a big expose would be a reason for doing so.

"Did she have others working with her in the organization?"

"There were a few people involved, but mostly volunteers. I think she was about to get somebody full-time and an office to work in. She was working hard to make it happen and when Charlotte set her sights on something, it happened most times."

Hunter saw sadness etched on his face as he talked about his ex-wife.

There didn't seem anything more to ask, so he stood up.

"I appreciate what you've told me. It's been very helpful. Sorry about knocking on your door so late with such tough news," he said.

"I appreciate that you came by." Mike's face was still drawn with grief as he walked to the front door with Hunter.

The rain was starting up again. It was wet and cold as Hunter hurried to his car in the now quiet, late-night darkness.

But he had a new lead. Mike had said that his ex-wife had been working on a big expose.

Tomorrow, he was going to find out where her sights had been set, and who had the strongest motive for silencing Charlotte and Guardians.

4
Top Secret Game Invitation

His unit was hemmed in, under severe enemy fire. The rapid stutter and crash of gunshots resounded in Daniel Bridges' ears. If they couldn't retaliate soon, then they would all go down.

His mind raced as he considered his options. They were trapped in a bunker behind an abandoned building, crumbling and derelict and pocked by enemy fire. But the building itself offered some cover, and if he could get there, then he could use the cover to get a clear shot at the enemy forces that were threatening to take them out.

"I'm going to do it," he muttered aloud.

It was risky, but that was to be expected. This was war, after all. And for the sake of his unit, he was prepared to try.

"I'm going into the building."

Taking his hands off the controls, quickly, he typed the words into the game chat that he used to communicate with his team; the others in the unit, who were fighting with him.

Immediately, the replies came flooding back.

"No, Captain Dan. Too risky."

"U're a hero if u try. But if u fail...?"

33

"Wait, if you wait I'll come with you."

More and more replies filled the screen. There were other responses from more far-flung members of their unit.

He took a moment to step out of his adrenaline-fueled immediacy and appreciate what a damned incredible game this was.

In all the eighteen years of his life, Commando Corps was one of the best and most realistic multi-player war games he'd ever known. He felt he'd changed a lot since playing it. He'd become more confident. Fitter, for sure, thanks to the physical challenges that the game forces players to complete. And with a noble mindset that fighting shoulder to shoulder with his brothers was the right thing to do – and there were so many of them! At any one time, he'd be fighting in a unit with twenty to fifty other soldiers. And there were tens of thousands of these units in the game.

He'd seen the numbers in the overview, and they were astonishing. The fact he was one of the top 10% in terms of his game performance was a real achievement.

He'd also learned very useful skills along the way. He'd earned himself a free simulation course in tank driving and fighter jet operation, and although he'd never held an actual gun, he knew how to field strip, load, and fire several of the actual Army models, thanks to tutorials he'd earned through his game credits.

Now it was time to prove his hard-won skills.

"None of you are close enough. I'm going alone."

Hands back on the controls, mind back in the game, he readied himself for the sprint.

And then, he burst out from the bunker.

His camouflage-clad avatar, which had dark hair and blue eyes like Daniel himself did, but who was way tougher and stronger, sprinted at full tilt toward that decrepit building, while gunfire exploded around him, the sound crashing in his Bluetooth headphones.

As he'd expected, a message flashed up on his screen and the game paused.

"One Hundred Skips. Press Start when ready."

He scrambled off his chair and reminded himself that he mustn't make a noise while he skipped. It was already after midnight and his mom, who'd come in an hour ago from her late shift though she hadn't greeted him, was sleeping.

His little brother, Luke, was also asleep in the next-door room in their tiny apartment.

He stood up, grabbed the skipping rope that he kept nearby, made sure his fitness watch was connected to the game and pressed Start.

Then, as quickly as he could, he did the skips, the rope curling above him, his arms and legs in coordination, each leap well timed. Making sure that the breath didn't gasp out of him but instead, came softly.

… ninety-eight, ninety-nine, a hundred, he counted down. There. Done.

Scooting back into his chair, he was breathing hard, but not nearly as hard as he had the first time he'd done those skips. He was much fitter now. He stabbed the Finish button and saw that he'd aced this challenge. And that allowed his character to run successfully to the building without being hit by enemy fire.

He crouched down, using a crumbling brick ledge for cover, gazing around him in the semi-dark. Back in the thrall of the game, he needed to get something, some visual guidance, as to where the enemy was. He needed to look out for their muzzle flash.

He scanned the trees and bushes that were on the opposite side of the bunker where his unit was hiding.

There! He'd got it. The flash was faint but definite. He raised his assault rifle, checked his ammunition, and aimed carefully. The higher ground made it easier to see from here. The visibility was far better.

He fired, holding the gun steady, moving it from side to side, still breathing hard from his exertion.

He was doing it! The kill count was mounting! Ten down, eleven, twelve."

Was that all? Had he gotten them all? He saw no more muzzle flashes coming from the dark ribbon of trees.

Watch out for tricks, he thought. That was what this game threw at you. Just when you thought you'd won, it would send a curveball your way that challenged and endangered you all over again.

Behind you, he thought suddenly. Check behind you, soldier. That's what you haven't done.

He swung around and caught his breath as he saw the gray-clad enemy soldier advancing toward him, gun raised.

Adrenaline surged inside him as he wrenched his gun around, aimed, and fired, throwing his avatar sideways as he pulled the trigger to avoid the hostile fire that would otherwise destroy him and take him out of the game.

The soldier fell to his knees, blood gushing from his chest. His gun clattered down, and knowing every weapon was important, Daniel rushed forward and grabbed it from him immediately.

He looked around him. Any other rogue soldiers?

It seemed like the coast was clear, and there was no more gunfire coming from the forest.

He'd done it! Every single one of the enemy forces had fallen thanks to his strategic and daring move.

"Level Achieved." The message flashed up on the screen, the game's victory tune resounded in his ears, and he slumped back in his chair, letting out an exhilarated sigh, finally allowing his intensive focus to relax.

"Congratulations, Captain Dan!" The messages flooded in from his team.

"You're our best leader."

"That was top class."

"It was a rush, man! So exciting, I want to do it over!"

"Me 2, but gotta turn in now, school tomorrow."

"You guys were great. We were a tight team this time," he praised the others.

"See u tomorrow nite to start level 8?"

"Yeah," he typed. *"See y'all then."*

Some of the boys in his unit were in the same part of LA where he lived, and a couple of them were his friends. Others were from elsewhere in California and even elsewhere in the country. All were brought together by the game. Strangers, fighting for a common cause. They'd become a brotherhood that he'd willingly kill for and die for. That's what Commando Corps, a spinoff from the wildly popular Carl Commando action figure that his little brother adored, was all about. For the first time in his life, Daniel felt he had a sense of purpose and a sense of belonging.

The messages tapered off and he reached toward the controls, ready to switch them off for the night at last.

But as he did, he saw another message had flickered onto the screen.

A private one this time, not viewable by the group. For his eyes only.

Curious, he read it.

"You did well there, Captain Dan. You're a credit to your unit. Congratulations, soldier!"

He felt a flare of pride as he read the words. But there was more to the message.

"We are inviting you to complete a new level of the game. Not with your unit. This is a personal challenge, and it is top secret. We only offer it to the top five percent of all players. It'll be the toughest yet. To accept, type in 'Yes.' If you accept, you may not tell your unit about this. Or you will be removed from the game permanently."

What could it be? And who were 'we'? It sounded like they were higher-ups in the game, maybe.

Frowning, he checked the chat again but nobody else was mentioning this challenge. That meant it really must be him alone.

A personal challenge? He'd never heard of such a thing in Commando Corps.

But if the game had invited him, there must be a reason for it.

He hesitated for only a moment before typing in *"Yes"*.

5

Detective's Feline Surprise

Hunter heard the sound as soon as he climbed out of his car that he parked on the apartment building's basement parking lot.

It had been a long, exhausting day. He'd hoped that by now he'd have a clearer lead to Charlotte Grace's killer, but all he had was a better idea of why she might have died. His right leg – still recovering after a bullet had smashed through the bone – was aching the way it always did after a long day. Rain was pelting down again, chilling the air with a wintry cold.

But the tiny yowl was audible above the drumming of the rain, and it attracted his attention immediately. He looked in the direction it was coming from but saw nothing. The corner of the basement, where a concrete shelf jutted out a few inches off the ground and some steel piping crisscrossed above, was dark and shadowy.

He moved quietly in that direction, feeling his tired leg protest anew. It made him think that even when it had fully healed, the bone would ache in the cold and damp.

There it was again. He homed in on it this time.

"Hey there?" Hunter called out. His voice was muffled by the sluicing noise of the rain outside, but another squeak came in response.

It was a mewing sound. He hadn't imagined it.

Hunter activated the flashlight on his phone and shone it into the shadows.

It picked up the flash of eyes, staring back at him. Wide, green, and scared.

"Psspsspss," Hunter said, stepping forward cautiously, his foot splashing into a puddle. How tame was this little creature? He didn't want to scare it, and have it hide away, going deeper under that concrete shelf.

"Psspsspss," he coaxed it, bending down. "C'mon. You'll be okay. Come here, little guy."

He leaned forward further, now going down on his knees in the puddle, his bad leg protesting, his pants instantly drenched, but he was almost there. Almost within touching distance.

The kitten cringed away, and Hunter stopped, staying still, keeping up with the coaxing noises. Then he twiddled his fingers and moved his hand closer, ever closer.

His fingers touched sodden, gray fur. Ever so gently, Hunter closed them over the kitten's scruff and lifted it out, staggering up to his feet again, holding the kitten in his hand.

"How'd you get there, little guy?" The furry creature was big enough to overflow his hand, but only just. It was shaking and drenched.

"We need to warm you up. Let's get you upstairs," he said.

Cradling the kitten to his chest, he returned to his car, got out his laptop bag, closed it up one-handedly, and headed for the elevator.

By the time he'd ridden up to his floor, the kitten had rallied and was starting to purr, a surprisingly thunderous sound that filled the elevator. Encouraged by this sign of recovery, Hunter got it inside and turned on the small electric heater in the living room.

He placed a blanket in front of it, put the kitten on the blanket, and went in search of some food.

A quick exploration of the freezer yielded a chicken breast TV dinner in a creamy sauce.

"Guess that'll do for us both," Hunter said, peering into the living room where the kitten was now energetically grooming itself. Its gray fur still looked somewhat ragged, but its long tail was now starting to look bushy, and not so much like a piece of wet reed.

The microwave pinged, and Hunter removed the dinner, separating a portion of the chicken and chopping it into small chunks. He put it on a saucer, poured some water into a bowl, and when he took it through to the living room, he was rewarded by a fresh spate of high-pitched mews.

He placed the food and water down and watched while the kitten devoured the chicken hungrily. Once every scrap was finished, it went back to its grooming routine for a few more minutes and then began chasing its tail. With his own meal on his lap, Hunter had to admit that the sight was far more entertaining than whatever random TV program he'd otherwise have ended up watching.

"Hopefully you're okay for the night, little fella?" he asked. "Tomorrow morning, I'll get up early and buy you what you need. And put some notices out in case anyone's looking for you."

Heading for the shower at last, Hunter acknowledged he didn't know a lot about cats.

Yet.

He had the feeling he might be going to learn fast.

*

Hunter woke up to the sound of the alarm and a warm, prickly sensation on his head. A quick exploration revealed the reason: the kitten was sleeping on his pillow, curled in his hair, its tiny claws kneading lovingly at his scalp.

Embarking on his morning exercises – his bad leg still needed intensive physiotherapy and strengthening – was more of a challenge with the small feline chasing his shoelaces. Finally working his way through the last set, Hunter realized that he hadn't laughed so much in the morning since – well, since as long as he could remember.

He fed the kitten the remainder of the chicken and printed out a few notices with the kitten's photo and his phone number. He put a message out on his apartment building's communication group for anyone looking for their pet. Then he went downstairs, placing the notices in the lobby, after which he headed to the grocery store across the road to buy some supplies.

Sand tray, scratching post, toys, food, bowls. He went through the aisles picking everything out, paid for it, and hurried back home. Once back in the apartment, he set out the kitten's entertainment center, meal station, and toilet facilities. All the while the small animal watched him from his chosen perch – Hunter's office chair.

"You'd better look after yourself for the day, okay?" he told the cat, scratching it behind the ears. "I'll see you later.

By the time I get back, I hope I'll have made some headway with my work, and found out what Charlotte Grace was so involved in trying to uncover."

He looked up the address for Guardian Moms, noting that the offices were on the other side of town and that according to their office hours, they should already be open. Deciding to call first, in case yesterday's tragedy meant they were closed, he dialed the office number.

It rang through to voicemail. And, listening to the recorded message, Hunter learned that the organization was indeed closed today. Whether this was because of the death, or for some other reason, he didn't know, and the message didn't say.

He'd have to try again tomorrow.

As he hung up, his phone rang.

It was Amy's landline number. Hunter's thoughts immediately veered to his son. Had there been a crisis? Having Amy call him first thing in the morning was very unusual.

"Amy? What's up?" he asked.

But to his surprise, it wasn't his wife on the other end of the phone. It was his son.

"Dad," Matthew hissed and Hunter's stomach instinctively clenched. What was wrong? Something was, that was for sure.

"What's up, champ?" he asked quickly, gripping the phone.

"Dad, I wanted to ask you something last night, but then you had to go. Can I talk to you now?"

"Where's Mom?" were his first words. Did Amy know about this call?

"She's in the shower. Dad, it's urgent!"

His son sounded stressed and anxious. Not the way that Hunter ever wanted him to sound. Whatever this was, he needed to know about it. And on the phone might not be the best way to handle this, especially if Amy came out of the shower unexpectedly. Whatever was going on, Matthew clearly didn't want his mother to find out that they were talking now, and Hunter had no idea why.

"I'll come around there." Hunter estimated the time hurriedly. Hopefully, when he was at the house, there'd be a chance to chat with Matthew in private. "I'll be there in ten minutes, okay? Then we can talk face to face, and you can tell me what's up."

6
Toy Trouble

Rushing downstairs and climbing into his car, Hunter remembered how unusually quiet and moody Matthew acted the evening before. He'd hoped to find the reason for his son's behavior, but the murder callout had thrown a wrench into his plans. Now, as he drove the short distance to Amy's house – a distance he could have run in half an hour before his leg injury - his concerns were at the forefront of his mind again.

Thinking that he should arrive bearing gifts to provide a reason for this impromptu visit, he stopped outside the bakery on the corner and bought a bag of cheese croissants. With these in hand, he then headed down the street and parked outside Amy's house.

It was a clear day; the air was fresh, and the sun was making an appearance after yesterday's downpour.

Amy opened the door after he knocked and stared at him, surprised.

"What're you doing here?" she asked. Hunter could already see Matthew hovering in the background.

"Well, I missed dinner last night, so I brought something for breakfast," he explained. "I've got a free half-hour as the place I was going to is closed. So I thought

I'd catch up with Matthew. He seemed upset that I had to leave so suddenly," he explained.

Amy was already dressed for work in a green blouse and a cream skirt, but her hair was wet, and her make-up wasn't yet done.

"He has been moody," she admitted. "Come on in. I haven't had time to fix breakfast yet, so those might just be a lifesaver this morning."

The smell of coffee filled the air inside the small, tidy house. Matthew had retreated into the dining room and was sitting at the table expectantly. Hunter noticed Amy's laptop was open yet again. She was clearly working overtime or else had some other project on the go.

"Morning, champ," Hunter said to him, giving him a conspiratorial wink and feeling glad to get a quick grin in response. He took the coffee jug and poured it for himself. Amy abandoned her half-finished cup and rushed to the bedroom, where Hunter soon heard the sound of the hairdryer.

As she left, Matthew's face changed. Now, he looked anxious and was frowning.

Hunter estimated they had five minutes. That was how long it usually took Amy to blow dry her hair.

He took the croissants out of the bag, put them in a bowl, and served Matthew one on a plate.

"You ready to talk?" he asked.

Now that he was here, it seemed Matthew had misgivings all over again. He shrugged, staring at his food, picking off a flake of cheese and nibbling at it.

"This is going to be our only time to talk, while Mom is drying her hair. I think we have three minutes left, max," he encouraged the boy. "So if you want to tell me what it is,

I'd suggest you don't wait any longer. Otherwise, your chance will be gone."

Hunter watched as Matthew considered his words. He could see his son thinking things over. Taking in the logic and also gathering his courage.

Then he nodded.

"Dad, I do need to tell you," he whispered. "It's important. Really important. I need you to help me. You have to help me change Mom's mind."

"Change her mind?" Hunter asked. "About what?"

He felt a flare of relief that he acknowledged might be premature, but at least it sounded as if this wasn't bullying or abuse or anything else that was potentially serious, although he knew that to a seven-year-old, even minor issues could feel very serious indeed.

Matthew grimaced as if the need to tell Hunter the whole situation in such a tight timeframe was simply too much stress for one morning.

"She's being unreasonable, Dad," he whispered, glancing at the bedroom door.

"Mom's not normally that way," he said. "What about?"

"There's this toy. It's really cool and almost all the other boys in my class have one. It's called Carl Commando."

"Carl Commando?" Hunter whispered back. "I think I've heard of it."

Something vaguely military was coming to mind. He had the feeling this was a military action toy. More than that, he didn't know.

"So you want one and Mom won't buy it?"

"No, she won't."

"Is it expensive?" Hunter asked, wondering what the reason was.

"It's not that expensive," Matthew argued with an expressive shrug.

"Is there any reason why she wouldn't buy you a toy? Did she say it was because of something you did or didn't do?"

"No. It's not that. It's just that she won't buy it for me. She gets really mad when I ask her. Dad, you have to help me, please. All the cool kids have this toy. They play together after school; they form units and – and it is really good fun. There's even a limited edition one, the Dress Blues Marine, that came out. Four of my friends have it, and it's not in the shops anymore now. Mom won't even buy me the normal one. And I feel left out."

He looked pained and Hunter felt a flash of empathy. Being left out, at the tender age of seven, could be excruciating, and again, the worries he had about bullying loomed in his mind.

"I'll speak to Mom," he promised. "I'll find out why she is against this. But I can't guarantee anything, okay?"

Seeing how drawn and tense Matthew's face looked, he tried his best to cheer him up, using his newly discovered trump card.

"I found a kitten last night. Want to see photos? And I took a video of it chasing my shoelaces this morning."

Now, Matthew brightened. "A kitten? Dad, that's so cool! Is it there now? Will you keep it? When can I see it?"

"I've advertised to see if anyone's missing it," Hunter said. "It might have owners looking for it. But otherwise – yes, I guess I'll keep it."

His words surprised even him. A cat owner? But the hope and excitement that was replacing the anxiety in his son's face told him that this might be a very good time to become a cat owner. Because if Amy's stance on the toy remained negative, it was a battle that Hunter knew he couldn't win.

*

Hunter finally got the chance to talk to Amy when she walked him out to his car, discussing Matthew's schedule for the week and finalizing who was doing what.

He made sure to broach the subject casually, "While we were chatting earlier, Matthew mentioned that he'd asked you for a toy." Already, he could see Amy starting to bristle. "An action figure called Carl Commando."

Now her eyes were blazing in true Amy style. "You didn't say yes to him, did you? Because I'm not happy that I said no, and he then went and asked you! He's playing us off against each other!"

Hunter hastened to clarify. "No, absolutely not. I saw he was moodier than usual, and asked why. He told me that it had to do with the toy. And I said I'd speak to you."

"Well, I'm telling you right now, Hunter, it's a no."

This wasn't just a no. This was an Amy-fueled, decisive, passionate 'no way'. Already, Hunter could see that there was no shred of a possibility that Matthew was going to get his toy. But he was going to push it further and ask why.

"Understood. And accepted. But your reason?"

Her eyes were flashing, her voice was forceful.

"That toy is an indoctrination tool."

"How so?" Hunter asked, blinking in surprise.

"I've done my research. Intensively so," she said. "The company behind it has an evil agenda – in my opinion, of course. Which a lot of other people share."

"Not everyone, surely?" he asked.

"Hunter, not everyone *thinks*!" She let out a frustrated sigh.

"You feel that way because it's pro-Army?" He was struggling to understand why she was so hell-bent on denying her son this action figure. "There are a lot of soldier toys out there."

"It's not just pro-Army, and I'm not against kids playing with soldier toys. Matthew has a collection of them in his toy box. And before you ask, I'm not against the armed forces as a career either. But I don't like the way the kids seem to be brainwashed into this Carl Commando mindset, forced to obey orders at all costs, to form a militaristic unit at such a young, impressionable age – that's bullying waiting to happen, right there."

"And you think the company has deliberately set out to create that?" he asked.

She shrugged. "I don't know. All I know is that this toy has an evil agenda behind it and what it is encouraging is completely unhealthy. And I'm not the only person who sees this. There's a big backlash against it right now, because of the brutality it promotes and the way it encourages unthinking obedience to violent commands."

Hunter thought uneasily of Guardian Moms and the murder he was investigating. Now might not be a good time to mention that to Amy, though.

"Okay. Thanks for explaining," he said.

"You understand? You see my point?"

Hunter shook his head. "Look, Amy, to be honest, I think the evil agenda might be veering into conspiracy theory territory." He remembered again what Charlotte's husband had said about the unreliability of the information that she had sometimes received.

"It is not! You're speaking from a standpoint of ignorance!" Now her anger was directed at him, her eyes like chips of steel. "There are people working on this expose, who are going to uncover it and show what this agenda is all about. But it's not easy. And in the meantime, this toy is not happening. Not for Matthew, not on my watch."

"That aside, I can see your reasons," he added hastily, wanting to avoid a fight at all costs even though he did feel that his wife's opinion might have been influenced by some unreliable theories.

Digging deep to summon up his best diplomatic skills, he said, "Perhaps we can research alternatives? It would be a shame for Matthew to be the uncool kid. There must be competing toys in the market that don't have such a strong military connection. Could I have a look and see what I can find out there?"

Her face softened. "That'd be great. There are alternatives. If you can help Matthew realize that they're just as good and that he's still a cool kid, I am happy to let him have those, but please, run the choices past me first."

"I'll do that," Hunter said.

He was surprised once again by the level of passion that blazed in her eyes. She really felt strongly about this, and he guessed that her stance on the toy was reinforced by her feelings on Hunter's job, and the dangers inherent in police work. Maybe this was a way of making sure Matthew didn't make the same choices as his father, he wondered.

Saying goodbye to her, he climbed into his car. He'd thought his next stop would be the LAPD police station, but he was wrong.

Hunter had only got as far as the cross street before his phone began ringing. It was the control room calling.

"You're needed urgently. There's a crime scene that's just been called in," the officer said, his voice tense. "A body has been found in the basement of an office park. Shot in the head. Twice."

7

Corporate Toy Clash

Amelia Evans quickly checked her lipstick in the compact mirror she kept in her purse. She tended to bite her lip when she was nervous and on the very first day of her new job with a blue-chip Fortune 500 company, it was no wonder she was feeling nervous.

She'd landed what would surely be anyone's dream job. She was the new PA to the CEO of Dreamland Creations, the astonishingly successful toy company.

"Remember, they're not going to look at your lipstick," she reminded herself, even though everyone else she'd seen this morning so far had been well dressed and well-groomed and highly glamorous looking. "You were hired for your skills. What you should be doing now is looking back over your notes so that anything that comes up in this morning's meeting will be familiar to you."

But it was too late. As she reached for the new, bright pink folder where she'd placed her printed notes, the CEO herself hurried through from her large, spacious office into the adjoining annex where Amelia worked. Slender and dark-haired, Olivia Montgomery was probably fifty, but she looked younger in a very sleek, well-maintained way.

"Let's go to the boardroom, Amelia," she said, checking her phone. "I see Sam's just arrived, and the others are there already. It's going to be important to record the meeting and take notes also, and I should warn you, things will probably get quite loud. They have been doing so recently." Amelia picked up an odd note of worry in her new boss's tone.

Scrambling up, patting her curly chestnut hair into place, and nearly falling over as one of her brand new, black pumps slipped, Amelia grabbed her folders and her laptop bag, putting her phone in the pocket of her jacket and checking again that she had everything she could need for this meeting.

"Is everything going well so far today?" Olivia asked her.

"So far, everything's perfect," Amelia reassured her.

Olivia was surprisingly nice and down to earth for the CEO of such a hugely successful company, she thought, as she walked in step with her along the wide corridor which had a stunning frieze of the company's bestselling toys painted on it. It was amazing to have landed a job in such a fun, exciting and colorful environment.

She recognized most of the toys. Here was the famous Hailey doll with her freckles and her curly hair which Amelia had always loved because she looked so like her. And here was the even more famous Carl Commando action figure with his wide shoulders and the heroic jut to his chin.

And then they reached the gray and white boardroom and were walking inside.

There were already eight people from the marketing and management team sitting around the table.

"Hi all. This is Amelia, my new assistant," Olivia introduced her.

"Hi, Amelia," the greetings chorused from around the table.

"Thrown in the deep end, starting your job on a meeting day," someone quipped as she sat in her allotted seat to the left of the table's head where Olivia sat.

Introductions were made and Amelia took special note of the most important names. Eleanor Ross, a platinum blond who looked like an ex-model, was the chief marketing officer. Sam Reynolds, a man in his early thirties with a trendy fade hairstyle, dark stubble and piercing, intelligent eyes, was the COO.

Cindy Royce, the chief technology innovation officer, looked to be in her late fifties, with spiky gray hair and funky, red-framed spectacles.

Smiling, working as fast as she could, she readied her laptop and her phone and her paper notepad, set her phone to record, and made sure all the right tabs were open on her machine.

"Okay all," Olivia said. "Let's get started." She paused, looking around the table and Amelia could feel the way the atmosphere suddenly changed, becoming tense. It was as if the polished wooden table had become the site for a battle.

"Now our first and most important point of discussion is Carl Commando."

Sam Reynolds sat bolt upright, opening his folder, gripping his phone as if it were a weapon.

"To give Amelia some quick background," Olivia glanced at her, "the Hailey Doll was Dreamland Creations' first huge success."

"That put us on the map," Cindy Royce agreed, nodding, and adjusting her spectacles.

"However, we didn't want to be known as a 'one trick pony', so we spent huge amounts of time and effort and innovation in looking for the next big success. There were a couple of excellent ideas that have created smaller product lines – Prehistoric Plushies, which was the brainchild of Eleanor Ross, is a line of stuffed dinosaur toys that's been doing exceptionally well on a smaller scale. But it was Carl Commando, Sam Reynolds' concept, that proved to be a smash hit when we launched it, which was four years ago now. It's created an entire culture."

Reynolds was looking oddly troubled as he took over the conversational reins.

"Carl Commando is a runaway success and it's not only because of the toy itself, which appeals to boys in the age group of five to twelve years. It's also the spinoffs that give the toy an even greater reach in terms of its target market," he said emphatically, counting off on his fingers. "The Carl Commando clothing line, which covers all ages from five to eighteen, is especially popular with teens. Military style cargo pants, camo jackets, tight T-shirts, boots, and the accessories – branded water bottles, laptop bags, gloves, scarves, lunch boxes."

"They are doing incredibly well. And then of course we have the action games. The board game, the video games, the Carl Commando exercise app," Olivia said.

"Which the kids love and also parents and teachers," Reynolds insisted, and now Amelia was surprised to pick up a note of defensiveness in his voice.

"Absolutely," Olivia agreed.

Sitting up straighter, Cindy Royce cleared her throat. "We're not here today because of the success of Carl Commando. Can we please move on to the point of this meeting? We're here because of the notable decline we've seen recently in sales and the massive groundswell of bad publicity that's developing in opposition to the toy's ethos."

Sam Reynolds pressed his lips together, glaring at Cindy as if she was personally responsible for the decline.

Amelia sat straighter. A decline? That sounded serious. She wondered what could have caused it.

"Yes. It is a complex issue," Olivia began, but Cindy Royce interrupted her – quite rudely, Amelia thought since Olivia was her boss.

"It's not a complex issue at all. It's incredibly simple and easy to fix. But you're not fixing it!" She glared at Reynolds and Olivia in turn, her expression hard.

Sam Reynolds turned to her, furious. "Sales always dip this time of the year, and they pick up just before Christmas. As for the bad publicity? Are you really going to rely on a couple of conspiracy theory websites that pick up inaccurate information and sensationalize it?"

"Sales have never dropped that much in the past," Cindy insisted.

"What you don't understand is that the military culture is the underpinning that the entire toy and its spinoffs are built on. The boys and the teens and the parents all buy into the ethos of the toy." He half rose to his feet, his voice passionate. "It's an ethos of discipline, of cooperation, with an emphasis on physical activity — which parents love, and bravery, and camaraderie."

"That's no longer what it is nor how it's perceived." Cindy thumped her fist down on the table, causing Eleanor

Ross's coffee cup to rattle. "There is very vocal opposition to what it stands for. Never mind the fringe sites, you've managed to make the activist groups mad."

"They won't stay mad for long!" Reynolds countered, and Amelia wondered what he meant by that.

Quickly grabbing a serviette to mop up her spilled coffee, Eleanor added her own input. "Look, it does seem to have become much more of an intensively military-focused toy over the past year, Sam. I mean, I'm in charge of the marketing and I've seen the change in focus, the changes you've made to the toy itself. It's in everything from the way it's marketed to Carl Commando's appearance."

Pressing a button on her laptop, she activated the big screen, and everyone turned to look at the visuals. "If you see here, two years ago, Carl Commando was sold with the following standard accessories. Backpack, handkerchief, iron ration lunchbox, Swiss army knife, and baseball cap." She touched the key again and a new screen appeared. "If we look at today, the standard accessories include a handgun, a machine gun, an ammunition belt, a helmet, and a walkie-talkie."

"That's in response to market demand," Reynolds insisted. "We did surveys, remember?"

"I'm not sure those surveys were widely enough circulated," Eleanor countered. "I had some suggestions for improving them that were never followed through. So I don't think you can regard them as the gold standard."

"Look at where the backlash is coming from!" Cindy argued. "It's coming from all the anti-gun groups and every time there's any form of gun violence in this country, Carl Commando is getting fallout from it. I'm telling you now, we need to backtrack on this. People are saying that Carl Commando is indoctrinating children into following orders blindly, into obeying violent commands, glorifying weaponry, and forcing them into a very dangerous mindset."

"That's ridiculous!" Reynolds argued back, his voice rising to a shout. "You're telling me that a toy designed to be a soldier can't have soldier accessories? Playing with a soldier toy does not encourage gun violence! I personally have had feedback that the discipline the toy gives and the structure it adds, might actually help prevent gun violence!"

"That's not what the anti-gun lobbyists believe! And you don't need to take away the discipline or the structure. You just need to remove the strong focus on the weapons."

"It's an essential part of the toy itself!" Reynolds roared. Now, everyone was shouting at once.

"You're going to see profits nosedive!" Cindy yelled.

"I disagree. I think it's modeling responsible gun ownership! Shooting on instruction from a superior officer? That's discipline!" Reynolds argued.

"Shooting at all is giving the anti-gun lobbyists a very strong argument. And all we need is one incident where any gun violence incident is shown to be linked to or inspired by, Carl Commando. We only need one of those and we're sunk!" Eleanor chipped in.

"We can't help that!" Reynolds said.

"But we need to speak against it in pre-emptive terms," Cindy insisted. "Did you not hear that the founder of Guardian Moms was murdered last night? If that's found to be linked to her stance, it could backfire."

"Oh, please! More than likely that poor woman was just a random crime victim," Reynolds pushed back.

"I've always thought Prehistoric Plushies could fill the gap more if we allocated more marketing budget to them," Eleanor ventured. "I mean, they're a really popular and non-violent toy."

But nobody was listening to her. The room was divided into pro-military and anti-military as the argument raged.

"The point is that you need to let go of your preconceptions about it, Sam. You positioned it a certain way but now the market's changing. And look at the damage our stance is causing in terms of marketing and merchandising!" Cindy emphasized. "It's leaving a gap for other toys to fill the market in a way that will placate the anti-gun consumer."

There was a short silence, filled only by the drumming of the keyboard as Amelia frantically typed her notes. She hoped the recording would pick up everything, but she was trying to keep track of who'd said what also.

"Look at what KiddoVerse Toys are doing. They're being clever," Cindy said, with an emphasis on the word 'clever' that caused Reynolds to look daggers at her. "They've brought out the Action-Adventure Hero. He's smart, he's skilled, he's fit, and he doesn't carry a gun. He uses technology weapons. He has a laser wand that dissolves his enemies and a matter transmitter that relocates them harmlessly."

"And there's also SparkleGrove Entertainment who've brought out Heroic Harry, who uses natural resources such as a fallen tree branch, a rope twisted from bark, and a piece of braided vine as a net. He's gaining a lot of ground and we're seeing a direct correlation in our sales falling and their sales rising," Olivia mentioned.

"Wonder Play Studios has also brought out a very strong competitor," Cindy added. "The Peace Defender is a figure that uses only mind power to control his competition. It's all about negotiation, smarts, and evasive action. That's tipped to overtake Carl Commando in sale numbers next season!" She was on her feet now and shouting the words across the table at Reynolds. "Your attitude is hurting the company and it's going to get worse!"

"It is not!" Reynolds yelled back. "The Peace Defender is going to fail! I've been tracking the stats and they're on a downturn. They're going to be history by this time next year."

"Your stubbornness is going to tear the company apart, and then *we'll* fail," Cindy screeched. "Can't you see that's what's happening here?"

"Enough!" Olivia shouted, and now the CEO was on her feet. "Enough. This meeting is adjourned. I can't listen to any more of this. And I won't! This is a Fortune 500 company, and the management team can't act like adults around the boardroom table?" She glared at them all, breathing hard, getting mutinous glares in return. "We come back next week. I want you prepared. Facts, figures, stats, trends. We're going to argue the facts, not the emotions behind them. And we'll make our decision from there."

Everyone was silent.

And then, one by one, they stood up and left. Sam Reynolds marched out first, his jaw clenched, giving Olivia a filthy look as if he had expected more support from her.

The others followed. Olivia, looking preoccupied and stressed, was already on the phone as she left.

Amelia switched off the tape recorder in the now quiet boardroom. She picked up her folders, feeling shaken by the unexpectedness of that flare-up. She stood up and headed out but before she could reach the door, her phone rang.

She picked up the call, only realizing as she answered that the incoming number had been withheld.

"Amelia Evans speaking?" she said, hearing the uncertainty in her voice.

"Amelia?" It was a man's voice, soft and furtive, so pressed her phone to her ear to hear him better. "Amelia, you don't know me. And I understand you're new there, at Dreamland Creations?"

She paused, suspicion flaring.

"I am. Why? How do you know? Who is this?"

"For now, I won't say. But what I will say is that we need to talk in person."

"About what?" she said, her worry intensifying.

"About what's happening at Dreamland Creations," the voice said quietly. "I need your help, Amelia."

She had no idea what this was, and right then, she didn't feel at all comfortable having this conversation. This was unsettling, especially given what had just happened in this very boardroom.

"If I meet you, I'm bringing my boss along with me. How do you feel about that?" she asked bravely.

He hesitated, then gave a frustrated sigh.

"Please, hear me out."

"No!" she countered reflexively, now angry that he was still arguing.

"We'll speak again. This is important and I can't leave it be. And soon, you'll see why."

Before she could reply, the anonymous caller hung up.

8
Toy CEO Murder

Hunter stared down at the slumped body, positioned on the concrete floor, midway between the Porsche Cayenne parked in the basement garage and the elevator going up to the building's lobby.

Another body. An identical MO. This time, one shot was in the back of the head and another in the forehead. Again, Hunter visualized the killer taking the man down and then making sure.

This time, the victim was a man in his forties – dark-haired, clean-shaven, and wearing a business suit. His briefcase was lying beside him, as were his car keys. His eyes were staring sightlessly at the flickering basement lights.

As Hunter had sped up to the scene, the radio had crackled with the news that the victim had been IDed. This victim was Brian Mitchell, the CEO of Wonder Play Studios, a toy company whose offices occupied most of the office park's east wing.

According to the police who were on the scene when Hunter arrived, his body had been found by the building's janitor, who'd been upstairs when he'd heard muffled bangs from down below. On heading down to investigate, the janitor met with the gruesome sight.

"I guess he got in early and there was nobody else around," Hunter said to Cody.

Cody, who'd arrived a minute after Hunter, nodded grimly. "It's identical to the other murder. I'm guessing the killer got here first, waited, and then he struck."

Was he waiting for Brian Mitchell in particular? Given that he was the CEO, that was a possibility, Hunter guessed.

The gloomy chill of the parking garage felt very far removed from the sunny, clear morning outside, but the forensic team was bringing in powerful flashlights so that they could search every inch of the space. Hunter and Cody were wearing full PPE – gloves, head cover, foot covers. They needed trace evidence, and they needed camera footage.

Hunter strode around the garage on the lookout for any cameras. There was one by the entrance boom and one by the exit boom. Since the booms were card-activated, he doubted whether the killer could have entered in a vehicle. But he could easily have come in on foot and then the cameras would give them at least a glimpse of him. Especially seeing there was no other way in and out.

"If you carry on managing things down here, I'm going to go upstairs now," Hunter said to Cody.

He headed over to the stairwell that led to the building's lobby, ducked under the first length of crime scene tape, and went up the concrete stairs to the second set of tape that had been put there as an extra precaution. Then, he exited into the lobby where a worried knot of workers was waiting, clustered near the reception desk.

This place was clean and clinical, decorated in silver and chrome and bright white. Very corporate, Hunter thought. The attires of the workers matched the building's environment. Formal and smart, rather than casual and relaxed.

"Morning," he said, staring around at their anxious faces. "I'm Detective Harden from the LAPD. Sorry about this incident, I know you must all be very shocked. We're going to work as fast as we can to get answers, but I'll need your cooperation."

Staring around, he saw a few cautious nods as he continued. "I need to speak to whoever worked the most closely with the victim, Mr. Mitchell. And I need to obtain your basement parking's camera footage."

A man in his forties with a round face, flushed cheeks and a perspiring forehead that belied the cool temperature of the lobby stepped forward. He wore a violet shirt and a pair of black suit pants over which his belly bulged.

"That'll be me," he said. "I'm Henry Pond, Brian Mitchell's chief operating officer. I've worked for him since the start." He hesitated. "However, I feel our lawyers should also sit in on this interview. I'm incredibly shaken by all of this. We all are. I don't want anything to go disastrously wrong. Not now."

"I understand," Hunter said. He could see the man's shocked demeanor and understood the weight of responsibility he carried. However, Hunter didn't want to have to wait for lawyers. He might have been here the whole day if that happened.

"How about we take a look at the footage first," he suggested, "and while we do that, I ask you some background questions? If there's anything you'd rather have your lawyers present for, we can always schedule another meeting for later."

Henry Pond thought about that, frowning, clasping his hands tightly once more. "I guess that'll do," he said reluctantly. "Come this way. The footage is in the office behind the reception desk." He turned, took a deep breath, and addressed the gathered group of workers. "I know this is difficult," he told them, "but right now, we need to get back to work. Please remember that nobody is to speak to the press or the police about this except me. Take messages on my behalf, and I'll work on a media release. We don't want this tragic incident to cause us any damage, and I know Brian wouldn't want that either."

Hunter picked up the next words that were muttered under his breath. "Not with the way things are at the moment and the tactics our competitors are using, and these damned conspiracy theorists with their rumors."

With this stern warning given to his team, he turned and walked with a surprisingly light-footed gait given his size and girth, to the door behind the lobby. He unlocked it and walked in, with Hunter close behind. He was feeling extremely eager to get a look at that footage. It might give him his very first sight of the killer.

The room beyond the lobby was small and had a musty smell. It was also much warmer than outside. The walls were covered in a bank of screens, showing Hunter that several places within the building had camera footage in place.

"You want the basement cameras?"

"Both of them, please. For the entrance and the exit," Hunter said.

Frowning, Pond lowered himself onto an office chair, which his backside overflowed, and which squeaked under his weight. He grasped the mouse, pulled the keyboard toward him, typed in a code so rapidly his fingers were a blur, and then went scrolling through the footage.

"I'm going to start from now in real-time and play the recording back," he said.

"That sounds good."

Hunter watched intently. This surely must yield something.

The footage, colorful but of average quality, played back. They both tensed as the first picture blipped up on the screen. This was Brian Mitchell's car, the Porsche Cayenne, entering the basement.

Where was the killer?

Hunter watched tensely as the footage unfolded. But there was no sign of the killer entering, nor had there been any sign of him leaving. Two earlier cars arrived, but that was all.

He was not invisible, Hunter reminded himself. He must have used the exit gate, not the entrance gate. Maybe he'd thought that at this hour, with everyone arriving, it would be the better choice.

"Let's take a look at the exit," he said.

Pond twiddled the mouse and adjusted the footage, breathing deeply, his actions still clumsy with shock.

The footage scrolled back – and there! Hunter caught his breath as he saw the man leaving. It was over in a split second. Aware of the camera, the dark-clad figure had kept his head low and gone out at a run.

"Oh, dear Lord, look at that," Pond muttered, horrified. "That's the man who killed him! I can't believe I'm seeing this!"

Hunter could even pick up the silenced gun, a solid, black object with its distinctively long barrel, held in his right hand. What else could he see?

He was broad-shouldered, wearing black. Black jacket, black pants, dark gloves, and a ski mask that effectively obscured his features. With his head kept down, there wasn't any chance to see his face clearly. But he was a fairly tall man, Hunter guessed, from the length of those limbs.

The footage played back and when the time stamp hit six forty-five, he saw the man appear.

Still fast, still furtive, slinking in so quickly that there was no real opportunity to see more at a glance. But forensics might be able to assess the footage more intensively. Hunter hoped that they would be able to visit the basement, plot the image, do some measurements, and perhaps give them a more accurate height estimate.

"I'll need this footage," he said. "Can you download it for me, please?"

Pond complied. While he worked, Hunter asked the questions that he hoped might shed more light on this.

"Seems like it's a very competitive market?" he asked by way of a lead-in.

"It is. Cutthroat, one might say," Pond agreed, busy with the download.

"And Mr. Mitchell was navigating those waters successfully?"

"He was an extraordinary businessman. He was able to read the market brilliantly. He innovated points of difference in all the major toy lines we produce that allowed us to get an edge when it came to sales and marketing." Pond nodded his head, looking sad. "But over and above his head for business, he was a very ethical person. He was a stickler for doing things the right way and playing fair."

"Have you had any threats in the past? Especially recently?"

Pond thought about it and shook his head. "Look, from time to time, there's been trouble, and there are situations that have to be handled. But there's been nothing on this level or even that would point toward it."

"What about your competition?"

"We kept a close eye on them but didn't know them well. We tried to take our own path." Ponds sounded evasive, and Hunter knew he was starting to think about what he might say and whether lawyers should be involved.

With Guardian Moms in mind, his next question was, "Did Brian Mitchell ever have any dealings with Charlotte Grace from Guardian Moms? Did he ever collaborate with her? Or the opposite?"

This was the important question and the one he knew would point to the killer. Hunter was sure that the canny businessman Brian Mitchell might have joined forces with Charlotte and caused damage to an opposition company. Knowing its name could lead him to the killer.

Pond sighed. "That's going to be something we'd need our lawyers to sit in for," he said.

Hunter nodded. He was going to take that as a yes, there had been interaction between them, but that he wasn't going to learn more about it now. Still, it confirmed the existence of a link.

"You mentioned conspiracy theory websites. Is there anything circulating that might be untrue or damaging?"

Pond's shoulders rose and fell as he sighed. "Always," he said. "We're not the main target but there's a relentless flood of misinformation and weird theories circulating all the time. We've suffered from the fallout in the past. And that's all I'm willing to say."

He handed over the flash drive with the footage and Hunter put it in his bag.

Thanking Pond, Hunter left the building. As soon as he was out, he got on the radio and asked for the Mitchells' home address.

His next stop was going to be one of those interviews he dreaded. He was going to have to head to Brian Mitchell's home and speak to his widow, who would just have received the devastating news.

But as he was about to climb into his car, his eye was caught by a brightly lit shop front across the road. It was a toy store which had just opened its doors for the day.

Curious to take his first proper look at the action figures that were stirring up such fierce competition and which might be connected with these crimes, Hunter crossed the road and went in.

9
Toy Industry Rivalry

Stepping into the brightly lit toy store, Hunter headed straight to the shelves where the action figures were displayed. They were near the front of the store. Prime retail display territory. These action figures were a huge draw card.

Carl Commando's marketing was dominant. The diagonal logo, the strong, square lettering, the grays and blacks and greens, it was all Army-focused.

Amy's warning rang in his ears. He heard again his ex-wife's passionate words as he stared at the figure in the display box behind the clear plastic. Gripping his machine gun, with a handgun on his belt and a helmet on his head, Carl Commando stared blankly past him.

Beside him was a different version of the same toy, with a blue box and a blue camo uniform. Same Carl Commando figure, but slightly different accessories.

Comparing this to the competing figures, who occupied the less prime space on the sides of the display, Hunter saw that those figures had a little more detail. He thought they were better made. He hesitated, raising his hand to the boxes, wondering if Amy would agree that this one, the Peace Defender, would be a good substitute for Matthew.

But as he did, he was shouldered aside by a determined-looking woman a head shorter than him, with a wild mane of dyed red hair and an equally frantic look in her eyes.

"Excuse me! This one's mine!"

Reaching up on her tippy toes, she grabbed the very last Carl Commando figure in the blue box. Holding it tightly in her hand, she turned to Hunter. "My boy's been looking for this for weeks! It's a limited edition and I thought they'd all sold out. My advice – if you see one, buy it! These are like gold! Sorry if you wanted it, but it's mine now!"

She marched straight to the till. By the time Hunter had gotten there himself, feeling rather bemused at what had just played out, the ferociously motivated mother had left the store

"You sell a lot of the Carl Commandos?" he asked the gray-haired woman at the till.

"Yes. They're our bestseller, for sure," she replied. "The others are also popular though, and in fact at the moment, Peace Defender is selling very fast."

"Has Carl Commando changed at all, over the past year or two?" he asked.

She thought about that for a while and nodded.

"You know, now you mention it, the doll itself has changed. If you can call it a doll, of course. I've noticed that the face used to have more expression in it. It looked as if Carl Commando was about to smile. He seemed happy. His eyes were defined, there was more contrast in his lips, and his cheeks were even lightly colored. I thought of it as a well-conceptualized face because it looked so alive. But now if you take a look, the face is very blank. I guess they might have done it to cut costs, but that's the biggest change I've seen." She smiled. "The customers don't seem to mind, though."

"Thank you," Hunter said.

It was a perceptive comment. The other dolls were far more animated. And Carl Commando? She was right. The face was strangely blank.

And it hadn't been in the past?

Interesting.

Feeling thoughtful, he left the store and headed to his car.

It was time to go and speak to Brian Mitchell's widow. He hoped that she might be willing to talk without lawyers present. If so, he might get the answers that hadn't been forthcoming at Wonder Play Studios.

He wanted to know more about what theories were circulating and if the people behind the conspiracy theory websites had issued any threats. Killing a toy manufacturer and an activist? He needed to find the common thread and who would have a motive for both these deaths.

*

"Whoever did this, they are sick. They deserve the worst death ever! Life imprisonment is too good for them!"

Hunter nodded sympathetically.

He was seated in the grand living room of the Mitchells' mansion, a beachfront property with a magnificent sea view, which Hunter barely noticed. All his attention was on the slender, fragile-looking woman who was in floods of tears on her designer couch, her hands shaking with shock.

"We're going to find out who did it," he promised Brian's wife, Suzy Mitchell, knowing that the words were cold comfort. At least she was talking. In her shock and grief, the words were spilling out of her, and he was listening hard.

"He was such a good man. Such an innovator. He was a workaholic and it drove me mad sometimes." She sobbed harder. "He was everything to me. Everything." She drew in a shaky breath.

"Tell me," Hunter probed gently, "was there any trouble in his life?"

To his surprise, she nodded. "I know something was bothering him."

"What was it?" he asked.

She shrugged. "He told me he'd be home late, the night before last; that someone had requested a confidential meeting with him and it seemed to involve the industry, so he was going to find out more."

"Did he say who it was?" Hunter asked. "Or anything about the meeting?"

"I didn't get the chance to ask him about it. I mean, I tried, but he said it was very worrying and that he'd need to take action. But I didn't ask more. It sounded like a long story, and both our lives are busy, so I thought it would be better to wait. He was definitely worried, though."

"So you don't know what it might have been?"

"No idea," she said, reaching into the box in front of her for yet another tissue.

"He talked to you about work?" Hunter confirmed, wondering if Brian was one of those men who'd kept home and work life strictly separate. But Suzy nodded slightly.

"He was a workaholic," she reminded him. "He talked to everyone about his work. It was his life."

So Suzy would have known something, at least, about his situation. This looked more promising. Perhaps he would get the answer he needed now.

"I need to ask you about Guardian Moms," Hunter said. "Did your husband have any interaction with Charlotte Grace?"

"Charlotte Grace?" Taking a wobbly breath, Suzy frowned. "She was – she was killed the same way, wasn't she? Now I remember. I heard the details this morning but didn't take them in. This is – it's crazy."

"Did she and your husband work together or collaborate at all?"

"Work together?" A note of incredulity now overpowered the shock in Suzy's voice. "Why on earth would they work together? She opposed the whole idea of military toys!"

"I believe there are some conspiracy theory sites that are spreading misinformation and wild theories. Did that affect you at all? Did your husband ever try to take action against any of them?"

But to his surprise, Suzy shook her head. "Not recently, no. We've been criticized but never targeted with slanderous comments like some of the others have."

So, who would have the motive to want to murder an activist and a successful toy manufacturer? Hunter realized that the logic was now pointing to a competitor in the market. But which one?

Thinking fast, he decided to try another question.

"Of all the opposition companies in the market, was there anyone whom Brian had particularly bad blood with?" he asked. "Or were there any of them who targeted your husband's company in a hostile way?" he asked.

She thought about that, frowning.

"Yes," she said. "That, I can tell you. It was a man called Nicholas Taylor whom Brian mentioned fairly often. He was Brian's biggest rival, he had a terrible reputation in the industry, and he hated the activists. Brian always said out of all his competition, he was the one he'd never trust not to play dirty."

Nicholas Taylor? An opposition toy manufacturer who hated activists and had a reputation for dirty tactics?

Hunter knew where he was heading next.

10
Virtual Reality

Daniel Bridges stared at the Play button eagerly, his finger hovering over it. He sensed this was a pivotal moment; it was the start of something that could take him to new heights.

He was in the top five percent of players and that was an honor. He wondered what it would mean. Maybe it would mean that he'd be able to attend one of the in-person Commando rallies that had been happening recently as a group leader. There hadn't been one in his area yet, but he'd seen photos, and they were amazing, with record numbers of kids and teens attending. They gave you a lot of free stuff. Jackets and Carl Commando water bottles and backpacks. His parents had already said that if he got free stuff, he could go.

Maybe this would be a lead-in to it?

The morning was quiet now; most of the people on his floor in the ramshackle apartment building had already left for work. He'd heard their footsteps and voices passing by through the thin walls.

He should be at school, but he'd decided to skip it today. He hadn't told anyone, of course. He'd gone out the apartment the same way he always did, and he'd walked his little brother across the road and seen Luke off on the bus to his junior school. He'd never shirk that responsibility, especially seeing nobody else, including his mother, cared for him.

But then, Daniel had doubled back and let himself into the apartment again because he couldn't wait. The temptation of the game's next level was too strong. He couldn't wait and play it tonight because he'd be back in the game with his team again. Now was the best time.

He needed to know what was going to happen in the combat zone.

Feeling a flare of excitement, he pressed Play.

"Are you ready, Captain Dan?" the words flashed up on the screen, crimson on black. *"This is your most dangerous mission yet. You're alone, in enemy territory. You have to fight your way back to your unit. This is a solo mission. No help, no support, no backup. Just you, alone. And you need to give it everything, to destroy every one of your adversaries."*

He swallowed, his hands gripping the game's controls as he watched the words slowly fade out.

Immediately, he was in the throes of battle.

But these weren't the game's usual visuals, he realized, adrenaline surging as he absorbed the unfamiliarity of it all.

This was *real*. Not game avatars, not game landscapes. It was as if he had landed in an actual battle scene. There was a man rushing him – not an animated figure but an actual man who looked like a real live human. And he was in the enemy's colors. That meant he had to die.

It felt weird doing this, different, and he hesitated for a moment as he raised his gun because firing it at an image of an actual human felt as if he was crossing a line. But he reminded himself this was war.

He fired. The hesitation almost cost him everything. Enemy fire crashed and stuttered back in his direction, and he wrenched himself sideways, sprawling down behind a chunk of concrete. More gunfire, this time from behind. With his reactions faster than thought, he twisted around and fired. One down, two down, but he felt a chill because the second one was looking straight into his eyes. It was almost as if he saw a mute appeal there.

And then, it got worse as a third stepped out from behind a crumbling pillar, holding up his hands in a gesture of surrender.

"Please, spare me! I'm out of ammo'!" he begged; his voice hoarse.

"No, man! Jeez, what is this?" Daniel muttered. His hands were trembling, his heart was racing. This was a situation he'd never encountered before. But he remembered his instructions at the start of the game. Destroy every one of your adversaries, he'd been ordered.

And out of ammo didn't mean he was any less of a deadly threat, Daniel knew. What if he achieved a new level and got fresh ammo allocated to him?

"Dude, I'm sorry, I'm really sorry, but I can't," he said, tight-lipped. "This is war."

It was not easy raising the gun and firing it directly at a man who was staring at him, his hands raised in appeal.

But he told himself in a moment it would be over.

He fired and watched as the man toppled over, clutching at his throat, looking so real, so human. Briefly, a wave of nausea washed over Daniel, and he breathed deeply to suppress it. Then the screen froze, and he felt anxiety flare, as if perhaps he was going to be punished for what he'd done, and it had been the wrong decision after all to kill that unarmed man.

But then a figure appeared on the screen and a voice ran out.

"Hit the floor, soldier! Forty push-ups!"

Daniel's eyes widened. This was Mike the Marine – again, a real-life depiction of a game avatar, his strong-jawed face filling the screen, his broad-shouldered stance strong and authoritative.

This was amazing!

Mike the Marine was an optional extra that you had to pay to subscribe to if you wanted his voice and his leadership during the fitness sessions. Daniel hadn't been able to afford that, so he'd gone for the plain avatar.

Now he was getting Mike the Marine, in real life and for free? How he wished he could tell the others! If only he could – but this was top secret, and he wouldn't be able to boast about what he'd earned.

He hit the floor, pumping out the forty push-ups as fast as he could, listening to Mike the Marine's throaty voice counting them down, feeling as if the tough marine was actually watching Daniel work his way through the physical test. Forty was a lot. More than he'd ever had to do before, and his arms were shaking by the time he completed the set. The last few were an uphill battle, his muscles screaming, his teeth clenching as he forced himself to keep up with the pace that Mike the Marine was setting.

His arms felt so weak he could barely grasp the controls again as he got back into his chair.

"Well done, soldier! You're the caliber we need. You've achieved the pace and the time. Now, give me one hundred jogs on the spot!"

And Daniel was up again, this time able to watch the screen and see Mike the Marine jogging with him, setting a relentlessly fast pace, getting his knees high in the air, his limbs working, his feet stamping. And Daniel – or rather, Captain Dan – jogged alongside, matching him stride for stride, thinking this was amazing, that it was like being in a real PT class. Normally there was only one challenge before the game commenced. This was very different. It was tougher in every way, and it was testing his caliber as no game had done before.

Gasping for air, he completed the set. Now both his legs and his arms felt like they'd had a major workout as he got back into his chair.

"Sit straight, soldier," the game control told him. *"You've got one more line of enemy soldiers to get through. Remember, you need to destroy them all in order to gain your level."*

At least nothing could be as hectic as what he'd just gone through, Daniel thought, preparing himself for the next lightning-fast round of battle. Or so he thought.

He fought his way through the enemy's frontline, now becoming used to the ultra-realism of the game. After the initial shock, it now felt more normal to be firing at real-looking humans. This was, after all, battle combat.

But then the last soldier appeared on his screen.

Once more he hesitated, thrown all over again by what he saw.

She was a woman. He'd never faced a woman combatant before. She was ultra-real, clearly human and she was beautiful with flashing, dark eyes, and hair in a thick braid down her back, and a curvaceous figure that he could see even through the dark gray camouflage she wore.

A woman! He didn't know how he felt about that. She wasn't carrying a firearm, only a silver-bladed knife.

But before he had the chance to analyze his feelings too closely, he lifted his gun, remembering the orders that the game had issued. It didn't feel right to shoot her, but it was only a game. Just something he needed to do to achieve this next level.

He was surprised by the lack of emotion he felt as his bullet tore into her chest and she was down, clutching at the wound with her hands, writhing briefly in pain.

And then he'd made it. He was through. The music was playing even as his adrenaline surged.

He waited for the congratulatory message to appear on the screen, feeling proud. But his high spirits curdled into anxiety as no such message flashed up.

Instead, the screen darkened.

"Captain Dan, your mission continues. You have a compulsory two-hour rest break. And then, you may resume at any time. You will be in urban territory and inside enemy lines. You will have to fight your way to the other side, destroying everyone you see. Fail, and your mission is over. Succeed, and you will be one of an elite few. Further opportunities will await.

Press Continue when you're ready and the two-hour countdown will commence."

So it wasn't over yet? Perplexed, he barely hesitated before stabbing Continue and checking his watch to see when the frustrating break would be over.

He wanted to see what would happen next and how far the game would push him, even though he hoped that the next phase wouldn't be as intense as what he'd just been through.

Surely it would be back to the avatars again.

But he had to admit, in a dark part of his mind, that he wouldn't mind if it wasn't. There was an adrenaline rush to be found in killing these real-looking humans.

He thought he might be getting addicted to it.

11
Corporate Intrigue

Hunter had never thought that a toy manufacturing company's headquarters could have an intimidating feel to them. But as he walked up to the steel double doorway of the square building where Sparkle Grove Entertainment was located, looking at the shutters on the first floor and the expanse of paving unpunctuated by greenery, he couldn't help feeling unwelcome.

He had the strong impression that this company held its secrets close.

When he walked in, the brisk and impersonal ambiance inside immediately reinforced that impression.

"Detective Hunter Harden," he said to the receptionist. "I'm here to see Nicholas Taylor, your CEO."

He showed his police badge to the young brunette woman, who raised her well-groomed eyebrows.

"Mr. Taylor is upstairs in the boardroom," she said, in a tone that clearly conveyed this area to be sacrosanct.

"I guess that's where I'll be heading then," Hunter said, and her eyebrows rose still higher.

"But you can't just walk in and interrupt a meeting," she protested with all the authority of her twenty-odd years.

"This is police business," Hunter said, his tone firm. "My team and I are investigating multiple murders. Mr. Taylor may have important information. So, either you call ahead and ask him for a few minutes of his time or else I'll start knocking on doors upstairs and see who can give me some answers."

"Let me – let me call him quick," she said.

She got on the phone and spoke rapidly, and then nodded.

"He'll see you in the downstairs meeting room," she said, still managing to imply that her CEO was bestowing an enormous favor upon the police.

"I appreciate it," Hunter said courteously, remaining gracious in victory.

She got up and headed along the corridor to a small, windowless meeting room equipped with a round table and four steel gray chairs. Hunter sat down and waited. He'd expected that Sparkle Grove Entertainment would espouse some of the ethos that he believed a toy manufacturer would have had. A sense of fun, for instance? That seemed notably lacking in this efficient and bleak-looking setup.

There weren't even pictures of toys on the walls. What Hunter saw was enlarged, framed posters that were milestones of the company's success. Reports, press releases, and financial news items. It was very clear to him that this achievement was the company's point of pride.

Footsteps outside signaled the CEO's arrival and a moment later, a man in his early forties with dark brown hair and a small goatee camouflaging the roundness of his face, swept in.

"I understand you're police?" he said, with a dubious look at Hunter's white button-down shirt and gray suit pants, as if he'd expected a uniform.

Hunter showed his badge. "LAPD detective Harden," he said.

"I'm Nick Taylor, CEO. And you're here why?" Hunter could hear in Taylor's voice that he already had an idea of why. He wasn't coming into this completely cold. But he didn't know how much of an idea. This man wasn't giving anything away. His eyes – a dark brown– were shuttered and Hunter couldn't read them.

Automatically, Hunter assessed his build, comparing it to the momentary glimpse he had seen on the cameras earlier. This man was within the attacker's physical parameters – he was broad-shouldered and probably five-ten in height. Could he have moved so fast and lithely? That was another question.

Right now, Hunter knew it was the mental agility of this suspect that he needed to test rather than the physical ability. Because if he was the killer, there was no way he was going to admit to it.

"There have been two murders in the past two days and they're both connected to the toy industry," he said.

Now, Taylor frowned. "That doesn't involve our company at all. I'm struggling to understand why you're here. You've called me out of a high-level meeting, and I'd like to make the best use of my time now if you get me."

His comment, borderline rude, was stated in the same flat tone that he'd used all along.

"Tell me about your relationship with the victims," Hunter said, ignoring the hint. "Let's start with Brian Mitchell. And please, sit down. I understand your high-level meeting awaits but I'd appreciate your full attention before you resume it."

Taylor's eyes narrowed slightly. He was annoyed at being called out on his behavior. Well, Hunter acknowledged, he was never going to have gotten this meeting off on a good footing. If Taylor revealed anything, it wasn't going to be because he was being cooperative. Rather, it was going to be because Hunter managed to trap him into letting something slip.

And he did, at least, pull out one of those gray chairs and sit down, with his left elbow on the table and his right hand on his phone, as if wanting to emphasize that he was simply too busy to let go of it.

"So," Hunter continued. "Brian Mitchell. Tell me more about your recent dealings with him."

Taylor's face was stone. "Mitchell was a competitor. There's not much more I can say. I don't believe we're in business to cooperate with each other and be nice. It's a tough, brutal market out there. A couple of bad decisions or unlucky breaks when your competition gets lucky, and you can go under. I had that happen to me in the past, years ago. I failed because I was too kind."

"You did?" That was interesting. Hunter didn't know how true this statement might be, but Taylor clearly believed it.

"I don't work with any of my opposition. I treat them as a threat. I don't collaborate and if I see a weakness, I'll exploit it."

"Who's your biggest rival?"

"The market leader, of course. Dreamland Creations, with that Carl Commando toy. Although my feeling is that they're going down the wrong road with it. Which is good." He gave a quick, sly smile.

"The wrong road?"

"That ultra-military focus is going to backfire on them and if they don't realize their competitors are also making sure that bad publicity comes their way, they're way more stupid than I gave them credit for," he said disparagingly.

"And how about Mitchell?" Hunter asked, remembering what Mitchell's wife had said about the particular animosity Taylor had shown toward him.

Taylor narrowed his eyes still further. "We were watching him carefully. He was making inroads into the market, and I'd be lying if I said they weren't affecting us. So yes, we had strategies in place. We do for all our competitors."

"Involving?"

Taylor shrugged, looking furtive.

"If you want to know whether they included murder, of course they didn't."

"Where were you this morning?" he asked, wondering if Taylor could account for his time when Mitchell was murdered. "Can you tell me about your movements earlier?"

"I was at home, then at the gym, then at work. I see where this is going. I wasn't running around with a gun if that's what you're asking. And I was nowhere near Mitchell's premises." His smile was more of a sneer and there was a taunting confidence to his words. Hunter had an inkling that he would, in fact, be able to account for his time – on paper, at any rate. He had the feeling that this sly CEO might take delight in trapping him and turning the tables on Hunter for having dared to suspect him.

"What about yesterday afternoon?"

"I was at work and then I went to the factory to sort out a few glitches. I was there until about five or six p.m., I guess. I didn't look at the time. I'm the CEO. I don't clock in or out."

Hunter was disliking Taylor more with every minute that passed – but he was also not going to make the mistake of underestimating him.

"Tell me how you feel about the advocacy groups – like Guardian Moms. Did you have any interaction with them? I'm sure you heard that Charlotte Grace was murdered?"

Taylor shrugged. "I am sorry she died," he said, not sounding sorry at all.

"Did she impact your business?"

He shrugged. "She was an irritation and yes, she cost us money. It's no secret that I hate those advocacy groups. They're attention seekers. They're the kind of people who would ruin the economy to prove their point. That's how irrational they are. I had a few clashes with Charlotte Grace. She was completely off the rails. Look, I know her son was killed in a tragic incident, it was sad and unfortunate, but she took the concept of payback way too far."

"You think?" Hunter asked, listening carefully.

"My lawyers knew about her and acted on my behalf when she got out of line. She knew she couldn't mess with me and that I would push back." He stared at Hunter unblinkingly. "And that goes for the others, too. That man from the National Peace Alliance is just as bad. He's fundraising nonstop, he's creating emotional arguments from nonexistent premises, and he's looking to enrich himself at our expense. That's just the way he's chosen to do it."

"That's an interesting perspective," Hunter said.

"And as for that other extremist, the one who's running that new local advocacy group, I'm busy researching them as well."

"Who are they?" Hunter asked, but Taylor shrugged.

"Some coward hiding behind the name of the organization, No To Violence. I'm not going to let someone's misguided agenda destroy me and when I find out more about that group, I'm going to crush it. And the same goes for the conspiracy theorists. They think they can hide under the cover of their sites. If their slander affects me, I root them out and make them pay." He let out a frustrated breath. But anyway, back to Charlotte Grace. Someone like that – an extremist, who's not prepared to compromise or see reason – is going to make enemies. A lot of them."

"The same enemies that Brian Mitchell had?" Hunter asked.

Taylor stared at him and this time, he saw aggression in his gaze.

"I did not commit that murder. And if you continue implying that I did, then I'm warning you, you're going to make an enemy out of me. Leave me alone to do my business, Detective. I don't think this conversation can go any further."

He stood up. But as he was at the door, Hunter's voice stopped him.

"One more thing, Mr. Taylor," he called out, also rising to his feet as Taylor swung around to face him.

"What?" he asked irritably. "What is it?"

"You do realize that you could also be at risk?"

"Me?" The word sounded guarded, but he caught a flash of surprise in Taylor's eyes.

"You might want to take extra precautions for the next while. Until we have a suspect in custody."

"Thank you for the advice." He didn't sound in the least thankful, though. "I'll do what I see fit. I doubt I'm at risk. I intend to carry on going about my work. And I suggest you carry on going about yours." There was a distinct note of threat in his voice as he turned and strode out.

Hunter let him go. For now.

Although this interview had increased his suspicions, he knew he'd have to dig deeper if he was going to get answers.

It was time to find out more about the company where all the trouble seemed to have originated and where all the outcry seemed to be focused.

Dreamland Creations. They were the market leader – but how far would they have gone to protect this position?

12
Corporate Interrogation

Just as Hunter arrived at Dreamland Creations' offices, his phone rang. It was Cody calling from the LAPD offices.

"Listen," he said. "I've got some news for you."

"What news?" Hunter waited in the parking lot, listening hard, looking at the afternoon sky which was clouding over again and at the offices of Dreamland Creations, which looked the most expensive and well-equipped of all the setups he'd visited so far.

"I've got the second lot of footage, or rather, the first. It's the one from the camera outside Charlotte Grace's house."

"The footage?" Hunter sat up straighter. "What does it show?"

"I've played the two sets," Cody said. "And my feeling is that they're identical. The one outside Charlotte Grace's house just shows the killer fleeing. There's a two-second clip of him racing into the frame and out again. Then he hotfoots it down the hill and out of sight. I'm getting forensics to confirm but it looks like the same guy. Same build, same clothing. Same ski mask."

"Any other identifying features?" Hunter asked, thinking again of the unpleasant Nick Taylor.

"Nothing so far. We're working on it."

"When you say, 'working on it', Hunter asked, "What are your chances of success?"

Cody had experience in forensics. Hunter trusted his opinion and when Cody gave a heavy, reluctant sigh, Hunter knew that this was not going to help them.

"The problem is that it will take time," he said. "The analytics can be done but you won't get it tomorrow. Maybe not even in a couple of weeks. They could find something down the line that helps prevent the case from going cold, but that's about it. It won't get you a quick result."

"What about the bullets at the two different scenes? Were they fired from the same gun?"

"They're still being analyzed. Might take another few days."

"Appreciate the information anyway," Hunter said. "In that case, what we know, we know."

Everything took time. Analyzing bullets, accessing phones. It seemed nothing would get done in the timeframe Hunter was hoping for.

Frustrating as it was not to have more answers yet from the evidence, Hunter headed through the doors, hoping that they would be found here instead.

Inside the colorful, cheerful, creative environment of Dreamland Creations, massive motifs of dolls were displayed on the wall. It seemed like the wall was a piece of history that followed the evolution of their most famous toys from conception to their current success.

"I'm here to see Olivia Montgomery," Hunter said, showing his badge yet again.

"This'll be in connection with – with the trouble?" the receptionist asked. She was a youthful, slender woman with a mane of dark, curly hair, and Hunter appreciated her forthrightness.

"Yes, that's right," he said.

"I'm going to call her now," she said.

Hunter didn't have long to wait. In a few moments, the elevator chimed and a regal-looking woman with shiny dark hair and wearing a power suit strode toward him. Behind her, following at a flustered rush was a younger-looking woman with curly chestnut hair, clutching at a clipboard and a notebook.

"I'm Olivia Montgomery," she said, holding out her hand. There was an air of assurance about her that Hunter immediately noted. However, she was most definitely not the figure in the camera shots. Her narrow shoulders and slim figure precluded that. She could have arranged the murder – not for a moment was he ruling that out. But she hadn't been captured in the frame.

"Detective Hunter Harden," he said. "Can we talk somewhere, for a few minutes?"

"Yes, of course," she said. "Come through to our playroom. That's what we call the meeting room. Company ethos, you know?"

A few yards down the corridor, it was a colorful and welcoming room, where again, the company's products and heritage were promoted front and center. He noted immediately the presence of Carl Commando, his figure imposing and subdued among the other, brighter toys.

"This is my assistant, Amelia Evans." Olivia introduced the younger woman. "She's only started with us today, so she's been thrown in the deep end." She smiled ruefully.

Amelia gave Hunter a wide-eyed glance and a quick, apologetic nod.

"Wishing you all the best in your new job," he said politely. "Now, I have a few questions about this unfortunate set of circumstances that's brought me here."

Olivia nodded. "With a competitor and an activist murdered, I'm sure you must be scrutinizing everyone. And we are the leader. We're the ones who take the lion's share of the criticism and the bad press."

"Do you have a lot of dealings with your competitors?" Hunter asked. "Do you ever collaborate with them?"

He thought he saw something in her eyes as he asked that question, but it was no more than a flicker.

"No. I never even contemplate that as there has never been a need," Olivia said, smoothing a hand over her sleek hair. She was calm and composed. "We are the market leader, we're the one who sets the trends. As such, I'm very aware of copycats and people who are looking to steal our intellectual property. So we remain apart and ahead."

Hunter was watching her carefully, interested in her reactions to his questions. She was a wealthy and powerful woman. Her company had a massive reputation to defend. She had already admitted that she was targeted in terms of criticism and negativity. But so far, he felt he hadn't got a clear answer from anyone else on the exact dynamic between these fierce competitors. He'd had hints and allusions, he'd had denials. But he was waiting, still, for the kernel of truth to emerge.

"It seems that your most famous toy, Carl Commando, has changed its focus over the past couple of years. Why was that?" he asked.

Olivia smiled, a bland expression.

"It was a mutually agreed progression. We're all behind the look and the ethos of the new Carl Commando."

That was what Olivia was saying and Hunter heard the words clearly.

But her assistant's face was saying something different, and he saw the discrepancy as he listened to her boss. Amelia's eyes were just about popping out of her head with surprise at her boss's words, even though her mouth was clamped tightly shut. As if to deflect any attention from her surprise, she quickly grabbed a pen and began jotting something down on a piece of paper.

Hmmm, Hunter thought. There were things he wasn't being told.

"So nobody in the company thinks otherwise?" he confirmed, watching Amelia turn bright red with the effort of concealing what he guessed was the truth.

"We, the management team of a leading Fortune 500 company, have mutually agreed on a direction," Olivia said. "It takes the toy more into the domain of the military than it previously was, and we did that to further differentiate it from its competitors and also to build on the expectations that people have for Carl Commando. There's a strongly positive brand awareness about the toy and in fact, a lot of our fans feel that it represents all the best qualities and attributes of the US military itself." She smiled. "Detective Harden, I want you to understand this. I am a single mother. My son plays with Carl Commando toys. All I see from the toy is positive results. He's outdoors, he's active, he's engaged with his friends. He's learning physical skills. I see why people love the brand and its ethos, because I love it too, as a parent. The military theme is secondary but it's what everyone latches onto."

So, Olivia – a single mother – walked her talk with her own son? That was interesting, assuming it was true.

"Even so, you must have attracted a lot of criticism from the anti-violence groups and the watchdog associations?" Hunter asked.

"Absolutely," Olivia agreed. "But that's inevitable. When you take a stance, you will attract criticism for it. We have chosen to maintain our well-loved brand in the style that the consumer wants and expects. Of course, it will attract some criticism. In a way, we welcome it because it draws attention to the product."

"No publicity is bad publicity?" Hunter questioned.

"Exactly," Olivia said.

"So you don't have any issues with any of these associations?"

"Not any issues at all. They are fringe organizations. They don't impact on us."

"I believe there are some theories circulating about military toys. From conspiracy theorists? Have you heard those?" he asked.

"I have not. I don't focus on irrelevant issues. People who believe conspiracy theories will find they're never short of new, flaky theories to chase after. I'm too busy for that. We know there is no truth to any of the rumors and we simply ignore them."

Again, Hunter was talking to Olivia, but he was watching Amelia, and her face was telling him something different. The mention of the conspiracy theories had made her concerned. That was clear.

This woman had been here less than a day. Why was she so anxious? And why was her face telling him that Olivia was lying?

"Does everyone in your company feel likewise?" Hunter asked, wondering if there was any conflict here.

"Although our executive team all have our own opinions and we retain agency for our areas of expertise when it comes to company policy, we think and speak as one," Olivia replied. Hunter watched with interest, wondering if steam was actually going to come out of the assistant's ears soon. Amelia's unspoken reaction was telling him so much more than Olivia's words.

"I heard, from a relative of one of the victims, that some of the companies resort to underhanded tactics. Have you ever had that experience?" As she drew breath, he raised a warning hand.

"Ms. Montgomery, I get the clear impression that you are trying to protect your company's reputation and your team. I understand that. But I can't sit here and listen to canned, generalized responses. If I feel that I'm not getting the truth from you, then I'm going to bring in a team of detectives and we're going to separately interview every single person who works here. It will probably be much more time-consuming than what we're doing now."

Even then, his threat didn't have quite the effect he hoped for. Olivia's face remained inscrutable.

"We need leads," he said. "If we don't get the leads we need, then everyone's at risk. The victims so far have been killed suddenly and violently. My main priority is to prevent that from happening again. It might happen to somebody else. Perhaps even yourself."

But still, Olivia said nothing.

"I wish I could help you, Detective," she said. "But I've told you all I know and there truly is nothing more I can say. I don't know who this killer is. I definitely don't suspect any of my team of being involved. And I don't know how I can help you further."

She might not be willing to talk but Hunter felt sure that the assistant knew more.

Dreamland Creations was a battleground, and as a new employee who was close to the CEO, she might be getting pressurized from outside sources.

He needed to find out if this was correct and to strategize how he could do it.

As Hunter walked out of the boardroom and headed back into the parking lot, his phone rang.

"Detective Harden?" The woman's voice was breathy and stressed. "Am I speaking to the right person? You're handling the – the murder case, for Charlotte? Charlotte Grace?"

"Yes," he said. "I am."

"I'm Debbie. I'm Charlotte's friend and the person assisting her in the Guardian Moms office. I've been on an airplane overseas and just heard this news. I'm sitting here in London now, for a friend's birthday party, feeling totally confused and stressed out."

Hunter was glad she'd called. Now he was speaking to somebody who hopefully did know Charlotte well. And more than that, Debbie might be able to shed some light on the wild rumors and misinformation – if that was what they were.

Given these two brutal murders, he was starting to think there might be a thread of truth in them.

13
Virtual Moral Dilemma

The clock was finishing its countdown and Daniel could hardly wait. He felt strangely exhausted – drained from the relentless action of the battlefield he'd been in, but at the same time, elated. He felt an adrenaline high.

And now, at last, the final seconds were ticking away, and he was permitted to move on to the game's next level.

He wasn't going to wait any longer but was going to dive straight in. He was desperate to know what would be next up in his solo game mission. He'd had Mike the Marine. Would he get him again? Or might there be something even better awaiting him?

Settling himself into his chair, he made sure that his phone was on charge and the bedroom door was closed. He checked his emails and messages, noticing he'd had a few junk mails come in, a couple of marketing mails, but nothing from school. He was keeping a close eye out for any school communications since he'd skipped today.

For the same reason, he was staying off social media. They didn't need to see him commenting and posting all over the place on a day when he was supposed to be ill. Even during the two-hour waiting period that the game had insisted on, he'd sat on his hands and refrained from commenting.

He'd had a couple of messages from his friends at school and he'd ignored those, too. He'd ignored the chit-chat on the group that he and a few others were in for remedial math.

He had also received a few new emails and messages from the Army recruitment offices, which he looked forward to reading when he'd finished this level of the game because they always made him feel excited. He'd signed up online a while ago to express his interest and since then, the guys had been following up. After the success he and his team had enjoyed in the game, Daniel was keen to join up and experience the real thing. He knew his passion and ability lay in that direction.

Hell, he wished he could do it now and not have to slog through this last year of school.

It gave him a sense of pride to know he was needed there, to know that there was a job and a future waiting for him when he was done with school. An exciting one with prospects. They wanted him and in fact, wanted him as one of the elite intakes. He just had to choose – would it be the Army or the Navy? One of the two for sure but he hadn't made a decision yet and was devouring all the information on both these career directions that he was sent.

He *wasn't* going to end up like his dad, a couch potato who kept getting fired from his jobs and went on regular alcoholic benders.

No, he was going to be different. He was going to be the strong, successful man that he knew his mother always wanted him to be.

Okay, skipping school today was a blot on his copybook, he acknowledged. Successful people didn't do that. He'd always told his little brother so. But he was doing it just this once, for this important reason.

It was time to play.

Feeling expectant, his pulse pounding, he pressed the button to start.

But then, he stared in surprise.

He wasn't back in the game at all. He was somewhere else entirely. He'd been routed to a screen on which a large message appeared.

"Psychometric Test Process is Commencing Now."

Psychometric tests? What were they? He didn't like the sound of that. The mere word 'test' struck fear into him because he knew he wasn't the best at them at school and the pressure always made him feel sick.

Was this, like, some kind of virus that the game had produced? Was it malfunctioning or had it taken him to a spam site by mistake? Anxiety flared and his finger hovered over the Escape button.

But then, the screen lit up again and he saw it was a personal message for him.

"Captain Dan," the words read, *"You've excelled so far. These tests are an essential assessment process so that the next level of the game can challenge your strengths as well as your weaknesses. Answer the questions immediately and honestly. Do not lie. Do not tell us what you think we want to hear. Note down your instinctive reactions. Only this way will the next level of the game be the truest challenge."*

He frowned. Well, okay. That made sense. It was weird and it might mean this next level was even harder. But he'd better not fudge the answers. Truthfulness was going to be key.

"Remember, respond fast," the message flashed brighter, in red, before fading.

And then, the questions began. A barrage of them, fast and confusing and with no seeming logic to them at all.

This was exactly like a school test, and he felt briefly terrified that he was going to fail. Then, gritting his teeth, he remembered that he was Captain Dan, fast and decisive and that he was not going to fail, but to succeed.

After all, this wasn't a test. It wasn't having to know the answers. It was only telling the truth, at a very fast speed.

"What's your favorite color?"
"Red."
"Do you believe in religion?"
He hesitated. *"No."*
"What's the furthest you've run in a day?"
"9 miles." It didn't sound like much.
"Pick one. Music or swimming."
Swimming.
"Height and weight, soldier."
"6 ft, 155 pounds."
"Have you ever stolen anything?"

His mind immediately veered back to the sweetshop when he was a kid.

"Yes."
"Do you hate your father?"

He stared at the screen in concern. How could he answer that? That was a terrible question. The response that he instinctively wanted to give was more shameful still.

A red light started flashing, counting down. *"You have not answered. Automatic fail in 5..4..3.."*

104

"Yes," he typed in, breathing hard. Might as well be truthful, he thought defiantly. You wanted it, you got it.

More questions. Questions about his love life or lack of it. Then about his foods, then about his sleep, then about his dreams, and the movies he watched, and every so often, a shocking one thrown into the mix. Like what he'd do in a certain situation, like if he'd kill if he had a choice, like *who* he'd kill if he had a choice.

And then, abruptly, the interrogation was over. And Daniel found himself flung back into the game without as much as a warning.

Just a message. In red, meaning it was one of the urgent ones.

To fight your way through this urban game level, your instructions are to kill everyone you see. You have no friends here. You are alone.

The words faded out. He felt his pulse accelerate, felt the dampness in his hands.

And then, he was in a street that looked like it had been shot to bits with machine gun fire and then had the guts bombed out of it. Crumbling walls, smashed windows, uneven paving stones. He was in the middle of the damned street! Like having a target painted on his forehead.

He dove right just as bright yellow gunfire crackled from the shadows ahead. One nanosecond slower and his special game would have been over, and all that soul-destroying and disturbing questioning would have been for nothing. Hands shaking, he huddled in the flimsy shelter of a doorframe. This game level was not going to play fair, that, he sensed strongly.

He grabbed for his weapon, noting immediately that he was low on ammo, remembering the stolen gun he'd gained at the end of the last game from the woman who'd looked into his eyes with a silent appeal before he'd shot her.

Grabbing that gun, he returned the fire. It was difficult to see in the shadows, but in between the volleys he took in his surroundings.

The door to his left was locked. He couldn't get into the building. And behind him was a pile of rubble so high he couldn't climb it. The only way out was ahead, down the street, from where that gunfire was coming. That was where he'd have to go. He wasn't sure how. It seemed impossible. Maybe it was, he thought, allowing himself to entertain the despairing thought for only a moment before his resolve took over. He was going to get out. He was going to make it through, even though he wasn't sure how.

Peering around the crumbling doorframe, he aimed and fired, looking for the muzzle flash, keeping low, because they would expect him to be at head height and would be returning fire at that angle.

A pause in the fire allowed him to burst out from his flimsy hiding place and sprint further down the street, getting to a broken wall that provided much better cover to shoot from.

Fire from another direction caused him to duck, his adrenaline surging. They were shooting at him from a window. Nowhere was safe! This game was rigged, they had a huge advantage. Was he being set up to lose?

But there was someone in the window. If he got them now… he aimed, fired, and felt a vicious surge of satisfaction as the man toppled out, landing in the street. Quicker than he'd believed possible, he rushed over and disarmed him, flattening himself behind the prone body and using it for cover until he'd subdued the fire from down the street, which allowed him to make yet more, hard-earned, headway.

"Okay, I'm going to get you. I'm going to get you."

Finally, a shaft of sunlight offered some watery illumination, giving him a view of what was ahead. He then saw the knot of enemy soldiers, clustered behind a broken-down water tank. Raising both his stolen guns together, one in each hand, he fired. This was tough, so tough. They were refusing to go down, and now he was getting hostile fire from another window.

With his breath ragged, and his hands tight on the controls, he battled for progress. And he made it! Finally. One soldier down, then another. Another body out the window. Then a third at the road's end. Breathing out, he rushed forward. He was at a crossroads now, staring left and right. Left, the road was blocked.

To his consternation, as he looked right he saw something he'd never expected to see.

He swallowed hard, his hands slipping on the controls, tension filling him.

This was not the battle scene he'd expected to find.

Instead, he saw an ordinary street with an everyday feel to it. There was a bicycle parked by a lamp post and a delivery truck nearby. A baker was carrying a tray of goods across the road.

A baker? He stared incredulously at the sight. He couldn't shoot a baker. He'd somehow strayed into civilian territory. He should turn back. But how? The other way was blocked.

The thought crept into his mind: was this a test?

Dread filled him as he considered his options. This must be a test. His instructions were very clear. There had been no room for doubt or second-guessing at all. He'd been told to shoot everybody, and that doing so was the only way to achieve the next level. He had not yet achieved the next level and he was still trapped in this urban battlefield.

And that meant he had to follow the instructions he'd received at the start.

He raised his gun. This didn't feel right. The ultra-reality of the scene wasn't helping. This was a real-looking, innocent-seeming man. He had a slight paunch that swelled under his apron, a round, pleasant face, and he was balancing the tray of bread rolls on his shoulder with both hands.

"It's just a game," Daniel reminded himself. "It's a test. Do it! It's only a make-believe figure. Pretend it's someone you hate."

Pretend it's your father...

The words flared unbidden in his mind and almost reflexively, he pulled the trigger.

The baker twisted, his face tautening with pain, the tray on his shoulder tilting and rolls spilling down everywhere around him as he fell, writhing on the ground, screaming for help.

"Jeez," Daniel muttered through gritted teeth, staring at the scene, unable to take his eyes off it as he processed what he'd just done.

And then, a new figure ran into view.

He hadn't thought it could get worse than what he'd just done. Now, he was questioning the wisdom of having done this at all.

This – this was as bad as it could get.

If he went ahead with what he was being told to do, he wouldn't feel the same about himself. Ever.

14

Government Visit Adds Tension

"Tell me, Debbie," Hunter asked as he walked across the parking lot of Dreamland Creations, heading for his car. "Were there any problems in Charlotte's life? Anything out of the ordinary happening, any threats, anything she was worried about?"

"Yes," she said immediately.

"What was that?" Hunter asked, his focus sharpening.

"She mentioned to me, just two days before I left, that she suspected she was being followed. That she'd seen someone whom she thought was watching her."

Now, Hunter's spine prickled. Followed?

"Do you know the details? When and where?"

There was a short silence during which he guessed that Debbie was trying to get her flustered thoughts in order.

"She didn't say but she spoke to me just after she'd come home at night. So I think it might have been there. I wish I'd asked her about it in more detail. I was so concerned by it, but she was the one who didn't want to talk about it and who moved on and started discussing work."

At home? That sounded likely to Hunter. What had happened? Had this killer been on site, staking out the home a day or two before committing the crime? And had Charlotte noticed him there?

Now, time to find out about the conspiracy theory sites and the project that Charlotte's husband had told Hunter she'd been working on when he'd last spoken to her.

"I know that Charlotte got her information from a number of different places and that she worked on various projects. Maybe you'd call them exposes?"

"Yes," Debbie said. "That's correct. That's exactly what she did.

"What was she working on a few months ago? I believe it was something big?"

Debbie sighed. "I wish I could help you but a few months ago I wasn't working with her. I only joined her full-time last month."

"And? Was there anything important that she was focusing on?"

He didn't want to mention Carl Commando unless she did. It would be better to leave this open-ended, he thought.

"She had a couple of projects," Debbie said hesitantly. "I don't know what they were, though. She didn't like to give out information like that until she had everything ready to go. That was because there were times when she did that that backfired on her. She ended up being criticized for spreading misinformation, fearmongering and being reckless. I know she even had a couple of lawsuits to handle a while ago, defamation suits. So she was very careful."

The information might be on her phone, Hunter knew. But they had discovered that the screen was broken when it was taken into evidence. Despite taking the pains to replace the screen, Hunter was informed just this morning that the phone lock was fingerprint-activated. All this to say that Charlotte's phone could not yet be accessed.

"In particular, anything about Carl Commando or Dreamland Creations?"

Debbie hesitated. "Yes," she said. "Yes, she was working on something linked to that. It's a familiar name and I did hear her mention it."

Hunter was frustrated that he was so close, but still so far.

"Were there any journalists or any websites or blogs that she used frequently to get her information? People she had a relationship with?"

"Yes, there were quite a few – but I really can't tell you offhand who or what they are," Debbie said. "I do have some of those links on my home computer but there's nobody at home. It's all locked up for the next week. There were a few people she dealt with regularly, but I just can't remember their names offhand. I'll try my best," she added. "I'll look back through my messages. Maybe there will be something to jog my memory there."

"Please, if you remember anything, can you call me? Or message me, and I'll call you." Hunter took her details and gave her his email address. After thanking her again for the information, he hung up.

It was a pity that the timing was so bad, and that Debbie hadn't been able to remember more. But what he knew so far was pointing to something. The pieces were not all fitting together but he was getting an idea of their shape.

He glanced up again at the windows of Dreamland Creations. From the outside, they were mirrored, and he couldn't see in at all. But somewhere behind those

111

windows was Amelia Evans, and Hunter knew that she knew more.

Maybe she would be able to fill in some of the missing pieces, but he would have to be careful and pick his time. She wouldn't talk if she thought it would get her into trouble, so he'd have to find a way to persuade her.

As he climbed into his car, his phone rang again.

This time, it was Gibson.

"Hunter? Are you heading back to the office now?"

Some research into these conspiracy theory sites might lead to answers. He could do that in the office.

"I am," he said.

"Good," Gibson said. He sounded excited. "We've got an unscheduled visit this afternoon. A high-level visit from the Department of Defense. They're inspecting a number of the police stations and we're on the list. Charles Harrison, the Secretary of Defense himself, is leading the team, so I need everyone back on site to help prepare."

Hunter cast his mind back to the earlier conversation he'd had with Gibson. This might be a positive move for the department. The mover and shaker, tipped to be President, was taking an interest in the police?

He felt curious about this man who'd made so many waves in political circles. Hunter was eager to meet him and learn why that was, and what exactly Charles Harrison was doing. Also, he hoped that he'd be able to get a moment alone with him and broach the topic of corruption earlier than he'd expected.

"I'm coming right back," he confirmed.

15
Cryptic Encounter

It was lunchtime and Amelia Evans checked her phone anxiously as she headed downstairs. There weren't any more calls from that strange number.

She was relieved that her day had veered back into the ballpark of normality again. Between the meeting this morning, that weird call, and the detective's questioning, it had all been super stressful and not what she'd expected at all.

Now, it was time for her lunch break. She had half an hour and Olivia had said that almost everyone at Dreamland Creations headed across the road to the local deli.

"They do very good sandwiches, excellent cakes, and smoothies. Go on, you need to get out of the office for a while," Olivia had encouraged her.

As she reached the lobby, she saw Sam Reynolds, the founder of Carl Commando, walking in. With his suit jacket on, he must have been out at a meeting and just gotten back. He was walking fast with a determined look on his face as if he didn't want to waste a moment of his working day.

She felt nervous remembering what had happened in that meeting. In fact, she was going to hurry past him with nothing more than a polite nod, but to her surprise, he greeted her in a friendly way.

"You had a lot on your plate this morning," he said genially.

"Yes," she admitted. "It wasn't what I expected."

She wondered if he'd say anything more or talk about why. He was frowning thoughtfully.

"I guess for someone coming in, it must seem strange, but the truth is that conflict always drives a company forward," he said. "There were arguments a couple of years ago about whether the toy should hit the shelves at all or not. Some people, like me, knew we had a bestseller. Others doubted." He grinned.

"I guess time showed them," she said, and his smile widened.

"Exactly. And time will show us again that we're still in the right direction. Gotta have faith in the decision, that's all."

"I'm heading out now. Do you want anything?" she said, hoping to build on the tentative steps that she thought they'd taken toward a better rapport.

"Where are you going?" Was there a note of suspicion in his voice now?

"Just across the road," she said.

"No. No, I'm fine." He paused, looking at her thoughtfully. "I have to mention this. I was walking past the office earlier. You didn't see me, but I saw you."

Amelia stared at him, surprised. This had veered back into 'strange' again.

"Was there anything wrong?" she asked.

"You were checking your phone a lot, I noticed," Reynolds said, and Amelia felt her face flush red with embarrassment – and guilt.

"I – I guess I didn't realize I was," she said. She'd been looking out for any messages, any more of those strange calls. She hadn't looked at it that much, but he'd seen.

"It's not advisable to do that," he said. "You need to check your personal life at the door when you get into work. And be careful what you say to strangers. There are always people trying to steal our intellectual property."

Her face felt like it was on fire now. There was a distinct note of threat in his words.

"Thanks for the warning," she said. "And I – I'm sorry."

She turned away and scurried out, feeling mad with herself now for having let that phone call distract her so much. This was her first day of work and Reynolds was right. She shouldn't have been looking at her phone at all.

What a terrible faux pas. She tried her best to put it out of her mind as she crossed the road and went into the deli.

The deli looked as luscious as she'd been told. Rows of glossy bread rolls filled sandwiches with cheese and meats and roasted vegetables, croissants and strudels and colorfully iced donuts.

Now feeling hungry, because she'd been too anxious about her new day to eat any breakfast, Amelia hovered over the display, narrowing down her selection to either a bagel with smoked salmon and cream cheese or a panini roll with roast vegetables and mozzarella.

She was aware of somebody beside her and moved over to give the guy room without really looking at him, her gaze focused on the food.

But he followed and sidled in her direction, and it was then that Amelia felt a quiver of unease.

She glanced at him. He was looking at her directly and now she stepped back from him, alarmed. He was an ordinary-seeming guy wearing a gray button-down shirt open at the collar, with short black hair and a goatee.

"You work across the road?" he asked quietly. "You're the new assistant, right?"

Suspicion flared. "Yes, I am." She could hear the defiance in her voice. "Why do you ask? Do you work there?"

Already, she was trying to figure out if his voice was the same as the one she'd heard earlier on the anonymous call. She couldn't be sure, though.

"I don't work there but I'm looking for some information," he said.

"I can't help you with that," she stated upfront, her sense of contentment dissolved. Instead, she felt threatened and exposed.

"Maybe you can. It's important. There's information we desperately need," he said.

"I am not giving away any confidential information. I have a job! And my job does not involve talking to you!" she said, now thoroughly upset.

He made a placating 'calm down' motion with his hands.

"I know. It seems rude. It seems intrusive. But please, listen to me." He lowered his voice still further. "Do you know what Day Zero means? Heard any mention of it?"

The weirdness of this conversation and his sibilant tone were causing goose bumps to prickle her arms.

"Day Zero? No, I – I don't. I have no idea. Why should I know?"

"Trust me, it's going to be a term everyone knows, soon. Unless we can stop this military onslaught."

"Stop it how?"

He was delusional. That's what she was telling herself anyway. But there was a serious intensity in his tone all the same.

"I need to tell you about it, but not here and not now," he said.

"I'm just an employee and I could get into trouble even speaking to you because you clearly believe something bad about the company."

"I understand and I know I need to explain myself better. Please, outside of working hours, would you at least be willing to listen? It's desperately important. Believe me when I say so."

"Outside of working hours, I don't have an interest in speaking to you," she snapped, teeth gritted.

"Look, there's a coffee shop a couple of blocks south of here, called Bean There. I'll be waiting there at six p.m. You don't have to speak to me but if company loyalty is what you're worried about, why not get both sides of the story at least?" he said, speaking fast.

"I don't think I can make it," she protested.

"You need to make it. Listen, there's a site called The Signal. They are publishing stories about what's happening. Read some of the content there, okay? Not on your company's Wi-Fi, just in case. When you're out of the office, please, just read it. And if it worries you at all, then you know where to find me. Tonight, six p.m. Public place. No risk. Bring a friend if you like. I'm begging you. Just hear me out there. And remember," his voice dropped even lower. "If we get to Day Zero, it's too late."

"Who are you anyway?" she asked, but he'd turned around and was already disappearing out of the door.

She stared after him, her stomach now clenching with anxiety.

Amelia still didn't know what this was about but the deadly serious note in his voice had caused the hairs on the back of her neck to stand up. Why had he approached her, outside of the office, in such a furtive way? How did he know who she was when she'd only just started? Had he been watching the place? Was this situation dangerous? She'd thought it was corporate espionage at first but then, she hadn't been so sure.

Now, Sam Reynolds' warning seemed to be more relevant.

Had he been warning her about something exactly like this? Did he suspect she would be approached?

Maybe she should go to the meeting place, she decided, trailing back to the display of food even though her hunger had all but vanished.

If she did, at least she'd know what was going on and what Day Zero was.

16
High-Level Station Buzz

Hunter arrived back at the LAPD police station to a feeling of excitement in the air. Preparation for this short notice, high-level visit was swinging into action.

The three parking bays outside the front entrance had been cleared and an officer was sweeping them, ready for the arrival of the official vehicles. Inside the lobby, three more LAPD officers were busy moving furniture and changing up three of the old chairs for newer ones. A sergeant, standing on a chair, was taking some of the scruffier and outdated notices off the big board behind the desk. A janitor was threading his way through the melee with a mop and a feather duster.

Hunter stared in surprise. These preparations were nothing short of frantic. It was just a visit! And surely, the police station had been clean enough to start with?

What was the need for this level of fuss? It felt as if a brand-new reality show, My Cleanest Police Station, was going to have a pilot run here, he thought, amusement cutting through the irritation he felt over all the song and dance.

Gibson, holding a clipboard and wearing a focused expression and a red tie, strode through. He scrutinized the list and then took in the lobby with a sweeping glance.

"Still a few things to iron out," he said. "That calendar at the back, can we straighten it? And I'd like the window cleaned. Also, there's an excessive amount of paperwork at the front desk. Put it away."

It's a *front desk*, Hunter thought, his irritation now spiking again. Its role is to have some paperwork on it. A police station with a totally clean desk looks like it's not in operation at all.

He wasn't a believer in petty attention to detail before a high-level visit. The damned place had been fine to start with. It was swept and vacuumed regularly. It wasn't like the Department of Defense contingent was coming in to perform surgery on the floor. Personally, Hunter thought that the focus should be on cleaning up what you couldn't see – corruption and incompetence – rather than what you could.

But now was not the time to start grumbling or showing a bad attitude. If the high-level visit had a good outcome and he could get this powerful Secretary of Defense to root out the corruption in the LAPD – then it would be a win-win. Worth putting all the papers away for a few hours, Hunter told himself.

Gibson's gaze homed in on him.

"Ah, Hunter, you're back. We're almost finished up here. They're due in half an hour. Will you straighten up your desk?"

"I'll do that," Hunter agreed.

Heading into the back office, he found Cody looking irritable, moving a filing cabinet far enough away from the wall to be able to get a broom behind it.

"One VIP visit on the cards and everyone loses their minds," his colleague grumbled, forcing the broom into the gap, and sweeping vigorously. "As if the Department of Defense contingent is going to get down on their hands and knees and peer at the floor behind our furniture?"

"If they do, they'll be pleasantly surprised. Promotions will be in order, I'm sure," Hunter quipped in an innocent voice, causing Cody to snort.

Hunter squared up the papers on his already tidy desk. Job done.

Now, with twenty-nine minutes to go until the high-level visit took place, he wanted to see if he could find out more about the bad press and the conspiracy theories surrounding Carl Commando.

"Want to help me with some research?" he asked.

"What research is that?" Cody asked, putting the broom down with an expression of relief.

"I need to get some background on what exactly people are saying about Carl Commando. There's bound to be some adverse publicity on the mainstream media sites, but I also want to dig deeper and look on the fringe sites, the wilder ones, where all the conspiracy theories are aired."

Cody made a face. "Just make sure to clear your screen before the Department of Defense walks in."

Hunter laughed.

He sat down and started his search, with Cody opposite on his own computer.

To Hunter's surprise, he found that there wasn't much negative press on Carl Commando. He thought that maybe

121

the negative comments he'd heard about had been overblown. The company did a lot of good. The toy manufacturer was a big contributor to children's charities and in particular, children who had physical challenges and disabilities.

The "Outdoor Health Drive" helped to supply crutches and wheelchairs to kids who needed them while the "Anti-Obesity Action Group" helped to supply healthy nutritious foods and exercise plans to kids who were suffering from being overweight. That, Hunter guessed, tied in with the Carl Commando video game and the spin-offs, such as a karate franchise and the paintball games, that he had heard of.

"They are also having gatherings," Cody said, sounding surprised, glancing up from his screen.

"Gatherings?"

"Yes. It seems that the Carl Commando enthusiasts are organizing – at any rate, someone's organizing – days to get together, do activities, outdoor games, and socializing. It sounds like a version of Boy Scouts, from what I'm reading here," Cody said. "They've held a few so far and they've been very well supported. I see here that they get lots of loot to take home. Branded everything."

"That's clever marketing for you," Hunter agreed.

Perhaps the negative news was hidden more deeply.

He tried a few different search topics and as he'd expected, once he probed further, there were some negative stories to be found. A Carl Commando games team was accused of bullying at school. There was a gun violence incident that seemed to be linked to a young man who'd been a Carl Commando paintball enthusiast. But the association with the brand was not strong.

Where were the theories he'd hoped to find, the ones that would contain wild accusations - perhaps with a grain of truth?

He looked carefully at the Guardian Moms website, wondering if there was any hint of this expose to be found, but there wasn't. Then, remembering what Nick Taylor had said to him, he went to the National Peace Alliance website.

There, he found more. There was an entire page devoted to the potentially negative effects of ultra-military toys. The National Peace Alliance had interviewed a few psychologists to get input and had issued a serious warning.

"Playing with ultra-military toys and embracing the mindset of following violent orders unquestioningly is an extremely dangerous combination that can lead to the manipulation of young minds. We feel that children should be encouraged to think for themselves and to act only after considering the consequences."

That was well and good, Hunter agreed. He approved of that argument.

What about the other site, No To Violence?

He searched for that, keen to take a look at what this site might have to say. This writer was much more outspoken. Immediately, Hunter saw a copy that was not pulling its punches.

"The Evil of Carl Commando and Why a Generation is at Risk," the headline read.

Now, that sounded intriguing.

But as he opened the article, he heard a commotion from the front office. Voices, footsteps, and greetings.

The high-level Department of Defense contingent had arrived and that meant he'd have to wait to read this fascinating piece.

Minimizing it, Hunter headed through to the lobby to meet the man who was tipped to be the next President.

17
Virtual Infiltration

Daniel's hands were tight on the controls. His breath was coming fast. This had gone bad, so very bad. He knew it was just a game, but it seemed that in the past twenty-four hours, it had suddenly expanded way beyond that. It *wasn't* just a game. And it didn't only mean that to him anymore.

But now, he was being asked to do the impossible.

Because, into the screen, a medic had run.

He had the red cross on his sleeve, clearly visible. Daniel couldn't see if he was armed at all, but he was definitely carrying no weapons. He had a stretcher with him and a medical bag, and he was bending over and tending to the baker – who must be severely wounded and not dead at all.

Daniel knew what this meant! There were rules about shooting medics in any combat situation. It was – what was it? He never concentrated in history classes but some guys on the group's chat had been discussing it the other day.

The Geneva Convention, that was it. It was an international regulation that you did not fire at a medic who had his insignia displayed.

He swallowed hard. He knew he was running out of time and that the wrong decision would be the fatal one. Was this another test, and if so, how was he going to pass it?

He was sure that a lot of times, the Geneva Convention was ignored in warfare.

And it wasn't like he was suddenly supposed to respect the rules of the real world, as opposed to the rules of the game. After all, in the real world, you wouldn't round a corner, having escaped from a deadly combat situation in a crumbling, shot-out alleyway, and find yourself approaching a baker carrying a tray of rolls. This game was just messing with his mind, that was what it was doing.

Ultimately the rules of the game, which he'd been told to follow, were to shoot anyone he saw in the street. From that perspective, they were very clear. There was no doubt. The game hadn't stopped when he'd shot the baker. No warning messages had flashed up on the screen.

So, that meant he'd been supposed to shoot the baker because that was what the game had demanded he do. Everyone meant everyone.

It was just that – in his mind – the concept of shooting an unarmed person tending to somebody who was seriously injured – that was unacceptable, and he knew it.

It was crossing a line but then again, this was a private level of the game and – for all he knew – all these people could be aliens in disguise or mercenaries undercover, or who knew what. It wasn't a real street, Daniel reminded himself. This wasn't a real situation. These were just figures.

He raised his gun and shot. He drilled two rounds into the medic's chest, breathing hard while he did it, his eyes wide, his hands tense, but his aim true.

And then, while he was in the zone, he drilled another two rounds into the fallen baker, because if he was dead and if he'd killed him properly the first time, then this medic would never have rushed onto the scene to try to save him.

And then, the street ahead was clear. He rushed forward, his mind racing just as fast as his legs and just as desperately, too. Please, no more, he begged the game. No more. That was like an unexpected horror fest, and he felt like a slaughterer now.

He reached the end of the street and abruptly, the game screen froze.

He felt weak with reaction. That had been hectic. He didn't know if he'd done well or badly. He didn't care. Lowering his head and finally letting go of the controls, he breathed out, taking the chance to decompress from that nerve-shredding situation that had tested his mind and his judgment far more than it had tested his skill.

Then, the brief blare of music got him looking up again in exhausted hopefulness.

"Congratulations, Captain Dan," the words flashed up. *"You've achieved the level, and your abilities have earned you Super Elite status. This has opened new doors for you. Doors that you didn't know existed. Are you ready to step through? Think carefully! There is no going back."*

New doors?

Wow, so that ordeal was actually getting him someplace that he didn't even know existed yet. But what kind of a warning was 'think carefully', he wondered. That was, like, pointless. Who was going to think carefully when a question like that came up? Of course, he had to know what would happen next. He had to. He'd been to hell and back, mentally, in the last few hours. This game had led him on an adventure so strange that he could never have imagined it.

He might need a rest before the next level, but he was sure as hell going to be up for it.

Even so, he hesitated before pressing *Yes*.

The game froze again. He didn't know why it was doing this. Was his connection faulty? He checked his phone, but it seemed to be fast enough. This building might have erratic heating, a water supply that tasted chalky and problems with dampness in the basement, but the one thing it did have was good, reliable Wi-Fi.

Letting out the breath, he pressed *Yes* again.

If it kept freezing, he could restart the game, he reasoned.

But this time, it didn't freeze. This time, the screen flipped straight to a picture.

He stared at it, frowning slightly. It was also a street scene, but weirdly familiar looking. He'd seen it before, he thought, but right then, and out of context, he couldn't place it.

Do you know where this is, Captain Dan?

The message flashed up on the screen again.

He waited, now feeling very disturbed because he didn't know where the hell this was heading. What if he didn't know? Did that mean a fail? What was he supposed to say? He couldn't think of any of the usual replies, the ones that would be accepted by the game and in line with its protocol. Although, Daniel acknowledged that the game protocol as he'd known it had been left behind a long time ago.

He decided on the truth.

"It's familiar."

"It's the start of a new mission for you. It's risky. Accept it, and you'll be entering a world of excitement. But it will take all your knowledge, all your skill, all your smarts."

There was a pause and then, in caps, *ONLY ACCEPT IF YOU ARE WILLING TO TAKE THIS ON. VERY FEW ARE CHOSEN AND EVEN FEWER WILL SUCCEED.*

Daniel considered the words. He felt queasy and very unsettled. There was something deeply strange about this. But he felt, now that he'd come so far, he had to go further. He'd fought his way through challenges that had seemed scary and dangerous and had tested him in every way. Really, how much worse could this be?

"I accept," he typed in.

And then, nothing.

The screen went blank. He wiggled the controls, feeling concerned. This was weird. It was like a glitch. It had completely booted him out of the game. This had never happened before. How was he going to get back in and resume the play tonight with his unit? Was this some kind of an experimental version and it had failed him?

What was he supposed to do?

He stared at the blank screen for far too long, anxiety rising. Then, as if remembering too little, too late, what needed to be done, he restarted his computer and went back in. Re-logged into the game.

But it didn't help. More of the same. More of nothing.

And then, his phone beeped.

He jumped at the sound, still focused on the screen and on solving what seemed to be an unsolvable issue with the game. Who could he contact? Was there a page where he could report a fault? Maybe he'd have to delete his software completely and re-download it.

Almost absently, he picked up the phone and checked his message.

And as he read it, he tensed, eyes widening, breath coming fast.

"Congratulations, Captain Dan. You have moved to a new level. Here is a pin drop. At the pin drop, you will find a black bag containing the items you need for your next mission. Further directions will be sent to you in due course."

With a sense of total unreality, Daniel tweaked back the window blind and stared outside. The pin drop was a mile down the road. It was in his own neighborhood.

Now, at last, he remembered where he'd seen that street view photo before.

It was at the park, a block down from his house.

His heart was banging hard in his chest. Was this a prank, or what was it?

Feeling mystified and scared and very exposed, he opened his door and quietly left the room. He headed downstairs and out, into the cloudy, chilly afternoon.

This was a time to be careful, he thought as he walked. He'd have to keep a lookout for his little brother who could be arriving home from school at any time and who mustn't know that Daniel had skipped school. He wanted to set a good example for the little guy.

But there was no one he recognized around as he set off on the walk.

On the way, he had a chance to think. Whoever was running this game – they must know about him. Well, he'd registered as a player and given his personal details. Had they seen those and were they singling him out for a reason? He hoped this wasn't something bad that would result in him being trafficked or grabbed or framed in a drugs deal or who knew what?

The answers weren't far away. The pin drop was closing in. And he saw it led to a park bench, under which was a black backpack.

"Open the backpack, Captain Dan," his phone beeped again, sending a shiver of dread through him.

Looking around him, nervous and furtive in case anyone was watching and thought he was stealing it, he picked it up and unzipped it.

Inside, he found a black baseball cap, a black hooded jacket, and a pair of dark glasses.

And a black wallet. He gasped as he opened it because it contained cash. A crisp, new, hundred-dollar bill. He stared at it in astonishment. This must belong to somebody else; this must be some kind of setup; this couldn't be for him. Could it?

Another beep. He grabbed his phone, anxiety flaring.

"This is for your project. It is a test," the message said. *"Tonight, you have to follow this person, track their movements, and take photos. Send them through. The money is your prepayment."*

A new pin drop flashed up.

And another photo.

This time, of a woman.

18
Uncomfortable High-Level Encounter

Hunter headed to the lobby followed by Cody, and as he neared it, the sound of voices grew louder.

"This is the largest of our central Los Angeles stations," he heard Gibson saying. "We have some of our lead detectives based here, and they handle crimes all over the wider area." Turning, he saw Hunter approach.

"Hunter Harden is one of our most senior detectives," he introduced him. "Detective Harden, this is the honorable Charles Harrison, Secretary of Defense."

It would be difficult not to feel a thrill of pride, Hunter acknowledged, even for an anti-establishment rebel like himself, as he walked over and shook the hand of the most powerful and senior figure in the US military, the Secretary of Defense himself.

Flanked by two members of his retinue, Charles Harrison was a tall man with sharply cut, graying hair and a hawklike face. His bearing, straight-backed and confident, spoke of long years of military service and it gave him a regal air. Walking forward, he pinned Hunter with a keen gaze.

"Pleased to meet you, Detective Harden," he said.

His handshake was firm – almost bone-crushing. Feeling that it was automatic rather than an attempt at asserting superiority, Hunter didn't turn it into a competition. He wanted help and support from this senior figure.

He hadn't known how difficult or easy it would be to speak privately with this man but to his surprise, Harrison put a hand on Hunter's shoulder and moved a few steps away from the other men, into a corner of the office.

"You've been doing some good work, I hear," he said quietly. "Stamping out corruption. That's a bold move."

Feeling encouraged to have gotten some face-to-face time with this powerful man, Hunter nodded.

"I'm doing my best to tackle it, sir," he explained.

Harrison stared at him, his gaze considering.

"It seems you've been doing more than that," he said. "You've been making waves."

He didn't sound particularly approving nor did he sound condemning. Perhaps he was just stating facts.

"I wasn't able to turn a blind eye to the situation," Hunter agreed, "but I need help. As we now know, there's more corruption within the LAPD. I don't know how high it goes, but it goes higher than Samuels. We need to root it out."

Harrison stared at him with a level gaze that Hunter couldn't read. The man would be an outstanding poker player, he guessed. Then he glanced behind him, beckoning over one of his retinues.

"I appreciate the fact you're getting involved. I'd like you to meet my assistant, Bryan Rogan, who is a key support person in our team, and who actions all our plans. He's my trusted second-in-command, he'd be heading up our massive Army recruitment drive and you'll be dealing with him mainly."

Bryan Rogan stepped forward. With a jutting jaw, a heavy brow, and an air of almost bullying confidence, he looked born for the role of actioning plans. His handshake was on the bone crushing side and he held Hunter's gaze while he did it.

"I'm planning on making big changes to the entire policing structure," he said in a low, grainy voice, shouldering in to stand in front of Harrison. "In our future vision, there'll be no room for corruption. In the restructuring, we're planning to create a roaming task force that exists solely to address it. Would you like to be involved in that, at a high level?"

Never say no to an opportunity, Hunter knew, even though Rogan's words gave him a moment's uncertainty, because would this mean he'd be completely removed from his day-to-day duties? What would roaming mean? Would it take him out of state, and if so, what would the implications be for his family, and for Matthew?

But he couldn't think of that now. It would be better to show willingness, at least until he knew more.

"I'd love to know more about it and to be involved," he said to Rogan.

"Excellent. There are going to be other changes too. In the next few years, I have a master plan which involves changing the police's focus, in line with other important changes that we'll be making." Now Rogan's voice was louder, including everyone in the room. "When our vision is realized, we're going to be living in a very different America, a better America. A more stable, wealthier, and more powerful country, that's for sure."

Rogan had an inspiring way of speaking, and as the words rolled richly off his tongue, some of the officers in the room burst into spontaneous applause.

Harrison nodded, his face stern. "I'm glad you share and support our vision, gentlemen. Now, I'd like to take a walk through this police station and see how much room for expansion in numbers we have here."

"Would you like to see our case list before we start?" Gibson said, opening a folder. "We've got a very good solve rate at this moment, especially for serious crimes. Our biggest case at the moment is the assassination crime, the multiple shootings, which Harden is handling with Cody Lamarr. Then, we have this nightclub shooting, the assault case, this domestic violence case…"

"Excellent. Rogan will take a look at it while I walk through. We need to see where we can direct this investigative potential," Harrison said. He turned and left the room together with the remaining member of his retinue while Rogan remained in situ.

Rogan's authoritative air was making Hunter wonder who was really in charge here. It almost seemed like the tail was wagging the dog, and Rogan was the boss of Harrison.

Rogan continued from where he stopped. "We intend to assist in restructuring the police and with the expansion in numbers coming up in the Army in the coming months, I daresay many vibrant and smart young men will be interested in joining the police too."

Expansion in numbers?

Hunter was intrigued, mulling over the words as Gibson quickly took Rogan through the major items on the current case list. It sounded as if Rogan had an extremely clear plan in place – but what, exactly, was it? How was he going to achieve it? And why only young men? He sounded like a relic from the 19th century. Had he forgotten that women police officers exist too?

At any rate, unclear though the methods were, it seemed that the Department of Defense was highly organized, had a very ambitious vision, and was supportive of the police – and of course, of the Army too. He could see from Harrison's confidence and demeanor why he was tipped to be the next President – but then, why was Rogan taking control here?

He hadn't given any opportunity for questions, but Hunter had one all the same. When Gibson closed the file, and before Rogan could leave, he quickly took a breath and asked.

"Mr. Rogan, what's the purpose behind the restructuring and how are you going to achieve this expansion when we currently have a hiring crisis?" he asked, wanting to know more about Rogan's thought processes. "Do you have a magic bullet or a new formula for success? I'm interested to know."

Rogan turned to him and regarded him sharply. Now, there was a very different look in his eyes.

Instantly, Hunter realized that this might not have been a good decision. Questions, it seemed, were not welcome at this time. In fact, Rogan was looking at him as if he might be an adversary.

"The plan we have in place is very complex and carefully thought out, Detective Harden," he said firmly. "It has been strategized at top level. I'll be honest with you. I find your tone critical and your question offensive."

There was a loaded silence in the room.

Gibson was looking daggers at Hunter. Everyone was staring at him with steel blades in their eyes. He'd just ruined the tone of the high-level visit with a poorly worded question whose tone had not been respectful enough for the Department of Defense's needs.

He was momentarily appalled and embarrassed by the outcome of what had been a genuine question.

"Detective Harden is by way of being a renegade," Gibson said in apologetic tones to fill the shocked silence that had descended. "Shall we go ahead with the inspection of the premises now?"

But Rogan kept staring at Hunter with that same expression in his eyes.

"Renegades have no place in the police force," he said slowly. "Still less, at a high level. I might need to have a word with the Honorable Secretary about your future role."

And with that, he turned and walked down the corridor to join his boss.

Hunter exchanged a glance with Cody, seeing that his partner was frowning deeply.

"Well, that went down like a lead balloon," Cody admitted quietly, as they turned and headed back to their office.

"Why, though?" Hunter argued. "Why couldn't he explain? Why did he get so angry? I don't want to taint the whole branch with my behavior and let Gibson down – but it was just a question, and I wanted an answer."

"Maybe it's not such a clear strategy as he would like to think it is?" Cody offered. "At any rate, one thing I've learned is that these powerful guys don't like their methods questioned. And you had – well, a challenging tone to your voice."

"I honestly didn't mean it that way," Hunter said, perturbed, sitting down again at his computer. "I was interested to know. I don't see why Rogan would have taken offense at a question like that. Do you?"

Cody shook his head. "Maybe he sees it as dissension in the ranks."

"It was weird," Hunter said. "It was like he turned around in a flash from being supportive of me to thinking I was the enemy. From one question? I don't see a reason behind it."

Feeling unsettled by what had played out and now regretful that his misguided question had painted the branch in a bad light after Gibson had been going to such efforts, he sat down and focused once again on the website, No To Violence, which he'd been reading earlier.

It might be too late to save his reputation in Harrison's eyes, Hunter thought, but at least he could turn all his attention to solving the case which was at the top of the LAPD branch's list of serious crimes.

"The Evil of Carl Commando and Why a Generation is at Risk," he read.

"The evolution of the Carl Commando toy has been a checkered one. From an innocent kids' plaything, it's as if Dreamland Creations has deliberately transformed their popular toy into a pro-military monster," the article stated. *"Through the toy itself and also the spinoffs, we have noted unquestioning obeying of orders, a focus on intense levels of violence, shoot-to-kill as a default, and the use of indoctrination techniques. These include repetition, restriction (the refusal to allow an alternative viewpoint), and socialization, where users are fully exposed to this*

shared culture. Emotional manipulation, reward and punishment techniques are used throughout the game."

Hunter looked up from the screen, taking in this critique. There were some very disturbing points being made here. Were they valid? Was there a way of checking, he wondered, refocusing on the text again.

"And there's more. Do you know that the game uses the screen's video cameras with AI analytics to ensure that only young people are playing the lower levels? Think I'm wrong? You go and try to log in as a parent and an adult. See how far you get. The game will freeze. What's in it and what's shared is only for younger eyes and younger users."

That was disturbing, Hunter thought.

But there, the article ended, with the promise of a second part to be uploaded in the next few days.

Hunter felt impatient to see part two, wanting more evidence to prove this theory right or wrong. But maybe he didn't have to wait for the article.

He checked his watch. Time to get going and see if he could sneakily find out what he needed to know.

19
Stalking Shadows

Amelia Evans glanced up at her boss, Olivia Montgomery, as she straightened out her desk, packing away the folders of order queries that they'd been dealing with.

She'd never expected to feel so anxious at the end of her first working day. It was as if she felt targeted.

She'd had two more missed calls on her phone from a withheld number. Luckily she'd switched her phone to silent, but even so, that buzzing noise was still audible.

And one of the times it had rung, Sam Reynolds had been in the office, having a quick conversation with Olivia. He'd heard the buzzing, and she hadn't been able to suppress a guilty jump at the low sound.

Reynolds had given her a suspicious look.

"Don't you need to take that call, Amelia?" he'd said. It had been like a challenge. Like he knew that she was being harassed by somebody who was pressurizing her to spill company secrets that she knew she didn't possess.

"It's just a telemarketer," she'd said, pretending casualness as she glanced at the screen, but she was a terrible liar and her face had turned tomato red.

He'd seen. He knew.

She didn't feel happy at all after what had happened that day.

Not only had she been targeted by this anonymous person, but she also heard of the death of the CEO of a rival company, a man called Brian Mitchell, during Olivia's interview with that detective. Shot twice, like a hit.

She'd thought the toy industry would be fun and exciting, a creative place to work. Instead, she'd landed in a strange, threatening territory with anonymous callers harassing her and people getting killed.

It was after five-thirty, and it looked like her first disastrous day at work was wrapping up. The sun, smothered by clouds, had just set and the weather was windy outside. It looked chilly and threatening out there which aligned perfectly with her emotions.

She should say something about that encounter in the deli. She should tell Olivia that she'd been asked to meet up with somebody.

That six p.m. appointment was hanging over her. It felt like a mountain in her mind. She shouldn't go to it, that she knew. But should she at least tell somebody that she'd been approached?

Right now, Amelia thought she was trapped in a lose-lose scenario. She might have gotten into trouble for saying nothing, but she was worried that saying something might lead to worse trouble. Maybe she should have handled it differently from the get-go, she fretted as she packed her papers away in a bag. What was Day Zero?

The phrase had been weighing on her mind all day, so much so that she'd been scared she'd inadvertently blurt it out. She was far too honest that way.

Of course, she could keep a secret as well as the next person. But hiding a guilty secret? That was something else entirely.

Playing devil's advocate, she argued with herself that Day Zero might be something that was intentionally being kept a secret by Dreamland Creations itself. She only had this strange man's word that it was disastrous. It could be a big launch or a blockbuster new product or something legitimate that they were counting down toward.

In any case, she was just the assistant. New and junior, what could she do? It might be better to ignore these calls completely, not say anything to anyone, and hope that the strange, dark-haired man with the goatee started bothering somebody else. Maybe if she just turned a blind eye, he'd look for a softer target.

Or – she could go to that coffee shop and find out what it was all about.

The scary thought made her stomach twist. Perhaps the most frightening thing of all was that despite everything she'd been telling herself, a small part of her was seriously considering going there.

Even though it could be dangerous. People had been killed. What if she was next?

Now Olivia was leaving too, looking preoccupied and focused, as if she had places to go and wasn't going straight home.

"See you tomorrow and thanks for your work today," she said as she rushed out.

"See you tomorrow," Amelia replied hastily. Would Olivia be thanking her if she knew what had happened in the deli earlier?

And why did she think that Reynolds already suspected something had happened?

Alone in the office at last, and since she didn't want to bump into Reynolds or Olivia on her way out in case her phone started ringing again, she dawdled over packing up, making sure everything was replaced correctly in the folder and then giving the office one last neaten up before she was done.

Feeling highly stressed, she picked up her laptop bag and her purse and put on her jacket. By this time, it was getting dark and cloudy. The wind was tossing tree branches around and rain was threatening. And she'd parked at the far end of the business unit's parking lot. If this weather was as bad as it looked through the window, she might get wet.

Amelia hurried downstairs, her feet echoing in the empty corridor. It looked like she was one of the last to leave. Even the front desk in the lobby was standing empty.

She headed out, catching her breath as the cold wind hit her.

With her head down to avoid the flying drizzle, she hurried along the walkway, treading over the concrete path flanked by grass and trees. Then she was past the lights of the building and into the semi-darkness of the lot.

That encounter with the stranger earlier had spooked her a lot more than she'd thought. What if he didn't wait for the coffee shop meeting but came back here now to confront her again?

Now, out here in the empty lot, on this dark and gusty night, she was feeling vulnerable. She couldn't wait to get into the safety of her car but as she scurried across the paving, she found herself looking around her nervously.

She remembered those murders as she passed a tall flagpole with the cord and the flag whipping loudly in the wind. Could she be under threat herself? Especially after what that man had said.

Her imagination was seriously running away with her now. In fact, she was thinking to herself that there was a dark figure standing there, very still, near the wall by the parking lot's gate.

It wasn't, of course. Just the shadows.

She must stop overthinking situations like this, she chided herself. All it would do would be to freak her out at a time when she needed a calm head on her shoulders.

It was not a person. It was just a pillar. Just a pillar on the wall.

Except, it wasn't.

When she looked again, she saw it was a person.

A tall, broad-shouldered man in a black jacket was striding purposefully toward her, his face invisible in the darkness.

Straight at her. Targeting her.

With fear boiling inside her, Amelia let out a shrill, terrified scream.

20
Company Secrets

Hunter moved quickly forward. Waiting unobtrusively in the parking lot, he had hoped to spot Amelia leaving. After seeing her shocked face earlier while he'd spoken to her boss and the way she'd reacted when the conspiracy theories were mentioned, he knew there were things she could tell him. But the poor woman was thoroughly spooked. Her eyes were saucer wide, and he could see real fear in them.

"It's Detective Harden, Miss Evans," he reassured her quickly, turning his head so that the little light there shone onto his face, and she could see him clearly. Recent events must have been highly disturbing for her."

At any rate, she was now looking more relieved than terrified.

"Detective Harden. I'm sorry. I'm on edge. I guess it's been a – a tough day."

"Tough all around," he agreed wryly.

"It's my first day here, believe it or not. Thrown in the deep end," she said. Now that she knew he wasn't a threat, the words were spilling out of her, and Hunter wanted to capitalize on her talkativeness.

"Your first day? That's beyond tough," he sympathized. "I came back to confirm a few things. Could I run them past you," he said, aiming for a tone that was serious but not threatening. "It's cold out. Shall we speak in my car?"

"Yes, that'll be fine," she said, seeming glad to be heading for the shelter of a car, although nervous at being under the spotlight.

He opened the passenger door for her and went around to the driver's side.

Rain pattered on the windshield as he closed the door, breathing in the harshly sweet scent of his car's air freshener and the faint but much more pleasant hint of Amelia's perfume.

"So, your first day?" he said conversationally, even though he already knew this. No point in starting out too hard-core. He wanted to gain her trust – as far as he could in the circumstances. "What did you think of it all?"

She looked at him doubtfully.

"This is for background," Hunter said. "Just interested in your impressions, that's all."

She was silent a while, then took a decisive breath.

"Well, I felt very overawed to be part of this company and I didn't know what to expect."

"Was it different than you'd thought?" he encouraged.

"Yes," she said.

"In what way?"

She hesitated again but then pressed forward. "There was a lot of conflict in the company," she said, sounding guilty. "I know it wasn't mentioned when you – when you came in."

"That's understandable." Hunter was quick to reassure her. "It's very common for people to not mention politics or negative issues when the police ask questions. But I'd appreciate a clearer picture because sometimes what isn't said can still be important."

"It seems like the company is split in two. Half of them think that the whole Carl Commando movement has gone way too far and the other half – well, they seem to want to push it forward."

He saw the tension in her face that hadn't been there before and wondered why this poor assistant was looking positively haunted.

"Who, exactly, wants to push on with it?"

"Well, Sam Reynolds, the COO, conceptualized Carl Commando, and he's the one who seems very set on keeping it ultra-military. I'm not sure why, though. Because it sounds as if sales have dropped."

She clamped her mouth shut, looking appalled at having let this slip.

"So sales have dropped but they're sticking to the strategy of going ultra-military?"

"Yes, that's right," she said uneasily.

With competitors flooding the market, sales might have dropped regardless, he told himself. And sticking to the military focus might be a strategic decision, Hunter reasoned. Or else, based on the beliefs of the founders. Emotion and tradition could play a role. But he was wondering if there was more to it.

"Tell me about the conspiracy theories you've heard," he said, interested to see her reaction to this question.

She looked appalled.

"There – there are apparently a few of them circulating," she said hesitantly. It was her glance at her purse that gave Hunter the lead he needed.

"Were you approached?" he asked. It struck him that she might have been. A new employee was always going to be a target for information. Maybe that was why she was looking so unsettled.

She was silent for a while. He sensed she was battling internally with telling him anything, and his theory was that whatever had happened today had set up a conflict of loyalties.

"This will stay confidential," he reassured her. "I won't mention what you tell me to anyone else at the company."

"Okay then." That seemed to reassure her. "In that case – it would be good to get this off my chest," she admitted. "I was unsure what to do about it or who to tell. But I've – I've been having these weird phone calls. Saying that there were things happening and they needed my help. And there was something else, as well.

Something that had scared her, he could see that. She was looking very disturbed.

"This guy – well, I went over to the deli at lunchtime. He was standing next to me, and he started talking. It was like he knew who I was. He was saying that I have to help them, and that Day Zero is coming. And that when it does, it'll be too late."

Day Zero?

Hunter frowned. He hadn't heard of it before. It hadn't been mentioned on any of the blogs or websites he'd looked at earlier. But it sounded significant. What could it be?

"Describe this man?"

"Well, I – I tried not to look at him too closely because this was all so weird," she admitted. "But he was a little taller than me, with dark hair and a goatee. Wearing ordinary work clothes – I mean, everything seemed normal until it wasn't."

"And he spoke about Day Zero, in connection with your company?"

"I think it might have been in connection with the Carl Commando brand," she said. "He mentioned the word 'military'."

"What else did he say?" Hunter asked.

"He wanted to say more," she admitted. "He wanted to meet with me at six p.m. He said he was going to be at the coffee shop down the road, Bean There. And that I should meet him there to find out what he wanted to tell me."

Hunter raised an eyebrow.

"Anything else?" he asked.

"Yes," she said, nodding. "I nearly forgot. He said there was a site with more information where I should go and look; that it would help explain things. But I didn't go to the site, of course. No way was I going to go there. What if they checked my phone or browsing history at work?" She grimaced, looking highly stressed.

"Did you tell your work about this?"

"No. No, I didn't."

"And the name of the website? Do you remember it?"

"Yes. It's called The Signal."

The Signal. Hunter mentally diarized it. It wasn't one of the sites he'd explored yet. He wondered what would be there to be found.

"I don't know what to do about this whole situation," Amelia continued. "I don't want to go to this meeting. It sounds like it could be too risky. But yet, I was wondering if I should go. If there might be something important for me to learn there."

"Yes," Hunter agreed. "I can see why you feel conflicted. But I have an idea."

"What's that?" she asked, hope dawning in her eyes.

"You go home and stay safe, keep out of this, which I agree is the best decision right now. And I'll go to this meeting in your place."

21
Conspiracy and Coffee

The coffee shop was small, with only eight indoor tables and a few more set out on the sidewalk. Its cheerful yellow and green sign, "Bean There", added a flash of color to the street. Walking in, Hunter felt expectant.

He knew that he'd have to be very careful. Amelia had been jumpy and nervous. The way she'd been contacted had been strange, to say the least. This man with the dark goatee, whoever he was, had gone to great lengths to connect with her discreetly and not to say too much about whatever information he had.

Hunter was there incognito, trying his best not to look like a police officer. He did not want to spook this man. Luckily, it wasn't hard for him to look less like a cop than he should. His hair always seemed to be longer than the LAPD preferred, for a start. To enhance the effect of being an ordinary person seeking coffee, he'd rolled up his shirtsleeves, unbuttoned his shirt collar, and made sure that nothing identifying himself as a police officer was visible.

He got there at ten to six and strolled in, taking a table near the front of the coffee shop that gave him a chance to see inside and outside on the sidewalk. He ordered an Americano and a bottle of water. And then, he waited.

There were only three empty tables, although the after-work rush seemed to be ebbing, and another table was vacated as he watched. Nobody fitting the man's description was at any of the tables. There wasn't anyone else who looked like they were waiting for someone. One gray-haired man, on his own, was busily at work on his laptop, engrossed in whatever he was doing. Everyone else was there with somebody, not looking around, not expectant, not waiting.

Six o'clock came and went, and Hunter started to have a bad feeling about this. It didn't seem like this man was going to be here at all. Had he been spooked, had he been in a car, waiting for Amelia to appear and only ready to show his face when she did? Or had something gone wrong?

He ordered another coffee and another water and gave it until six-thirty. Then, reluctantly, he admitted defeat. Almost all the tables were empty now and the place was getting ready to close up. Whoever this man was, he hadn't had the chance to speak to him and Hunter doubted that he'd even arrived.

This was all becoming curiouser and curiouser, he thought, leaving the money on the table, and heading out again. But he now had a new lead, and he wasn't going to go home.

He was going to go back to the LAPD and look up The Signal.

Hunter wanted to know what the content of that site was. And also, who was behind it.

*

He walked into the LAPD police station warily. The last time he'd come in here, things hadn't played out so well.

He'd managed to antagonize the next president-to-be. Hunter thought that not being able to handle tough questions from the lower ranks was a worrying trait, but it was one he'd rather not have found out about in that situation.

Hunter was worried that a guy like him, who had an ego, might go out of his way to make sure Hunter got repercussions for his actions.

Briefly demoralized, he wondered why it was so damned difficult to keep a good relationship with his superiors. He needed to try harder. Even Gibson's attitude toward him would have been soured by the scene that had played out earlier.

He was nobody's yes man though, and that was the hard truth of it.

As he walked into the back office, he saw Gibson at the far end. He'd been poring over a laptop, but as soon as he saw Hunter, he got up and headed over. Cody wasn't there and must be out on a case. The only occupant of the office was Gibson himself and Hunter now realized he'd been waiting for him.

"Harden," he said, in tones that combined frustration and concern, "you need to quit making enemies."

"I didn't do so intentionally," Hunter said.

"For an unintentional action, it was surprisingly effective," Gibson told him. "Was it necessary to question a plan that is still in the early stages and most likely, highly classified?"

"If it was classified, all he needed to do was say so," Hunter countered. "I'd have not minded that answer, but I didn't get it. And I was, and am, curious about his strategy and his vision. What's wrong with being interested?"

"From your tone, it didn't come across that way. It came across as critical. Disbelieving. Like you were ready to trash his theory."

Hunter shook his head. "Maybe my tone was challenging?"

Gibson sighed. "And maybe there are some people who don't like that type of challenge from a police detective who's many ranks their junior and who they've just met. Harden, you're a damned intelligent guy, but sometimes, when it comes to reading the room, you just don't get it."

"I'm sorry if it didn't come out the way it was intended," Hunter said.

"Too late for sorry. I think the wheels are already in motion."

"What?" Now, Hunter could hear the concern in his own voice.

Gibson stared at him grimly.

"I've been told that the anti-corruption task force will be expedited. They're working on it and will have it up and running in the next couple of days. And if and when it goes ahead, you'll be a part of it. Not in charge, just a part of it. You will have to give up your cases and you won't be working here anymore. You'll be relocated."

"Relocated where?"

"Somewhere more central. Atlanta was mentioned."

"Atlanta?" Hunter's mind reeled at the impossibility of this. The corruption he'd been concerned about was right here, in LA. He wanted to root out the rot he knew was lurking within the LAPD itself. Now he was going to be relocated, supposedly to fight it, thousands of miles from where he'd picked it up.

This wasn't redeployment, it was punishment.

For one misguided comment? How fragile was Rogan's ego? Why was a powerful man so offended to be questioned?

He replayed that scene in his mind, remembering every moment of it, how he'd asked the question, how Rogan had turned away from the list of cases and stared at Hunter, his expression changing.

The decision he'd made, seemingly on the fly in response to that question, and was now pushing through, was completely unfair.

Opening his mouth, Hunter got ready for an angry retort, to tell Gibson exactly what he felt about this. But then, he decided against it.

He closed his mouth. Now was not the time to speak his mind and to say what he wanted to say. He already knew there was no way he'd accept that order to redeploy, which would mean he'd have to move away from his son. Family commitments kept him here. And there was nothing more important than his son.

Resigning from the police?

He felt utterly floored by the twist that this situation had taken.

Would he end up taking up that career in literature as a teacher or a professor that he'd turned his back on so many years ago, and had never really missed?

Would he even still be employable in that field after so long?

Hunter swallowed down his anger and concern, and simply said, "Noted, sir."

Gibson strode out, and with a heavy heart, Hunter turned back to his screen.

He tried to tell himself that power, in some cases, was fleeting, and its might and influence could be overestimated. There might still be a way to fight this decision.

As he took his laptop out of the bag, Hunter tried to comfort himself by remembering the words of the poem Ozymandias, by Percy Bysshe Shelley.

The last lines of that sonnet, both powerful and true, had consoled him many a time when he'd been up against somebody or something, who thought they were all-powerful and all-enduring.

"And on the pedestal, these words appear:
My name is Ozymandias, King of Kings.
Look on my Works, ye Mighty, and despair!
Nothing remains. Round the decay
Of that colossal Wreck, boundless and bare
The lone and level sands stretch far away."

Sighing, Hunter hoped that Rogan would be ousted from his influential hold over Harrison and that justice – poetic or otherwise – might trump over unfairness.

For now, though, he had two days at most on the case. There wouldn't be time to get the forensic evidence. All of those would be handled by other detectives if Rogan went ahead with his redeployment plan, forcing Hunter to quit the police.

There wasn't much he could do now but what he could do, he was going to.

He had a name. The Signal. That was the website where he might find more information on the theories nobody seemed ready to speak about. He might even learn what Day Zero was.

Opening his laptop, he began to search.

22
Kitten Compromise

There it was. The Signal. At last, after an intensive search and trying many different names, Hunter had found it. It was surprisingly well hidden. No search optimization here and the URL was different from the site name.

Focusing intently on the screen, shutting out the background noise of the police station and the occasional person coming and going, Hunter began to read.

"America's Truth – Exposed!" the flashing tagline read.

A bold claim and one that automatically got Hunter's eyes rolling. He had a feeling that searching through this site would be tedious in the extreme – but he needed to because if a grain of the truth was hidden anywhere, it might be here.

It was a search. The website was poorly configured, the clash of colors made Hunter's eyes bleed, and there were an infuriating number of pop-ups exhorting readers to 'Donate! Subscribe! Act Now to Save America!' Nothing was logically categorized and most of the articles were poorly written. There didn't seem to be an overarching theme and the publisher of the site seemed ready to expose anything. Reading some of the articles – with difficulty – Hunter picked up that they seemed to be written by different people and not all by the same author. There were various styles, mostly chaotic.

For a while, he wondered if he would find anything at all here, amid diatribes on Big Pharma, Big Agri, Big Government, and more.

Hunter was about to call it a day and go to stare at a blank wall for a while to let his retinas recover from this onslaught when he stumbled upon an article headline.

"Day Zero – It's Coming!"

He clicked on the article, seeing that – like most of the content on the site – it didn't have a date attached, so there was no way of seeing how recent it was.

"Day Zero is approaching fast," the headline read. *"Plans are being set in motion now for a chain of events that will change America as we know it. And it will change the world. What would you say if you knew that children all over the country were being brainwashed, prepared to become part of a new wave of militia that is as dangerous in its mindset as it is in its actions? What if your child was one of these and you didn't even know?"*

Hunter frowned as he read the words.

What set this article apart was that it was, at least, semi-coherent. It wasn't out-and-out delusional like some of the others were. He wondered where it had come from, as he continued.

"Day Zero is not a possibility. It's not a probability. Day Zero is a certainty and when it occurs, there will be no going back. Life as we know it will be over. Want to know more about it?

Stay tuned to this page, because we are working on getting more information so that this deadly chain of events can be stopped before it starts.

In the meantime, what can you do?

Monitor your child's online activity. Do not allow any online games associated with the military.

Do not allow your child to play with action toys that promote the military.

Do not allow your child to attend any activities, sporting events or gatherings that occur under the name of any branded toy or have any military agenda.

Please, be aware and spread this message. This is a matter of life and death. The stakes could not be higher. More information will follow soon."

Hunter stared at the article thoughtfully.

The first thing he noticed about it was that it did not mention Carl Commando. Not anywhere, not even once. He wondered if this was deliberately done to keep it under the radar. Or avoid a lawsuit?

Remembering Matthew's pushback when denied a Carl Commando toy, he didn't think that the instructions issued to parents about military toys and games would be easy to follow – or that many parents would even bother. How many parents would even find this article hidden away in a sea of others? Comments had been disabled; he saw. But the page itself had been viewed a few thousand times.

Who ran this site? Was there any way of finding out?

There was a regular column, called Coburn's Comment. That was all he could find. Was the site owner called Coburn? It sounded like a last name, but Hunter could find nothing more.

Not at first glance or second glance. He was going to have to dig deeper and make some calls. After hours that might not be possible, and this could end up being tomorrow's job.

But, as Hunter started to make an action list for the next morning, his phone rang.

Seeing it was Amy, he picked it up quickly.

The stress in her voice got his heart rate spiking, even before he'd taken in her words.

"Hunter. I'm sorry to have to ask this. I've got a crisis unfolding here. Please, could you take Matthew tonight?"

He didn't even hesitate for a moment.

When Amy said 'crisis', it meant just that.

"I'm on my way," he said.

*

When Hunter arrived, Matthew met him at the front door, grinning from ear to ear, carrying his overnight bag which was packed and ready to go.

"Hello, Dad!" he said. "Can we go? I'm ready!"

Hearing him, Amy rushed from the dining room, still in her work clothes and wearing a headset.

"Enjoy your evening, champ!" She hugged Matthew and gave Hunter a quick, stressed smile. "Thank you so much. This evening ran away with me completely, there's been an unexpected delay in getting info, I've got hours of work ahead and I may have to go out to another meeting either tonight or first thing tomorrow."

"Is this all your job still?" Hunter asked incredulously. But Amy shook her head.

"No. Different issue. Got to go." Clearly preoccupied, she turned and rushed back to the dining room. In another moment he could hear her talking the way she did when she was in a meeting, formal and authoritative, though he couldn't make out the words.

He felt concerned about her working so hard on this nameless issue, and also that she didn't want to speak about it. But there was nothing he could do. He was just glad he'd been available to take Matthew for the evening and drop him at school tomorrow.

"Dad," Matthew asked, as Hunter closed the door, making sure the lock clicked into place, as they walked quickly through the drizzle to the car. "Dad, have you named the kitten?"

"I haven't named him yet." If it even was a 'him'. Maybe an androgynous name would be wiser, he decided, until he'd had a chance to take the tiny feline to the vet to get checked out.

"Is his family looking for him?"

"Nobody's gotten in touch yet. I've advertised him and I've been checking the local groups, and I called around to the vet clinics today also," Hunter said. "It seems nobody's looking for him, so I think he's ours to keep."

"I can't wait to see him!"

Eagerly, Matthew scrambled into his booster seat and after fastening him up, Hunter got into the front.

"How was school?" he asked.

"School was okay," Matthew said, giving the words a spin that told Hunter the matter of Carl Commando was not forgotten or forgiven yet.

He could imagine the difficulties, the peer pressure, the need to have what the other kids did and play those games—to be one of the crowd. To not be singled out and bullied. And yet, what he treasured most about Matthew was his individuality. He never, ever wanted him to lose that. He never wanted his son to become just one of the crowd.

As he pulled up outside his apartment building, Hunter put the thoughts out of his mind. He helped his son out of the car and the two of them ran over to the elevator. Hunter was grateful to be able to run. The injury from the bullet wound that had shattered his leg a few months ago could have ended his career. There had been a time when he hadn't known if he'd walk again. Now, running was painful but possible.

The elevator doors opened, and they raced to the apartment's front door.

Already, Hunter could hear excited mewing coming from behind the door. He unlocked it, eased it open, and Matthew went in first.

"OH, Dad! It's so cute!" Abandoning his bag in the hallway, Matthew dropped to his knees and began stroking the tiny feline, who was rubbing his whiskers against Matthew's fingers and rolling on the floor. Soon, he began purring thunderously.

"He's a cutie, isn't he?" Hunter moved the bag into Matthew's bedroom, switched on the dinosaur lamp, and then headed to the kitchen to fix cat dinner and make a start on human dinner. He'd decided on a firm household favorite, DIY pizzas. He'd bought the bases and some toppings, and he and Matthew would each decorate their own. Last time they'd even given them silly names as well. He hoped they'd do the same this time.

It was a lighthearted end to a tough day. He couldn't forget his worries but at least they'd been relegated to the back of his mind for the time being.

As he fixed himself a beer and Matthew a soda, his son came into the kitchen with the kitten now atop his shoulders, balancing precariously but looking as excited about the arrangement as Matthew was.

"I think this kitten should be called… should be called…" He stroked its head as he considered the possibilities, while the kitten gnawed tenderly at his ear.

With a flash of fear, Hunter dreaded that he was going to suggest Carl Commando as a name. He didn't know why that thought occurred to him. But luckily it hadn't occurred to Matthew.

"I think he should be called Merlin."

"Merlin?" That was a name that Hunter hadn't expected.

"He's gray, like a wizard's beard," Matthew explained.

Hunter was pleased that his son's mind had turned to the Arthurian legend that he'd read to him and given him some picture books of, earlier this year.

Setting out pepperoni, tomatoes, ham and bell peppers, Hunter liked the logic behind that choice. And he was elated by how happy and distracted Matthew was.

"There's only one problem, Dad," his son explained as he took the bowl of kitten food from the counter and put it on the floor for Merlin to devour.

"What's that?" Thoughts of military toys were uppermost in Hunter's mind once more as he waited for his son to explain the problem.

"I'm worried about Merlin being lonely," Matthew confided. "Because you're at work all day and I'll only get to see him a couple of days a week." He put the kitten down in front of the food bowl, which it attacked with gusto, still purring loudly.

"Well, I'm not really sure that's something we can fix right now," Hunter protested feebly, but Matthew, showing a remarkable similarity to Amy at that moment, forged ahead with his argument without even taking in Hunter's words.

"I have an idea!" he announced. "We can get Merlin a friend! And then, you and I can have two kittens, Dad!"

Two kittens? Already, his son was negotiating upward. The thought of an ever-growing band of felines occupying his apartment was worrying. If he had to resign, he and the two cats might end up looking for different accommodation, a cheaper place, somewhere further out of town. After what had played out today, Hunter had to acknowledge that was a possibility.

It wasn't a time to go acquire any animals, let alone more.

Then again, if Hunter agreed to this, then he'd have a strong bargaining chip if and when the subject of Carl Commando came up.

He could then play his two-kitten trump card, telling Matthew that he'd compromised on the cats and that *he* needed to compromise on the toy.

It was worth it, he decided.

"Great idea," he said, and saw his son's face light up. "I'm going to take Merlin to the vet tomorrow for a checkup – we'll go before school, so you can come with me, and we can find out then if there's a friend that we can adopt." And if Merlin is really a 'he', he thought wryly.

Now, he let the seriousness be audible in his voice as he set out the bargain. "But I need you to understand something, hero. Are you listening?"

"Yeah, Dad. I'm listening," Matthew said. Having finished his dinner, Merlin was listening too. Two sets of eyes were on Hunter as he spoke.

"Two kittens is something within my power to do. It's helping animals, giving them a home, getting us a little furry family. But buying you a toy that your mother disapproves of is something I can't do. Understand?"

Matthew made a wry face.

"I guess I do."

"One's more important than the other. One's a toy you'll play with for a few months. The other is an animal that we'll care for and enjoy for years. So, which is more important to you? Carl Commando, or getting Merlin a friend?"

"Getting Merlin a friend," Matthew said instantly, and Hunter nodded his approval. His son had gotten it. There might be bumps in the road ahead – but for now, he'd gotten it.

"Now, we need to get these pizzas decorated and cooked. I'm going to name my pizza ' Pandemonium'. What are you going to name yours?"

But as he spoke, despite the happiness of the evening and the elegant solution that the second kitten had enabled, Hunter felt a cloud of worry darkening his thoughts again.

There was an unsolved crime still looming. With two dead bodies so far and no real leads, he feared for another death. He was worried that the mystery man hadn't pitched up for his meeting with Amelia. That made Hunter uneasy, and it made him think that things were happening behind the scenes.

With a day left to solve this case, the pressure was on.

First thing tomorrow, he needed to find out who Coburn was and if he was the man behind that website.

23
Journalist's Demise

The call came in just as Hunter was heading from Matthew's school to the police station the next morning.

"There's been another body found," the control room operator told him. "Same MO. It's a male victim on a property out of town."

Already, Hunter was veering off the road to the police station that he'd been following. Instantly, his heart rate was spiking.

"On my way. Send the coordinates," he said.

A third murder in as many days? He shook his head, turning right and right again to backtrack his route as the coordinates came through.

Surely there was no way that Rogan could redeploy him or tell Gibson to pull him off the case now. Could he? This was now a murder epidemic. He had no idea who this latest victim would be. But he was sure, with a cold certainty, that the man would somehow be linked to the others.

A toy manufacturer? An activist? He didn't know and could only guess. The happiness of the early morning's activities – the visit to the vet, the pronouncement that the kitten was in good health, Matthew's fascination as the vet had given Merlin his shots – all this now faded into the

166

background as he sped to the scene. At least he'd gotten Matthew to school. Now, he followed the road out of town, thankful that he was going against the floods of traffic coming in.

The victim has been identified as Mick Coombes; the radio told him as he drove. That was all he had. He didn't know who Mick Coombes was. All he had was a name and an address – which was leading him to a quiet housing estate that juxtaposed a larger tract of land where development was taking place. Bulldozers and cranes were hard at work creating a high-density estate backing onto this quiet road.

Hunter swung into the street, seeing police lights ahead. Parking behind them, he got out of the car and hurried up to the house – a modest, double-story home with a shabby look to it and a garden growing wild. The front door was open. Outside were a few people gathered, with a police officer keeping them back from the doorway.

Briefly, Hunter greeted the officer. He put on foot covers and a head cover and went in.

The hallway was a bloody sight. He guessed this man might have been ambushed there on his way in or out. Car keys lay on the floor near him. Blood streaked the white wall tiles and spattered the floor. The coroner was already on site, bending over the body.

"Morning, Hunter," he said, glancing up, brisk and businesslike as he went about his examination. "This victim was killed yesterday afternoon. Probably around three or four p.m. I believe one of the witnesses outside, from a neighboring house, has just confirmed this. She heard a bang, but thought it was work being done on the construction site."

So he'd been killed yesterday? Hunter considered that fact as the coroner worked.

And then, he moved aside, and Hunter saw the body clearly for the first time.

Two head wounds, one on the side of the head, one on the forehead. On an upward trajectory, the bullet had blasted out of the top of the man's head. His skull was a bloody ruin. But his face, below the forehead, was undamaged.

Hunter hadn't thought he would recognize him but to his astonishment, he did.

He had black hair and a short goatee.

He was wearing a gray button-down shirt.

Blinking in surprise, Hunter took in the facts as he knew them.

Without a doubt, this was the man who'd approached Amelia Evans in the deli. He'd asked her to meet him after work because he had important information involving Day Zero. And this was why he hadn't arrived at the coffee shop.

He'd been desperate to tell Amelia. He'd known something, and he'd been taken out.

He returned to the door. Looked out at the shocked group of people who were still standing a few yards away. Two men, three women.

"Any of you know more about this victim? What he did?" he asked.

"I know," one of the women said. She was in her forties, with a drawn, lined face that told Hunter her life had been hard. "We used to talk to each other every few days. He was a journalist. He was a freelancer who wrote pieces for a few different publications."

"What did he specialize in?" Hunter asked.

"He was a very good investigative journalist. He worked on some big exposes, and he also did regular pieces. I think his areas of expertise were politics and business."

Politics and business?

Hunter shook his head. He was too late to get the information directly from this man and he felt sick inside. Whoever was doing this was a step ahead, and now he suspected that they were cutting off information sources about whatever this was. The knowledge had died with this man before he could tell it.

So far, an activist had been murdered while she was busy with a big expose. A toy manufacturer who had a social conscience had been murdered after he'd had a clandestine meeting that had left him deeply troubled. And now, a journalist had been murdered – and Hunter was sure he'd been busy with a story.

He was too late. Too late in joining the dots and now, too late in finding out what he needed.

Was there anything to be found in his house, he wondered suddenly. A freelancer would have done his work from home. If Mick Coombes' notes were on his phone then Hunter wouldn't get them today, but maybe he'd also kept a record somewhere else?

He went back inside and stepped carefully around the site where the body lay. Then he headed upstairs. The stairway was narrow, and the wooden steps creaked as he trod on them. Upstairs, the air smelled faintly of cigarette smoke. There were two rooms – a bedroom and a small room he guessed was the study, furnished with a desk and an overflowing ashtray.

There was a laptop on the desk. Hunter moved the mouse, but a screen came up asking for a password. Another job for forensics, another few days' delay. He might not even be on the case by then.

Didn't this guy keep jotted notes somewhere, he wondered. Anywhere? Maybe on that messy desk pad that was full of scribblings and random names and numbers.

He only had one lead left and that was The Signal, the conspiracy theory site that had published some of the information and that warning, which now, he was wondering if Coombes had written.

He could understand, given the body count so far, why the contact details of that site owner were so difficult to obtain. But he needed a break here. He desperately needed a break.

Sitting down in the hard, squeaky office chair, he scanned the notepad closely. Looking at every small jotting, every squiggle of the pen. There was nothing that tied up with this, though. Just random notes that didn't mean anything.

However, Hunter now saw that there were a few pieces of paper stuck under the edge of the desk pad as if wedged there for temporary safekeeping.

One by one he took them out and had a closer look.

The first two meant nothing to him, they seemed nothing more than venues and dates for meetings.

But the third had a name. A name he recognized from The Signal.

"Harvey Coburn", was jotted, in Mick's inky scrawl.

And it was followed by a phone number.

Hunter breathed in deeply, getting up from the chair. He'd found the lead he needed, and there was no time to lose.

If Coburn knew something, then he was in danger. Hunter needed to get to him fast before the other side did.

24
Desert Chase

He had a name, a last name, and a phone number. And even better, Hunter had Cody Lamarr as a partner.

His partner's expertise in sifting through the databases and getting information was second to none.

Hunter called him before he'd even left the crime scene.

"I know who runs the conspiracy theory website The Signal," he said. "And we need to reach him, fast. Because other people are going to be trying the same."

If there was ever a time when he needed Cody to work his magic, it was now.

"Send it through," his partner said, sounding confident. Hunter wished he shared his assurance. Everything that had happened in the past twenty-four hours had shaken him and now, he wasn't sure of anything anymore.

Or rather, to put it another way, he was now deeply distrustful of everything.

With the details sent, Hunter focused on his driving, catching the tail end of the traffic coming back into LA and taking a few shortcuts to try to bypass it. As he drove, he tried to think through what he'd learned.

People who knew something – presumably about Day Zero – were being murdered. Day Zero seemed to be linked, somehow, to Carl Commando, although nobody was explicitly saying so. Not publicly, anyway. But the assistant had been approached. There was an attempt being made to get information. And people were being killed for doing it.

Somebody at Dreamland Creations might know something, especially since Amelia had been approached. But without more knowledge of the situation, Hunter knew he'd be stabbing in the dark. He'd already been stonewalled by Olivia Montgomery and a second visit would only mean more of the same unless he could get a break on the case.

Now, to find out if this would give him the break he needed.

When Hunter got into the back office, Cody was at his corner desk, speaking on the phone. He didn't see Gibson anywhere, to his relief but he did see a couple of the other team members. They returned his quick greeting with a level of restraint that told Hunter they knew exactly what had gone down at the high-level inspection by the Department of Defense.

He was a pariah all over again, without even intending to be. Through one innocent question, he'd made a very serious, very influential enemy. And he still did not understand how exactly it had turned so bad, so fast.

"You got anything yet?" he asked Cody in a low voice, bending over and seeing that the cup of coffee on Cody's desk was virtually untouched. If that was a sign of how hard he'd been working on this, then Hunter was impressed.

Cody turned to look at him, an expression of determination on his bulldog face, his stubby fingers flying as he updated him.

"I have checked three normal databases. I found an old address. He's moved."

"Don't blame him, given the attrition rate so far," Hunter said.

"I'm now looking in alternative databases and I've made a few calls."

Cody had informants in a couple of key companies, who were sometimes prepared to give him information they shouldn't. His powers of persuasion were second to none and he had a lot of friends in strange places.

Cody could sit down for a beer with anyone and within a half-hour he'd know their family history and their mother's problems, and be offering them advice on how to sort out their car repayment discrepancy or pointing them in the direction of a guy who could help. He was well-networked.

Now, Hunter saw that it was getting results.

Cody's phone rang. He answered briefly.

"You got it? Excellent. Appreciate it."

Hunter's pulse quickened as his partner scribbled down an address on his notepad, before hanging up.

"Someone who shouldn't have told me gave me an updated address. Seems legitimate but it's far out of town. We'd better get going."

Hunter was already turning for the door, car keys in hand.

*

Coburn lived twenty miles beyond the city limits. Hunter guessed that the area would be rural, bordering the desert; a tough, arid environment. And it was.

Nearing the place where he lived, they sped along a dirt road with a deep gully a few hundred feet away, jagged mountains on the horizon, and rocks, tufts of grasses bushes, and Joshua trees lining the road. Every so often along the way, a house came into view. They all looked dilapidated and some even seemed deserted.

It was the kind of environment where he'd expect to find a man who fit Coburn's description of a conspiracy theorist – and a man who was, rightly, probably quite paranoid.

"We'd better keep a lookout early on," Cody said, as Hunter slowed the car, checking the map. They were close by, although the satnav was not totally accurate in this remote area.

"Yes. We need to be on the alert," Hunter said. Who knew who else was looking?

"Seems a couple of miles further," Hunter said. The satnav had rerouted, and he hoped this time it was more accurate. There was a narrow crossroad a couple of hundred yards ahead that matched up with the map, at any rate.

"Straight out of a Western movie set," Cody commented. His oftentimes partner always kept things lighthearted at such moments, even though Hunter knew that he was scanning the surroundings with a watchful and experienced gaze.

"Yes. Feel like every time we turn a corner, we might bump into a film crew at work," Hunter joked back.

"As long as Buffalo Bill doesn't end up grabbing our car to make his getaway," Cody quipped.

And then, the map zoomed in and the time for tension-easing jokes had passed. Harvey Coburn's recorded address was ahead. Hunter was praying he'd be there, and be alive, and be willing to talk. Right now, nothing at all was certain.

It was a low, brick building with a tin roof that Hunter guessed would be sweltering in the heat of summer. On this cloudy, cooler day it simply looked ramshackle and forlorn. There was a shed behind the building that might double as a garage. There was no car in sight, and no clues as to whether Coburn was home or not.

Hunter eased up to the house and stopped the car on the road, before climbing out and walking the twenty-yard distance over stony ground where a faint path had been trodden, to the front door.

Hunter knocked on the weathered wood, noting that the film of dust on the only visible windowpanes at the front of the house made it impossible to see in.

He might not be home.

Or else he might be home but no longer alive.

He waited, hearing the tiny rustle of fabric as Cody shifted beside him, a throbbing truck engine from the main road a couple of miles away, and a clanging noise as a loose piece of sheet metal was blown by the wind.

Then his head jerked to that dusty window. Had there been movement there? He hadn't been in time to clearly see it, but he sensed that someone had peered through briefly.

Was that the sound of footsteps inside? Cody tensed at exactly the same time. Who was in there? Were the footsteps Coburn's – or had somebody else gotten there first?

A few tense seconds passed. Hunter made himself breathe slowly and easily, listening hard.

And then there was a loud, banging noise.

It was so sharp and sudden that Hunter jumped, his hand instinctively moving to the grip of his gun. Then his brain caught up.

The noise had come from the far side of the house. It was the back door slamming.

The pounding of footsteps told him that yet again, this case had taken a disastrous turn. Coburn had heard them arrive and had assumed the worst. He was not waiting around.

He was a scared, paranoid man, and now, he was fleeing.

"Go after him!" Hunter shouted.

This was a man they couldn't afford to lose. Terrified as he was, they had to catch up with him. If he ran from them, somebody else would get him. That was a certainty.

Hunter sprinted around the side of the house, the uneven, stony ground already taking its toll on his leg. He could feel it starting to throb and knew he'd need to tread as carefully as he could.

But the chase was more important. The man – a lithe, dark-clad figure, had already vaulted the wire fence and was now racing into the desert. Shrubs, trees, rocks, and boulders provided far more cover than Hunter would have liked.

"Coburn! Come back! We want to help!" Hunter yelled, but the wind whipped his voice away, and he didn't know if Coburn had heard it at all.

He was weaving through the harsh terrain with such familiarity and dexterity that Hunter wondered if this was a preplanned route. Had this website owner mapped it out, thinking about the eventuality of a killer arriving?

At any rate, worryingly, he'd already vanished from sight by the time Hunter and Cody had leaped the fence.

"I'll take the right," Hunter yelled, seeing that the faint track branched in two directions at the junction of an enormous boulder.

Cody pounded on, heading left, and Hunter veered right, following the trail, glancing down for any sign of footprints on the rocky ground that might show where their suspect had fled, keeping aware of his surroundings in this unfamiliar terrain.

What could he hear? The wind was still blowing strongly, muffling ambient sound, and he couldn't pick up the thud of footsteps now. It was as if he was alone. He could just see the track in front of him, a faint indentation among the stones, but Hunter acknowledged there were lots of places where somebody could simply have left the track and headed across the wild desert terrain.

But scrambling over the loose boulders and among the rough grasses would have slowed Coburn down, so Hunter was going to gamble that he wouldn't have done that, not when he was running scared.

What was that? He skidded to a stop, listening hard. It had sounded like a clatter of rocks, a mini avalanche. If so, then it was coming from the right- and looking closely, he saw the trail veer off, no more than a flattening of the ground, into a right-hand branch.

Hunter ran along it, seeing that the path was narrowing fast, and the ground was dropping off steeply to his right. This chase was veering ever closer to the edge of the steep gully they'd glimpsed earlier.

And then, his heart accelerated.

There was his suspect – but not as he'd expected to see him.

Racing along the edge of the precipice, Coburn must have slipped and fallen. And he'd gone right over the edge.

A yard below the precipice's rim, he'd managed to grab hold of a jutting tree root. He was grasping onto it, his face pale and taut, his body dangling over the sheer drop.

As Hunter ran up, he saw the root loosen, jerking downward in a shower of sand.

"Help!" Coburn gasped, glancing up, his face gray and his knuckles white as he gripped the bark.

The root slipped again, loosening further and Hunter's stomach clenched. He didn't have long. Just a few more seconds and that root was going to rip free from the sand.

When it did, Coburn would plummet down the cliff face onto the jagged rocks far below.

25

Cliffside Rescue

Hunter could see the root tugging away from the cliff face, a shower of sand accompanying each weakening. Coburn was hanging on for grim death, his gaze pleading as he stared up.

"Help me," he muttered, his arms quivering with the strain of holding his own weight, his legs flailing helplessly as he fought for purchase against the sandy cliff.

"Cody!" Hunter yelled. Another pair of hands in this perilous situation might save the day. In the meantime, though, he had to act fast.

Coburn was too far down the cliff for Hunter to grab him on his own. What could he do? Throw something at him? He had nothing with him that could work. What could the environment offer?

Turning away from the sheer drop, Hunter stared around the arid landscape, hearing another panicked shout from the cliff face. Any moment, that flimsy root would tear out completely.

What about that branch lying there? It was an old tree branch, gnarled and woody and about a yard and a half in length. He didn't know if it was strong enough – but it was more solid than the root. If nothing else, it would buy him some time.

Hunter grabbed the thicker end of it, wrapping his hands around it, making sure his grip was as tight as possible, and using a rough knot in the wood to help secure it.

"Cody!" he yelled again, as he rushed back to the cliff face. He needed his partner now. He hoped Cody could hear his shouts.

Grasping the tree branch, he lowered it over the edge, his boots slipping in the loose, stony soil. That rock, there. Would it be solid enough for him to brace on? He locked his hands around the wood and pushed the sole of his right boot against the rock, trying to anchor himself strongly enough that his position would hold when Coburn took his weight off the loosening root and grabbed the branch.

"Go on!" Hunter shouted. "Get hold of it!"

He didn't want to think about that sheer, plummeting drop to the jagged floor of the valley far below or of the treacherous, crumbling cliff edge that had already given way once.

He just had to think about what would happen when Coburn grabbed hold of the branch, and how he would try to hold him.

With abrupt suddenness, the branch was all but jerked out of his hands as Coburn abandoned his grip on the flimsy root and threw all his weight onto the tree branch. Hunter's arms were nearly jerked out of its sockets. The wood scored his palms painfully, but he held on for grim death.

While his right foot was keeping its braced position on the rock – just – his left one was skidding on the stones, slipping inexorably toward the cliff edge.

Hunter fought to retain his grip, wishing he'd been able to do this the other way round because his right leg was the weaker one thanks to his old injury.

The stones slid again. Now his left leg was all but useless. It was about to slide over the cliff face too. As Coburn did his best to clamber up the tree branch, Hunter knew that all their hopes rested on his quivering right leg, which was starting to burn.

Worse still, the rock it was braced against was beginning to shift. He didn't know how long it would stay secure but feared its time was short. Coburn was scrambling up the branch, he could hear his ragged gasps, but it was happening far too slowly.

Deadly slow.

The rock was wobbling now, and Hunter gritted his teeth, seeing that this was a race against time that they were going to lose.

And then, with a thudding of feet, Cody appeared, sprinting toward him up the hill.

"Got you! I got you!" Cody yelled.

Rushing forward, he flung himself flat on his stomach, throwing his arms out to grab the branch below where Hunter was holding it.

Instantly, the dead weight on Hunter's arms eased. His muscles were still quivering, the branch shifting and tugging as Coburn struggled up it, inch by painful inch.

Then, with a jolt, the weight came off the branch as Coburn grabbed Cody's arm in his. Now, Hunter stepped sideways, grabbing his other arm, hauling as hard as he could. And, in a shower of sand and pebbles, they dragged Coburn back onto solid ground and away from the treacherous edge.

For a moment, they simply stood, breathing hard.

"Mr. Harvey Coburn?" Hunter confirmed in breathless tones.

"That's me." He paused, looking from Hunter to Cody and back again. "Thank you for your help there." Looking at them more closely, he said, "You really police? Not that it makes much difference," he said sourly. Right now, I don't trust anyone, police or not."

"Appears there's a fair reason for that," Hunter admitted, showing Coburn his LAPD police ID. "But we need some information from you urgently."

The man they'd just rescued was tall and broad-shouldered and in his early forties. He had the look of someone who'd spent time outdoors, with tanned skin, a tough-looking jaw, a short beard, and the curling edge of a tattoo protruded from the collar of his gray plaid shirt. He was wearing slippers. Hunter guessed he'd run without having paused to change his footwear, and that was why he'd slipped as he'd traversed the stony path.

Poor footwear choices aside, it was clear that this man had been ready to run. He'd been on the alert, and he hadn't wasted a moment when he had thought Hunter was after him. He hadn't even paused to change his shoes. He knew more about this, and Hunter wanted to know what he knew.

Coburn shook his head. "Right now, I'm not in the mood for talking. Seems if you say anything, you don't last long in these parts."

Hunter considered the problem.

"Shall we walk back down?" he asked. Willing to talk or unwilling, the cliff face wasn't the best environment to conduct this discussion.

The wind was strong up here, cooling Hunter's hair and scouring the fresh grazes on his forearms from his cliffside struggle. Perhaps the walk back down to the house and being in a more comfortable environment would settle this man's fears and make him more willing to talk. Surely the fact that Hunter and Cody had saved him might also count in their favor?

Hunter decided, as they picked their way down the stony pathway, that it might not actually count in their favor because fear might override this logic. Three people who knew something about this had been murdered.

Harvey Coburn was a frightened man.

As he slipped and skidded his way down the path – it hadn't seemed so steep when he was running up it, in desperate pursuit of his target – Hunter tried to work out the best way to approach the situation.

Police protection? He didn't know if it was within his powers to offer that currently, and more worryingly, he wasn't sure how effective it would be. Hunter's confidence in his own police department was badly dented. The presence of corruption eroded the integrity of the police, and it made him cautious about suggesting that.

Promising confidentiality? That might also not be persuasive enough.

Asking for other sources? That might work.

He knew there was an undercurrent of information flowing. The website No to Violence seemed to have been tapped into it, but not yet to the same degree. What about the man from the National Peace Alliance, whom Nick Taylor had spoken about in such a derogatory way? He might also know some but not enough.

Perhaps there were others.

Approaching the small house, Coburn led the way inside and when Hunter followed, he was surprised to see what awaited him.

The small living room, which contained a scuffed leather couch, a large television, and a writing desk, was filled with the evidence of hasty packing. There were folders lying on the couch. A travel bag on the scuffed blue carpet was standing open. Another black carry-on was standing in the doorway that led to the bedroom. It was closed up and looked full.

"Yeah," Coburn said, seeing the direction of Hunter's gaze as he took in the state of the room. "I'm going. I'm not waiting here for them to find me. Not after what's happened. I got a friend north of San Francisco who lives on a farm, and he said he'd put me up for a few weeks."

"Why a few weeks?" Hunter asked. "What does this timeframe depend on?"

Coburn gave him a sidelong glance. "It might be longer," he said. "You think I'm going to hide away and let things happen? I'll be working to stop it, just from somewhere else. Somewhere they don't know where I am."

He lowered himself down on the couch next to his pile of files and clasped his hands so that his weathered fingers were knotted tightly together.

"If you're working to stop it, why not tell us what you know?" Cody reasoned.

Coburn stared at him with narrowed eyes.

"Because I don't want my leads evaporating," he said. "I'm busy getting information. Quietly, patiently. I have a couple of sources who are passing it on to me. They trust me. Just as I don't want to be killed, I sure as hell also don't want any of the people who are helping me to be killed either."

"I get that. Without giving them up, what can you tell me then?" Hunter asked.

Coburn nodded. "I like it that you respect my loyalty," he said.

"I understand how fragile it is. But this thing – whatever it is – sounds big. It sounds like it might be difficult to stop. You might not be able to do that on your own. And if exposing it is so difficult and dangerous and time-consuming, then it's gaining momentum with every day that passes?" Hunter reasoned. "I'm guessing here, I know. I'm inferring things from what you have said. But if I'm right, then surely it's a danger that's getting ready to explode?"

"Yes, you are right. And it is a danger."

He paused.

"Look, I was getting most of my information from Mick. He was feeding it to me."

"Mick Coombes? He's the journalist who was killed this morning?" Cody confirmed.

"Yes, that's right. That's why I was packing up now. That was a massive shock to me. For the best part of an hour, I was paralyzed, sitting here with my mind spinning, feeling that there was a target on my back already and anything I did would be the wrong move. Then I started planning," he said. "I had to because I knew if he had been taken, I might be next."

"Why was he targeted? Because he was writing a story?"

"He was busy with a massive expose, although it wasn't as detailed as it needs to be. But he was finding it difficult to get the story out. He said it was being suppressed."

"Suppressed how?" Hunter asked.

"He said the mainstream media – excuse the term, I know it's used a lot on my website – he said they've been pressured not to publish anything. I'm not sure how. Whether it's a financial incentive or a threat or the fact that at top level they're all an old boys' club, who knows."

"You think a senior person in mainstream media could be bought?" Cody asked, sounding surprised.

"I don't think. I know."

"Happened before?" Cody asked curiously.

"It happens more often than you would believe," Coburn said. "But my feeling is that this isn't one of those occasions. I think this time, it's a threat. I don't have a reason for thinking that. I guess it's just aligned with the character of everything else that's been going on. This is something bigger, worse, than what I've had to deal with in the past."

He was talking more freely now. He was relaxing somewhat, Hunter saw. But he hadn't yet given any details; that he was still being cagey about, and Hunter needed to figure out a way to break through that resistance.

"What is it?" Hunter asked again, but Coburn shook his head.

"Man, if I could tell you I would. But I don't know. Genuine. I was hoping to get answers from Mick and now, Mick's dead. I've got to backtrack. Go back to my sources. Look, I understand this needs to be solved."

Hunter waited, forcing himself to be patient, remembering that frightened men didn't talk freely, and it was clear that Harvey Coburn was a frightened man.

"Okay. This is what I can do," Coburn finally said. "I'll give you the contact of the very first person who gave Mick the heads-up. I think that'll be safe because he left the hotel, and they never knew he was involved. So he's a cutout now and they won't know how to find him. That I can do. His name's Drew Gonzalez. And I'll tell you his cell number because I don't want you calling the hotel and finding it out."

He looked through his phone. Hunter saw that his hands were shaking.

Hesitantly, he read out the number and the address.

"But be warned," he said when Hunter had taken it down. "You must go easy with him. You think I'm scared? Gonzalez is terrified. He knows they're going to come after anyone who tries to stop this. And he doesn't want to be next."

26

Apartment Chaos

As Hunter drove off, he saw Coburn had stationed himself at his front door like a statue. Staring into the hazy distance, watching the quiet road, the bearded man was going nowhere until he and Cody had left.

Hunter couldn't even label his behavior as paranoid. Three people so far, had been murdered. Perhaps the reason Coburn was still alive was that he had stayed so alert.

"We need to go straight to Gonzalez," he said. "Straight there."

A delay might be costly.

"The address is on the other side of town," Cody keyed it into his GPS. "It'll take us half an hour."

Hoping he could shave a few minutes at least off that estimate, Hunter made tracks for the highway.

Getting there fast was the easy part. The tougher part would be to find Gonzalez, and then, to see if he would talk. Given the deadly implacability of what was playing out, Hunter didn't feel too optimistic about any part of this.

"Media suppression?" Cody asked as they drove, interrupting Hunter's troubled thoughts. "I was surprised by what Coburn said. You think it happens a lot?"

Hunter nodded, grateful for the distraction of the question. "There are very few media houses who are truly impartial. Nobody can afford to be in an industry that relies on advertising income. It's not even about the old boys' club most times, it's more a case of not biting the hand that feeds you."

"I guess there's a lot more competition for advertising dollars these days," Cody agreed.

"What would you do if you were a media owner who was tipped off about misdoings in one of the companies owned by your biggest advertiser?"

Cody nodded thoughtfully as Hunter sped along the highway, away from the barren desert fringes, heading once again toward the city.

"You upset them; they withdraw their support? And there are other choices these days?"

"Exactly," Hunter agreed. "They have businesses to run, employees to pay, lifestyles to support. Stories are put on the backburner or killed these days for that exact reason, or else, they allow the other side enough of a response that they can sow doubt or discredit the source."

And that, he knew, was where the fringe media played a role. They would publish what the main media houses wouldn't, but without the checks and balances and editorial know-how in place, they were less creditable, their stories often unbalanced, and sometimes incoherent, as he'd seen on Coburn's website.

Nope, Hunter acknowledged as he neared the suburb where Gonzalez lived, it was a complex topic. The truth was never easy to find and often impossible.

They were heading into a densely populated part of LA that was the polar opposite of what they'd left behind.

Weaving his way through increasingly narrow streets, between high-rise buildings, the crush and noise of traffic seemed loud and intrusive after the eerie quietness of the desert.

Which building was it?

"That one, there," Cody said, checking his GPS yet again.

Hunter squeezed the car into a space – the road was crammed with cars, mostly elderly and dented, a sign that the residents here were mostly struggling. Climbing out, he smelled the air, dense with fumes with an undertone of acrid smoke. Usually, Hunter felt a sense of sympathy when he investigated places like this.

These people were on the fringes, living paycheck to paycheck, their lives a fragile and vulnerable struggle for survival.

At any stage, Hunter believed that the average person was only a couple of bad decisions away from being on the streets. He'd seen it often enough in his police work.

But now seeing this environment drove home to Hunter the fact that at the moment, his job was in jeopardy, and he had tough decisions to make.

Now, he couldn't help wondering if asking Rogan the wrong question at the wrong time had been bad decision number one for him.

Looking at this ten-floor apartment building was causing his own predicament to weigh heavy on his mind. It might not be too long before he was looking for a cheaper place. Without his salary as a senior LAPD detective, there was no way he could stay where he was for more than a month or two.

He and Cody headed up to the entrance. The doorway was barred by a large glass door, with streaks and smears on the cloudy glass. On the wall beside it was a long keypad with numbered buttons and an intercom.

There was a short queue at the door, the only access point for visitors. The buzzer made a harsh, shrilling sound when it rang up to the apartments. The intercom on the wall was crackly, making it difficult to hear what either party – downstairs or upstairs – was saying. It was a tedious and noisy process to get in.

And it was clear that the system didn't work so well, because when one person was buzzed in and the door was opened, other people often grabbed it and went inside as well. And then, the adjacent doorway, which was for residents only, accessed by key card and also frequently used, was also an opportunity to get inside without being invited.

The cameras positioned above the door looked elderly and Hunter guessed that the footage wouldn't be clear enough to pick up facial features clearly.

Security here was porous, and that was worrying.

At last, after an impatient-looking, dark-haired man in a courier's uniform had buzzed at one of the third-floor doors and been let in, it was Hunter's turn.

He pressed the bell, hearing the now familiar buzz. Would there be an answer?

Hunter waited, listening only to silence, trying to tell himself that he shouldn't get suspicious. That more than likely, Gonzalez was at work. Hunter didn't know if he'd quit his hotel job or been fired, but either way, a man had to put food on the table, didn't he? Logically, it was likely he was at work somewhere else.

"Let's call his number now," he decided, stepping away from the door.

He dialed and waited, but it rang straight through to voicemail. The phone wasn't even turned on, and Hunter didn't like any of this. Not one bit.

"I know this might all be innocent," he muttered to Cody, "but I'd still like to get upstairs and check."

Cody nodded. Then, he edged his way over to the other door as a resident approached.

The dark-haired man had a handlebar mustache and a preoccupied air. He buzzed open the door and headed swiftly for the elevator without looking back.

The door swung closed again, but just before it closed all the way, Cody stuck his shoe inside. A moment later, quietly, and not drawing any attention to himself, he opened it again.

It was a master move. For a big man, Cody could move like a dancer when he was executing a stealthy action. He slipped in like a shadow and held the door open for Hunter.

Hunter checked behind him. Nobody was watching, nobody had even noticed what Cody had so sneakily done. He hurried over and followed Cody.

They crossed the lobby's scuffed floor and headed to the elevator.

The elderly elevator bumped and rattled them up to the sixth floor. When they stepped out, Hunter immediately noticed it was quieter. Up here felt removed from the noisy street below.

The corridor windows had a view of the streaked and grimy back end of the apartment block next door. Its proximity gave the corridor a surprisingly claustrophobic feel.

Apartment 601's door was tightly shut, and the curtains drawn. Same for 602.

Glancing at the window of 603 as he hurried past, Hunter saw it looked totally empty. No blinds, no furniture, just a view of a bare living room through the dusty glass.

Then he reached 604. Raising his hand, Hunter knocked.

The sound made the door rattle noisily.

Glancing at Cody, who was looking surprised by the sound, Hunter waited. No reply from inside.

But it wasn't that which was bothering him so much as the unsteady feeling that door had given him when he'd knocked on it as if it was rattling on its hinges. It hadn't sounded stable.

He pushed down on the handle to see what would happen. Then he grabbed at it as the whole door tipped sideways, accompanied by Cody's cry of "Watch it!"

It didn't open so much as half fell off its hinges, leaning sideways as the wood let out a cracking sound. Hanging onto it, easing it open until it stabilized, allowed Hunter to see the damaged lock clearly.

His eyes narrowed as he saw how it had been forced open and then closed again in a way that had concealed the damage done.

Beyond that, the apartment was a destruction zone.

Hunter caught his breath as he stared inside, taking in the open drawers, the ripped cushions, the torn papers, the smashed glass, and the crockery that littered the floor.

The place hadn't just been raided. It had been torn apart.

"Where's Gonzalez? Where the hell is he? Did they get to him?" Hunter said. The sense of dread that had simmered ever since he'd heard that unanswered buzzer boiled inside him as he strode into the apartment and headed straight to the open bedroom door.

27
Intruder Panic

A tuft of grass under Daniel's shoe almost tripped him up and he hurriedly turned his attention away from the fancy double-story homes lining the road to the quiet sidewalk in front of him.

Now was not the time to draw attention to himself in any way, not even by stumbling. Invisibility was an imperative. This wasn't a game any longer. This was reality and what happened now might set him on a new path in life.

Or else it might have disastrous consequences.

He couldn't let himself think about that because the flashes of fear were overwhelming. So Daniel firmly curbed his imagination as he headed along the quiet sidewalk, wearing the hooded jacket and the sunglasses that he'd been given yesterday, and that he'd worn the last time he was here. He was keeping a lid on his fear but now, guilt thrummed inside him.

Last night, spying on the woman – or rather, surveilling her – had felt like an exciting adventure, even though his conscience had been prickling him. After all, it wasn't illegal to take photos of somebody and to follow them.

But this – what he was about to do was illegal. There were no gray areas. He was plunging into a scenario that could land him in serious trouble.

If the setup was real, of course. Maybe it wasn't. Maybe this was a – a test setup. Something that had been designed to assess not only his skills but also his ability to follow orders.

Entering somebody's house when they weren't home wasn't a bad crime, he reassured himself as he paused near the crossroad on the pretext of checking his phone, but really checking around him to see if anyone was looking.

But he hadn't been told to do just that. He'd been told to take photos and steal something. No way around it, that was a lot more serious and could land him in bigger trouble.

What about cameras? His head swung around again, scanning the houses as anxiety resurged. He knew what these fancy neighborhoods were like. There were cameras everywhere and he had heard some of them even had facial recognition.

Captain Dan might be scared to death and feeling way out of his depth, but he was still a thinking man. He had been smart enough to look out for those cameras on the way here.

There had been some earlier, at the main road but he'd been on a bus at the time. And since then, no street cameras had been around that he could see. He couldn't see any here. Some of the residents would have them inside, of course, but he hadn't seen any outside the house he'd been told to target.

Maybe that's another reason they picked that place, he wondered, the little voice trying again to reassure him that this was, in fact, a legitimate setup.

Even though he knew, deep down, it wasn't.

But then, a hundred dollars was a hundred dollars.

Somebody was paying him to do these fairly innocuous, basically harmless, though increasingly disturbing tasks. Did that mean some kind of contract was in place in other ways? Would he be offered any protection, any immunity, if the worst happened?

That, he didn't know.

Trying to scan his surroundings while appearing casual and nonchalant was challenging. He wished he had eyes in the back of his head as he walked, making sure to keep his demeanor as relaxed as it could be, even though inside he felt so taut and nervous he could twang.

Here was the house. Now, he had to get in.

Fear and a sense of premature defeat swirled inside him so strongly the sensation was almost crippling.

In here? No, he couldn't do it, he should turn and run, he should give this up now. It was wrong, and he'd mess it up and he'd end up in prison, his life ruined.

But there was no turning back when he was already committed. He accepted the money. What was he going to do, go and leave that hundred-dollar bill under the bench where he'd found it again? These people who were paying him and messaging him knew who he was, and he didn't know who they were. The situation was already stacked against him.

Glancing left and right, he grabbed the top of the home's chest-high wall and vaulted over it, feeling a dizzy sense of triumph as his feet landed on the neatly mowed grass, as if he'd broken a barrier he didn't even know existed.

Heart pounding hard, he tiptoed around the house. He needed to think strategically now, even though this was unfamiliar territory to him. He had to find an undetectable way in. That meant he'd need to do exactly what he did in the Carl Commando game. It was really no different. Stay alert, be aware, and take stock of his surroundings. Look for an opportunity and when he sees one, grasp it with both hands, just as if he was on the battlefield.

Where were his opportunities? And where were the threats?

It was strange, Daniel thought, how playing this game – especially the higher levels – had taught skills that he hadn't even known he possessed. Now, as he drew on them, he focused on the upper window of the house next door, separated from this one by a few square yards of well-tended garden on either side of the wooden fence. That was a threat. He could be seen by a neighbor. How to overcome the threat? Hug the fence.

As he did that, he was in a good position to check out the target house, searching for weak points. It seemed quiet and he didn't think anyone was there. Last night there had been activity as he'd crept around and taken his photos. The woman inside had been moving from room to room. She looked like an executive because she'd still been working on her laptop and phone. A wealthy executive woman. He hated that corporate world. Executives had made the decision to fire his dad from his low-ranked office job a few years ago. That had started his dad's downward spiral. Top management, fat and wealthy and insulated, didn't care about the people, only about the numbers.

A sense of resentment toward this homeowner flared and he tended that flame. If he could convince himself she was part of the unfairness of life, then it would make this easier.

Daniel's mind veered away from these resentful thoughts as he saw an opportunity for access, the bathroom window on the first floor.

It had been open the last time he was here, and now he saw that it was open again – just a crack, but he thought he could push it wider. Better still, the bathroom window was on the side of the house and there was no view of other houses nearby. So strategically it was a good choice.

He pushed it up slowly and carefully, easing it wider. He was a tall guy, but he was supple and flexible. Now, it was wide enough for him to wriggle through.

Don't leave any scuff marks on the wall, Daniel told himself.

He hesitated for just a beat. This felt like the point of no return.

Then he was up, grasping the top of the window, easing himself through, making sure to keep his feet well away from the wall. It was harder than he'd thought to wriggle inside. His legs were clumsier in their job than he'd have liked them to be.

And, as he swung his leg around, disaster struck.

He felt his foot brush against something he couldn't see and that something shifted.

And then, with a smashing sound, a glass container that had been on a shelf above the basin fell onto the bathroom floor and shattered in an explosion of glass.

Daniel let out a hissed, desperate breath. His heart was in overdrive, and he was shaking as he threaded himself the rest of the way through the window and clumsily lowered himself down to the floor while trying his best to avoid those gleaming shards.

It was a glass jar that had been filled with potpourri. Fragrant, colorful petals were strewn on the shelf, in the basin, on the floor, and a few floating in the toilet.

This was a catastrophe. He had messed up, he had failed, his mission was over, and he was no longer in the top five percent.

No more praise. No more prospects. And he dreaded what might happen now. Would there be payback from the anonymous person who'd sent him here?

For an entire minute, he stood in the small bathroom, frozen with despair, unable to move or even think.

But then, Daniel drew on his reserves - on what he'd learned in the game. This might not be a defeat but only a setback. Setbacks could be overcome if soldiers took swift action. That meant he was going to have to fix it, and fast. That was what Captain Dan would have been tasked to do and he was going to do the same.

He needed a broom and a dustpan to sweep up the glass. Then he'd have to throw everything in a bag and get rid of the evidence. He wouldn't be able to leave it here. If she checked the trash, she'd see it. He'd have to take it with him and then she'd just think it had disappeared.

No, Daniel told himself.

That's *stupid* thinking.

Reality check! You broke in and smashed something and when this woman gets home, she's going to be mad. She's going to want answers.

So, right now, think smart, Daniel exhorted himself, staring around at the destruction scene. You need to be able to give her answers.

Creating a plausible scenario, Captain Dan whispered in his mind as he stared around, firmly clamping down on the panic clenching at his insides.

That window blind—It looked loose on the left side. If it had dropped down, then it could have knocked the potpourri out of place. So all he had to do was loosen the blind a little more and then this woman would simply think that an accident had occurred.

Annoyance would be her main emotion, rather than suspicion. He could unfasten it now and then once he was out, he could tug it down and close the window, and nobody would suspect a thing.

He breathed out. Then he inhaled sharply, standing there like a statue on the bathroom floor as he tried to avoid standing on any of the shards of glass.

This had almost made him forget his mission. He'd been tasked with a job and that was to take something from the house.

Dan was tempted to bend down and just grab one of the petals. That was something, right? But as he considered the tempting possibility that his mission was almost complete, he shook his head. He didn't think a dried petal would be enough. He needed to go further, to take something that would prove to them that he'd been inside.

Stepping very carefully, Daniel traversed the messy bathroom floor and walked out, now treading on soft carpet as he moved through the interior of the home he'd seen from outside last night.

It was large and spacious compared to his place. The bathroom led into a corridor with a blue carpet and pictures along the wall. Everything was neat and in place, making him worry even more about the breakage he'd caused. At the end of it was a flight of stairs, leading up. He guessed the bedrooms were up that way. Breathing hard as he stood in the corridor, feeling terrified and confused and way too much like a criminal, Daniel considered his options.

He didn't want to go upstairs. That felt too much like an invasion. It would be better to take something from down here. Realizing that his hands had steadied now, at least, after the shock of knocking that container off the shelf, he walked through.

This was a spotless kitchen. A world away from the disaster zone of his own house. Clean, sterile-looking surfaces with gray granite counters and cream tiles that gleamed. Nothing in the sink. Nothing easy to take, but getting his phone out of his pocket, he took a photo to prove he'd been there.

How about from the living room beyond? Heading in there, Daniel saw immediately that the room had more potential. It had ornaments on the mantelpiece, paintings on the walls, and a few framed photographs that were arranged on a side table in the corner.

He took another shot of the room. In it, he could see his own reflection on the edge of the mirror. That was good, right?

Never mind taking photos with his phone. Stealing an actual photo from this display would prove he'd been here. That might be the best choice. The most strategic one, he decided.

He moved forward, looking at them. It felt like peeking into someone's life. This was the woman, and now he saw she had a son too. There were a few family pics near the back of the display and behind them, there was one photo of the little guy, right at the back. A small one of him on his own, crowded out by the others. That might be the best one, he decided. It wouldn't be immediately missed.

He reached for it, pride and satisfaction surging inside him that he'd completed a difficult, dangerous, and illegal task without being caught. It made him feel strangely powerful, like society's rules didn't matter and he was above and beyond them.

But as Daniel's fingers closed around the small steel frame, he heard a noise that spun his mind into panic, shattering this feeling that had so briefly and pleasantly filled him.

A key was rattling in the front door.

In a moment, somebody would walk inside.

28
Secret Dealings

Hunter strode to the bedroom, stepping over the debris, dreading that Gonzalez had been murdered here and he would see a worse scene inside.

He exhaled slowly as he stared into the small space. This room was just as badly trashed. The bedcovers had been ripped away and were on the floor. The mattress was askew. All the drawers hung open; contents strewn on the floor.

But there wasn't a body.

Now, analyzing the scene with a calmer mind, he didn't think this looked like the scene of a struggle. He was guessing Gonzalez hadn't been taken.

Walking carefully, Hunter retraced his steps.

"He's not there?" Cody asked anxiously, and Hunter shook his head.

"He's not there."

"I think someone broke in hoping he would be here and then tore the place apart." Cody stepped forward, staring at the papers on the floor, a cushion ripped out of its cover.

"I don't think this is just vandalism. I think they were looking for something."

Those drawers dragged right out of the desk, those cupboards hanging open, the cushions pulled off the chairs. It spoke of a frantic search done by someone who'd desperately been looking for something.

"You reckon they found it?" Cody lifted an edge of the rumpled carpet with a thoughtful expression.

"They sure didn't stop looking," Hunter said.

Would a desperate and fearful man have left compromising evidence in his apartment? Hunter thought that he might not have done so, but if he had, it would be very well hidden. Especially seeing how easy it was to bypass the building's basic security and get up here.

As intensively as this intruder had searched, Hunter had to look even harder.

"What are we looking for?" Rolling up his sleeves and closing the front door softly behind him, Cody stepped inside.

"My guess is information relating to this, something explaining Day Zero, but I don't know in what form we'll find it," Hunter said. "Flash drive, physical papers? If it was on something big, like a laptop, I'm sure they would have taken it."

"Something smaller sounds likely then," Cody agreed.

A frightened man would have hidden his secrets well. But how thoroughly had somebody searched? There had been anger here as well as intent.

Cushions were ripped. A kitchen knife had been used to pry open the locked desk drawer. He had no idea what had been in there, among the scattered contents that littered the carpet.

Gonzalez might already have fled, taking whatever was with him. He hadn't picked up his cellphone – it wasn't even turned on. They couldn't trace the number because they would need to set it up and provide reasons. It would mean sharing the information on Gonzalez's whereabouts. And Hunter had promised Coburn that he would not blow this thing out of the water. He couldn't do it. Not without knowing more about it, and not while being unable to trust people higher in the LAPD command chain.

Think like a frightened man, Hunter told himself.

He checked the underside of the bed, wriggling under it and shining his flashlight up. He found a lot of dust for his efforts and one discarded sock, but nothing more.

There was nothing behind the stove. Nothing taped to the top of the cupboards. Nothing in the dining nook apart from some cracked and shattered crockery.

Cody was continuing the search in the small bedroom and Hunter knew there was no way his sharp-eyed partner would miss anything – if there was anything to be found. He was becoming less sure now.

Although – there was one more place he hadn't yet looked. One more place where people did sometimes hide things that they wanted to keep secret.

Hunter walked over to the refrigerator and opened the freezer door.

It was pretty iced up and needed a serious defrost. A big chunk of fluffy ice crashed down onto the floor when he opened the door, sending frozen shards scattering over his feet. Inside the freezer was an ice tray and a half-finished bag of oven fries with a clothes peg around the top.

Determined to take this down to the wire, Hunter unfastened the clothes peg and untwisted the bag. He peeked inside.

There were a double handful of frozen fries, looking pale and unappetizing and as if they'd been there a long while.

And something else – a dark object that was barely visible among all those fries.

Hunter reached into the bag's cold recesses. And his fingers closed around a small, battered flash drive.

"Cody!" he called out, hearing the excitement in his own voice. "I've got something!"

*

Driving away from the tumbledown building, Hunter felt encouraged that something had been unearthed.

Best case, this flash drive might shed light on Day Zero, but its storage conditions were a worry. The drive had not been protected by a cover or a plastic sleeve. It looked like it might have gotten some moisture inside it while sharing space with the fries in that unreliable freezer.

Let it not be corrupted or damaged, he pleaded with himself as they turned onto the main road.

"I don't want to head back to the station," he said, and Cody nodded his agreement.

"Your name was mentioned there earlier. I think this transfer might be happening sooner than later," his friend and partner admitted. "The chief of police was in a meeting with Gibson when I left. I don't know if this is Charles Harrison's idea or if it's coming from elsewhere."

"His second in command, Rogan, must have influenced the board of police commissioners, and I guess he has allies there now," Hunter remembered his conversation with Gibson a couple of days ago. "Who's going to argue back when a bigger budget is on the table? And when the consequences of arguing are so disproportionate?"

"Nobody except you, it appears," Cody said wryly, as Hunter nodded grimly.

Why don't we park up someplace quiet and just watch it in the car?" his partner suggested. "That might be safest. My laptop is fully charged."

That was a good idea. Hunter carried on along the main road for a few minutes and then turned in the direction of a small shopping center. The mall looked to be struggling. The shops were dilapidated, half of them boarded up. The parking lot in front was only about a third full. And the basement parking around the back looked like a morgue.

"I'm pretty sure we won't be interrupted here," Cody said, as Hunter drove down the ramp and into the gloomy environment. Hunter parked and opened a window and the smell of damp concrete that he'd been expecting filtered in.

"Let's see what we can get," Cody said, in tones that told Hunter he also wasn't sure about the integrity of an uncovered flash drive in that environment.

He reached down, got his laptop out of the bag, and powered it up, pushing his seat back as he did so to give it more room. Cody turned it slightly so that he and Hunter could both see.

Hunter found himself holding his breath as Cody plugged the flash drive in. They needed information so desperately. They needed to catch a break on this damned case. Let this be a start, he pleaded silently.

The flash drive took a long while to appear on Cody's machine. For a while, Hunter feared it was totally corrupted.

And then, finally, it popped up. The expectation in the car felt like a physical force as he and Cody stared down at the contents.

One video file. That was all it contained.

Hunter took a deep breath. "Let's watch," he said.

Whatever was on here, it must be important. It might be a game-changer. Gonzalez had gone to great lengths to hide it away.

The footage began playing.

Hunter watched it closely. A fuzzy image came into view – it was wavering and poor quality, but it looked to him like a hotel meeting room. It had that impersonal yet luxurious feel to it. He saw a section of table, plush, red-upholstered chairs, a generic landscape print on the wall, and a tea and coffee station with an urn, and a row of white cups.

Then, the camera swung slightly, and the new angle revealed a person at the table. A man he recognized. He was sitting with his profile to the camera, talking to somebody that Hunter couldn't see. Someone who was out of the frame.

Would he come into the frame? Hunter waited and watched, willing the image to move and for him to see who this man was speaking to.

And even more importantly, what was he saying? Why was this recording completely silent?

Cody made an annoying noise, fidgeting with his laptop's volume button, but it was like watching a silent movie.

"Either the storage in the freezer has damaged the sound," he said, "or else it didn't work to start with."

Hunter wondered which it was. Perhaps this had been an attempt that had only half succeeded and there had never been any sound at all.

Sideways on, he doubted that a lip reader would be able to pick up the words. He couldn't, but he could see the body language.

It was tense, intent, focused. Whatever this conversation was about, it was incredibly important. The body language gave him no room for doubt.

It wasn't only that which convinced Hunter that it had been a matter of extreme urgency. It was the fact that this had clearly been captured at some effort, and in secret. Had there been a hidden camera? He guessed there might have been one, cheaply bought and concealed on a shelf or in a plant pot.

This was important evidence, and he knew it because somebody had gone to great lengths to film and then to hide this footage.

"Wonder if we'll get a glimpse of whoever he's talking to?" Cody asked as they watched. "Pity the sound isn't working."

Hunter didn't stop hoping that it might, but disappointingly, the sound didn't work the whole way through. Neither did the camera angle widen to show the other person. It was static, and whoever had placed it there had moved it as far as it could go.

All they got was a glimpse of a hand that hand appeared in the frame toward the end of the footage.

It looked like a man's hand, with a white shirt sleeve at the wrist, and it was holding a manila envelope which was passed over to the person being filmed.

Hunter watched carefully, scenarios and ideas crowding his mind, as the man who was in the frame opened the envelope.

It was full of hundred-dollar bills.

Cody hissed in a surprised breath when he saw them.

"Hell, that's a lot of money," he observed. "Some kind of corrupt or underhanded deal playing out there, that's for sure."

Counting them out took a while. It took a full five minutes for the thick wad of cash to be counted. Hunter guessed that there must have been a hundred thousand dollars or more in that tightly stuffed envelope.

Just before the footage ended, the other person's hand appeared in the footage once more as the man, after stashing the manila envelope in his briefcase, stood up.

This time, it was to shake hands.

A deal had been concluded and an agreement made for a handsome price.

Hunter didn't know much. He didn't know where this footage had been filmed, although he could guess it was at the hotel where Gonzalez had worked. He didn't know who the disembodied hand belonged to or who'd given this incentive or what the money was for.

But he knew who'd accepted the money.

Without a doubt, Hunter recognized the man in the frame, whose profile had been visible throughout the filming.

It was Sam Reynolds, COO of Dreamland Creations and the founder of Carl Commando.

"Mr. Reynolds," Hunter muttered. "You have some explaining to do."

29
Unforeseen Consequences

Daniel froze. He stared in the direction of the opening front door, adrenaline pulsing through him so powerfully it felt as if the world was in slow motion.

He was in here illegally, his mind screamed. He would be caught and arrested. He had to get out!

He'd never dreamed he could move so fast.

Turning in one flowing movement, he left the living room and raced back along the corridor in the direction of the guest bathroom. The carpet twisted under his foot as he veered inside, and his knee whacked agonizingly into the doorframe.

Though intense, the pain was a minor consideration compared to the rest of his predicament. At least he was in, he'd made it, just as he heard the front door handle turn.

Picking his way through the glass felt like navigating a minefield that was due to detonate at any moment. He reached the window, hauled himself up, and got his foot over. Then, with a muscle-burning flail and a scissoring of his legs, he was out. He dropped headfirst onto the grass, breaking his fall with his hands, and rolling.

Just in time, he remembered to complete his mission. Good soldiers think under pressure. They don't panic.

He stood up, reached into the window once more and tugged down the side of the blind to complete the scenario that explained the smashed jar.

Then, he wrapped his fingers around the sill and pulled the window as far closed as he could.

Paranoia surged inside him, and he felt at any moment that he might hear a shout or running footsteps, or see somebody appear around the side of the house and race toward him.

None of that happened.

He waited a while, flattened against the wall, just in case anyone was looking out of a window.

Then, calmly, he walked across the grass, leaped over the wall easily, and strolled down the street letting out a long breath and then another.

He put a hand in his jacket pocket. Miraculously, despite his headlong dash, that framed photo he'd taken was still there, still in place.

Although Daniel's legs were cotton wool and he felt sick with the aftermath of the adrenaline, a strange elation bubbled inside him. It remained there, buoying him the whole way home. He'd done it. He'd achieved his mission. Now, he'd earned that money and since he'd taken a very personal item that belonged to the homeowner, he knew he'd excelled.

He waited until he was home. The house was empty. His little brother Luke was still at school, his mother was out at one of her two jobs, and his father was who the hell knew where.

Daniel went to his bedroom and, once there, he collapsed on the bed and simply lay there for a few minutes, finally decompressing after the most stressful situation of his life.

Then using his phone, he took a shot of that photo in the frame and sent it off to the number he was communicating with.

"Take that," he said, in a hoarse voice, the first words he'd spoken aloud since going into that house. "Take that. It couldn't have been done better."

He waited for the response, checking his phone expectantly. His nerves were still so on edge that it did not take long for expectations to become anxiety and then veer into serious worry.

What was happening? Why hasn't this person acknowledged what he'd done?

He needed that confirmation, needed to know that things were okay.

But there was no reply. Nothing. Not even an acknowledgment. He stared at his phone and then, with unexpected speed, the guilt rushed in and the enormity of what he'd done began to hit home.

He'd stolen something from a house, he'd broken in, he'd smashed an item. And now, the person he'd done this task for was not responding and he had no idea if everything was okay or if there had been some catastrophe.

When his phone finally buzzed, he grabbed it so frantically that he almost dropped it.

He stared at the message, first with concern, and then with horror.

"Daniel," it read. *"You made a mistake. Now, you have a huge problem."*

30
In Pursuit

Hunter had suspected from the get-go that the founder of Carl Commando had to be caught up in this somehow. That strange, furtive footage had just confirmed it. He was not going to allow the COO to hide behind canned responses like Olivia Montgomery had done. If necessary, he was going to bring Sam Reynolds in and question him until he gave answers.

Day Zero. The more he thought about the words, the more ominous they sounded.

Cody was back at the police station. He was doing research, trying to discreetly find out where Gonzalez had worked. Knowing which hotel it was would help them a lot. Perhaps there was other footage or bookings or records they could request.

Hunter was heading back to Dreamland Creations alone. He wanted answers and he was going to fight for them.

He got there shortly before two p.m. Not bad going, considering what the day had been like so far, but it felt suffocatingly slow all the same. This case needed to be solved, fast. Someone was killing fast to suppress information and if Hunter didn't keep pace, it might end up being too late.

Sam Reynolds. The founder of Carl Commando. What in hell's name had he been involved in? What bribe or payment had he been accepting in that footage and from whom?

Had he done these killings, Hunter wondered with a chill. It could have been him. He was physically similar enough. He'd know more when he sat down with him, face to face.

With so many unanswered questions surging in his mind, the drive seemed endless. Finally, he pulled up outside Dreamland Creations and rushed inside.

In the lobby, to his surprise, he saw Olivia Montgomery herself. The CEO was at the reception desk and looked to be briefing the receptionist. Her dark hair was sleek, and her blue power suit was immaculate, but even so, Hunter picked up that there was a crisis. Olivia looked stressed. She was speaking rapidly and as he approached, he could hear the words.

"I'm not sure when I'll be back. Amelia can take notes in my meeting. I'll ask the marketing department to stand in for the early afternoon briefing. I'll be available on my phone."

She turned, hearing Hunter approach and looked at him with an expression that told him his arrival represented one problem too many in an impossible day.

"Detective Harden," she said. "What is it? Do you need something from me?"

She didn't sound defensive. Hunter had no idea if she knew what was happening.

"Ms. Montgomery," he said. "Is there a problem here?"

"Yes, there is," she replied. "My little boy is sick. The school just phoned. He's throwing up and is running a fever. I'm leaving now to fetch him and rush him to the doctor. Then, I'll take him home."

Much as he needed answers from her, Hunter acknowledged that he wasn't going to get them now and he would have to wait before talking to Olivia. But that was okay if the more important suspect was here.

"When will you get back?" he asked. "This afternoon?"

She shrugged. "I hope so. I have a housekeeper who works in the afternoons. If he seems better after the meds, then I can leave him with her for a few hours and come back." She shook her head. "I also didn't want this to happen on such a busy day. But family comes first. It's something my employees know, and I try to live by."

"Is Sam Reynolds here?" he asked.

"Yes, he's upstairs," she said, sounding distracted. "He is probably in a meeting, but you can speak to him if you like. Just please make it quick if you can."

Looking frazzled, she turned and walked out to go to her boy.

Now to confront Reynolds.

He headed upstairs. On the second floor, the bustle of footsteps, the murmur of voices and the ringing of phones proved Olivia's words about it being a busy day. He walked down the corridor, glancing into every office as he passed but keeping an eye out for the one he needed.

Here it was.

The door was closed but the nameplate on it, "Sam Reynolds, COO," told Hunter he was at the right place.

He knocked and waited. No answer from inside.

Knocking again, Hunter tried the door.

He found it locked.

Was Mr. Reynolds in the habit of locking his office door every time he stepped out to head to the boardroom or the bathroom? Hunter guessed such habits would be easily adopted by men who were filmed accepting large manila envelopes with wads of cash inside.

He carried on along the corridor, now peeking into all the offices and knocking on all the doors. But he didn't see the COO inside, and nobody seemed to know where he was.

His final stop was Olivia's office suite. Amelia was inside there, her head down, working on a long list that she seemed to be typing up.

Her head jerked up when she saw Hunter.

"Good afternoon," he said.

"Good afternoon, Detective Harden," the young PA replied warily.

Hunter guessed that she would have no idea that the man she'd been supposed to meet yesterday had been killed. She'd only seen him briefly and hadn't known his name. If she had known, he was sure she'd look a whole lot more unsettled.

"I'm looking for Sam Reynolds," he said.

"I don't think he's here," she replied, with an apologetic note in her voice.

"Ms. Montgomery said he was in a meeting?" Hunter queried.

"Yes," she said. "I thought so too, but about ten minutes ago, I heard him rushing out. I don't think his car is in the parking lot any longer."

Getting up, she went to the big window on the east wall and peered out. "You can just see the empty bay from here," she said. "He drives a red Corvette."

"Does he now?" Hunter mused, thinking again of manila envelopes and the vehicle upgrades that their contents provided.

"Can you see it there?" he asked. At least it was a fairly distinctive model, even in LA where there was no shortage of gleaming sports cars.

She shook her head. "No. That parking bay is empty." Turning to the calendar on her computer, she checked the schedule. "I see here that he's got another meeting here in two hours. That's with the marketing team, so he'll definitely be back for it."

"I'll come back," Hunter said. "But in the meantime, what's his address and his cell number?"

"Do I have to give that to you?" she asked, sounding worried.

"Yes. It won't get you into trouble. The information is not privileged. It's available elsewhere, but it'll be quicker if I get it from you. And I won't say you gave it to me," he added, remembering that he'd sensed a tense dynamic in the company the last time he was here.

"If you're sure about that," she agreed, but she now looked anxious as she collected the information for him. The printer whirred.

Here was Reynolds' address and his phone number.

"Do me a favor," he asked her. "Can you try to call his cell?" An incoming call from the office would be more likely picked up than an anonymous number if Sam Reynolds was guilty of involvement in this and running scared.

"What must I say?" Amelia asked, her brow knitting.

"Ask if he'll be back for the meeting," Hunter said.

"I don't usually confirm that kind of thing with him," she protested.

"Tell him you're doing it because of Olivia's emergency," Hunter said.

She was wary of Reynolds, he saw, as she dialed. But as soon as the call connected, Hunter could hear the voicemail message.

"He's not picking up," she confirmed. "His phone is off."

"If he calls back, just stay calm, and ask him that question," Hunter said, noting that Amelia didn't look calm at all now. She looked stressed and nervous, and he didn't blame her.

Feeling extremely worried that Reynolds was out of contact, he left Dreamland Creations.

He didn't go back to the police station. Instead, he headed to Sam Reynolds' home address.

Hunter had a nasty feeling that Sam Reynolds might have gotten a heads-up that the police were on his trail. What if he was hiding out somewhere or on the run?

His eyebrows rose when he saw that the home was located just outside the Pacific Palisades. That wasn't just expensive, it was stratospherically priced. Even for a COO, this was pushing it big time affordability-wise. A whole stack of manila envelopes would have been necessary for Reynolds to have afforded this place if he didn't have generational wealth backing him.

Hunter drove through the quiet, tree-lined streets, noticing the presence of street cameras and private security. He stopped outside Reynolds' large, sumptuous, double-story home and rang the doorbell.

After a pause, the door was opened by a housekeeper, a dark-haired woman wearing a gray smock and a surprised and suspicious expression as she saw him standing there.

"Mr. Reynolds," Hunter asked. "Is he home?"

"No," she shook her head.

"Was he home this morning?"

She too looked conflicted, as if she wasn't sure she should be talking to the police, but Hunter's deliberately innocent question was difficult not to answer.

"Yes," she said eventually. "He left here just as I arrived at seven a.m."

"Everything normal inside? He left for work, not for – for vacation?" Hunter was thinking of hastily packed bags and boarded airplanes.

"He left for work," she said, sounding confused.

That was something, at least. Hopefully, that meant there weren't plans in place – yet – for him to skip the country. Or maybe he'd never intended to run. It could be that the killing off of these information sources would mean he didn't have to.

Suppress the sources and he could walk away with his hands clean from whatever he was caught up in.

Thanking the housekeeper, Hunter turned away. As he headed back to his car, his phone pinged. Glancing down, Hunter saw that he'd received an alert for one of the blogs that he'd researched.

This one was the local, LA-based site, No to Violence, the one that was anonymous but clearly written. And there was a new piece up on it.

Was it a follow-up to the one he'd read earlier? That one had hinted there was more to come. Was this going to take him further?

As soon as he was back in his car, he opened the blog post.

The heading pulled no punches and Hunter's eyes widened as he read it.

"Day Zero: What it is, and why you should be very afraid."

31
A Desperate Bargain

The phone was shaking in his hand. Daniel could see it trembling. He couldn't stop it. Nor could he stop the frantic acceleration of his heart as he thought about what he'd done. He'd broken into a stranger's house, he'd taken one of her belongings, he'd smashed a glass jar and left petals, pink and white and blood red, strewn over the tiles.

Now this text was harshly stating he had failed, and he didn't even know why.

How should he answer this?

As he considered his options, he stared around his bedroom, which no longer felt like the safe, boring place it had done yesterday, with the peeling walls and the old posters of action movie stars he'd stuck them on a while ago and never taken them down.

Now, it felt like a flimsy shack that could be breached at any moment. It felt like a place where he could be arrested, where the cops might break in and take him. That could happen, right?

He didn't know how to handle this or what to say. Would there be any further information coming through? Should he reply now?

The screen stayed silent. Nothing else beeped onto it.

That meant he would have to respond. He needed to know.

Gritting his teeth in an effort to pull himself together, he typed, *"What is the problem?"*

Let it be nothing bad, he prayed, as he pressed the button to send it.

Then, after a wait that seemed endless, the message came back.

"There were cameras in the living room. Your footage is captured. Your face can be clearly seen. This woman will go to the police when she sees the footage. No question. They will use facial recognition and find you. It's happened before when people fail their tests."

He felt sick. Never mind that, he felt paralyzed. He'd been caught on camera. The worst had happened. He was a criminal now, his life was ruined, and one terrible mistake had brought him down. From such success, doing so well in the game, this was an abrupt and shocking reversal.

"But why did you let this happen?" He typed the words and pressed Send angrily before he could think better of it. Whoever this person was, they must have known. Why had they let him go in there when there were cameras? They were the ones who ruined his life, not him! He'd just been going along with what he was told!

Regretting it almost instantly, he stared at the screen, breathing hard.

He'd had one person on his side – one person – this anonymous message sender. And now, he'd replied in a way that would make that person mad. Not an intelligent move. Now, he had nobody on his side. Nobody at all.

He guessed he was done now because that woman had come home as he'd left – or at any rate, he supposed it was her – and would have seen the smashed bowl. Of course, she would check the cameras. Of course.

He'd been too rushed to realize they were there. Now, he was all alone and in deep trouble. The police were going to come for him and whoever this person was, they wouldn't have liked his answer.

Was he going to get a reply? The screen seared his eyes as he stared at it. Empty. No messages.

Then he nearly dropped his phone as his familiar, rap-tune ringtone blared out.

Frantically clutching it, he saw to his astonishment it was the same number that had been texting him.

Now they were calling him! Whoever this was, they wanted to speak to him.

"Hello?" His voice was high and wobbly as he picked up the call.

"Daniel?" The voice on the other end was exactly what he'd supposed it would sound like if somebody who controlled this game was ever to find his number and call him. Authoritative, calm, confident. The voice of someone who gave orders and had them obeyed.

"Yeah," he said, hearing again how breathless he sounded. This wasn't the way Captain Dan would sound in the game. Now, in real life, he was frantic and tense, and in this mindset, he always ended up saying the wrong thing. Always.

"How could you send me in there?" He clenched the phone tighter. "Did you- did you know there were cameras? You must have known! How was I to know? I didn't see them?"

"The footage was copied by ourselves."

The voice was harsh and emotionless, but the words were so shocking they drove the breath right out of Daniel.

"What – what do you mean?"

"The homeowner has cameras in place. We hacked into them to record you. Not difficult to do."

It was like he couldn't breathe, like he was suffocating.

"Why did you do that?"

"Why did you choose to break into somebody's home and take a personal item of theirs, Daniel?"

"Because – because – you told me to!"

"Knowing it was illegal?"

"It felt like a dare," he stammered, unsure what to say. "You paid me, and it felt like a dare. I – I didn't know it was a real house. I thought it was a test house."

He swallowed, hearing an audible click in his throat because his mouth was very dry.

"Exactly. A test. You dared to do this, and we taped you because we want evidence."

Horror simmered inside him as the man continued speaking. "Now we have it. Evidence that could give you a criminal record. You know how hard that makes life? Your future will be very different than you think. Job prospects will be problematic if they exist at all."

He was going to end up like his father. He'd never, ever wanted to follow in his old man's footsteps, become a loser like him. Now he was set on this path, and it was too late.

"What can I do?" he asked, clearing his throat. "Is there a way out of this?"

"Now you're asking the right questions." The voice was more approving. "We saw potential in you from the start. You have the promise to become one of the elite. So now, you have the choice. You go forward with us, or else that footage will ruin your life."

"But – but – wait. You said you hacked into the homeowner's cameras. What if she – what if that lady finds the footage anyway?"

"That is another good question. She might well do that when she gets back, later this evening."

So it was somebody else who'd been at the door earlier then, he guessed.

"You can't – you can't get in and erase it? If you hacked it, can't you wipe it?"

"We can. But before we do, you must do something for us, in turn," the man said. "This woman is no friend of ours or yours. She's recently made decisions that will cause us damage. Her actions must have consequences, Daniel. This is the real world."

"So – what do I do?"

"There is a package waiting for you in the usual place. The contents will make it clear what you need to do. We will not accept failure and there is no turning back. You have the choice to take this opportunity. Within the hour, if you accept, your future with us is secured and we will erase the footage. If you don't accept or don't reply, then the police will be knocking on your door."

The call ended abruptly. Not even a goodbye, just silence.

Daniel turned, gripping his phone. This was a desperate situation but there was a glimmer of hope at the end of the tunnel. He needed to do something, and they would erase all of this.

Then he'd be theirs. He thought about that as he rushed down the stairs, taking them two at a time, he burst out of the building and ran along the road to the bench he knew so well.

Perhaps he was already theirs and he'd have to accept that he was now working for this guy and that he needed to continue. There didn't seem to be a way out. The only option was for his future to be destroyed and he had no doubt that threat was very real.

It was like they'd led him into this. Now he had to decide whether to go willingly or to fight and let them destroy him.

Daniel was breathless by the time he reached the bench. Not so much from the run as from sheer tension.

There was another black bag hidden under the bench like a lurking shadow. Checking around carefully first, wondering who was watching or who was filming, he bent and pulled it out. It felt heavy. He grasped it tightly, turned, and ran back the way he had come, his feet pounding along as fast as he could go.

He powered up the stairs and burst into his parents' apartment and back into the shelter of his bedroom that didn't feel safe or familiar anymore.

Only then did he open the bag.

Gasping, he stared at the contents, feeling the world shift under him. It felt like going into a skid on the highway, a bad one, where you knew life would never be the same.

Inside was a gun. A real gun, a Sig Sauer like the handguns the Army used. It was one he had never actually touched but knew from the game and from the special training exercises he'd done. And affixed to the end of it was a silencer, making it long and heavy.

The only other thing in the bag was a sheaf of hundred-dollar bills.

It was more money than Daniel had ever seen before in his life.

He picked up the weapon, weighing it in his hand, seeing that it was loaded with two bullets.

Its message was clear, leaving no room for questions or doubt.

32
Unraveling Web of Secrets

What was Day Zero and how had the writer of No To Violence found out about it? Would this connect to the brainwashing that The Signal blog had recently mentioned? To the Army link that Hunter suspected was so important?

Arriving at the police station, he rushed inside, heading straight to his desk.

At last, somebody had exposed the facts and now, he would know what they were. He hoped the article was detailed enough. That title had sounded promising.

He sat down in front of his computer, glancing around him briefly. The only other cop in the office right now was Cody. He was so busy with his research that he hadn't even heard Hunter come in. Only when he looked at Cody, did Cody glance up, his brow wrinkled.

"Got nothing on Gonzalez so far," he said. "Not sure where that hotel was yet. I've ruled out the big ones. I'm now trying the small ones, of which there are hundreds."

"Keep trying. I may know more soon," Hunter said. "I've got something here."

He signed in. Navigated to the site and sat forward in his chair as it loaded, waiting expectantly.

The site refreshed.

For one confused moment, he stared at the screen.

Bodies pumped, meaty buttocks thrusting, breasts bouncing. The lens panned over a woman's face, twisted in mock ecstasy, with a man behind it, his face taut, misted with perspiration. Close-ups of genitalia, filmed by a wobbling camera, filled the screen. A fake, ululating cry of orgasm resonated from the speakers and Hunter grabbed the mouse, muting the volume as Cody glanced over curiously.

What's going on there?" Cody asked.

Hunter shook his head. He closed the site and tried again, refreshing the link, hoping it was just a glitch. But it wasn't, and when the screen refreshed, he saw more of the same.

"No To Violence just brought out an expose on Day Zero. I got the notification for it as I left Reynolds' place. By the time I'd gotten here, it'd been hacked. Someone's gotten in, and they're running porn on it."

"That's fast work," Cody said.

"It's extremely worrying."

He closed the pornographic footage, wishing he'd read the blog immediately. If only he'd taken the chance and gone in immediately on his phone. He hadn't known it would vanish. That response, that hacking, had been lightning fast.

"Whoever they are, if they're good enough to hack the site, they're good enough to track the owner. We need to get there first. Or else, there's going to be another killing."

Hunter left the office and headed upstairs to the LAPD's IT department.

"Is Officer Brixton here?" he asked the tech at the desk as soon as he walked into the busy, bustling environment.

"He's in a meeting," the tech replied, barely glancing up from his keyboard.

"How urgent is the meeting?"

There must have been something in Hunter's voice, because turning to face him, the tech gave him his full attention.

"It's a scheduled weekly meeting. Troubleshooting issues, general maintenance," he said.

"Can you pull him out of it?" Hunter leaned forward, his hands on the desk. "It's an urgent issue linking to a multiple murder case."

Thankfully, the tech wasn't going to give him a hard time after hearing that.

"Sure," he said.

He got up and strode out of the office. A few moments later, he was back, followed by the man Hunter needed.

Brixton's dark hair was mussed as if the department head had been far too busy with his coding to brush it this morning. He wore three silver earrings in his left ear, one of which was a tiny skull. And he was the only person in the LAPD who routinely wore jeans to work.

"Hunter," he said, coming straight over. "My office?"

"We need somewhere quiet," Hunter agreed.

Brixton led the way through the lobby, down a corridor, and through a door at the end. His office was small, with the blinds closed and four big screens on the wall opposite the desk.

"What's the situation?" he asked.

"There's a blog, privately owned. It's one of a few publishing insider information on these murders," Hunter said. "The hits that have been happening."

"Two bullets each?" Brixton was already scrolling through a list on one of his screens. "I heard about that case. And that you were heading it."

"Yes. Those."

Now wasn't the time to mention politics. For the time being, he was heading it and he'd fight to keep it that way.

"So, what do you need to know about the blog?"

"It's just been hacked. It published an expose piece on the murders and on what Day Zero is. Day Zero seems to be an integral part of this whole business."

"Did you read it? See it at all?"

Frustrated, Hunter shook his head. "That piece vanished within twenty minutes of me being notified. Now, there's just a porn show there."

"That's very quick work." Brixton leaned back in his chair, his hand still on his mouse. "They've got skilled people if that's been done."

"If they've hit the site, I'm worried the owner is next. They are doing whatever it takes to suppress this information."

"You want me to do some research through the official channels?" Brixton tilted his head sideways as he asked the question.

"Of course," Hunter said. "But if it will get a faster result, can you hack it, too?"

Brixton glanced at him slyly. "How much do you want to know?"

"I want to know who the site owner is, first. That person is the one who's in danger. Then, is there any way of finding out the content of that blog post? Before the post was erased?"

"It might be. Partially at least, I'm not sure." Brixton paused, tapping his finger on his mouse thoughtfully. "How about the hackers themselves?"

"You think you can find out who the hackers are? Is that even possible?"

"It's worth a try. You say they're hacking sites with information on this? I could set up a honeypot trap and see if they take the bait."

"Whatever you can do." Hunter paused. "Can you do it now?"

Brixton frowned, turning to another screen, and scrolling through it.

"I'll need ten minutes to wrap up some other business. Then, I'll focus on this. I'll work as fast as I can. If it's possible to track down this website owner, I'll do it."

Grateful for his expertise, Hunter turned away.

While Brixton searched for virtual facts, Hunter was going to dig for answers in the real world.

And he was sure that Olivia Montgomery had some of them.

She needed to be jerked out of her denial and he was going to go hard on her now. Pulling his phone out of his pocket as he strode out of the station, he dialed her number.

33
Intrigue Behind Corporate Veil

Olivia Montgomery was waiting for Hunter in the boardroom when he got to Dreamland Creations. She was standing by a window, staring out at the parking lot. When he came in, she turned to face him.

Looking pale and stressed, she seemed different from the polished, self-assured woman who'd given him such bland responses on their first meeting. Now, the reality of the situation was hitting home.

"Your COO is AWOL, and we suspect him of criminal activity," Hunter said, striding inside. Time to cut to the chase and see if she, too, had been hiding things.

"I – I was shocked by what you told me on the phone. I don't think he's AWOL. He organizes his own day and has meetings all over town. He's due back here later," she said.

"Later isn't good enough. Why's his phone off?"

"He's in meetings! He has the right to turn it off."

He walked closer. Around the boardroom table up to where she was standing.

"What's Day Zero?" he asked, watching her closely.

Her face was very still. "I don't know," she said.

"Really? You really have no idea what it is? Have you ever heard the term before?"

"No, I –"

"Truth, please!" Hunter's voice rose and she flinched. "People are being murdered! If you know something, anything, then say so!"

She was breathing hard. "Look, I don't know! I really don't! But in the past day or two, a few people have mentioned it. They've heard about it. One of my marketing people told me there was something online, my accounts manager said the same. And I researched it! I also got my lawyers to have a look. You see, I keep my eyes open for damaging information, but the blog posts didn't mention our name. They linked the name to military action figures and the related activities, and we're the leader in that field, but we chose to leave it be for now." Anger in her eyes, she glared at him. "I'm the one going through this huge stress here. Our brand could be damaged by this. And now you're implying I know about it? What the hell do you take me for?"

Her emotions were genuine. What she'd said made sense. This didn't seem to be a carefully constructed lie; she was too angry for that now. Hunter believed that she didn't know more.

"Sam Reynolds does know more. And he is deliberately damaging your brand."

Unable to stand still, she turned and walked across the room, looking out of the other window, and then back again. Her hands were tightly clenched.

"You've suspected him from the start and it's nothing but a witch hunt!"

"Did you ever consider that Sam Reynolds could have been selling your company property? The names and addresses and contact details of all the users of the Carl Commando spinoffs."

"Sam would never do such a thing. Why would he? There's no reason for him to do that."

Hunter wasn't going to tell Olivia about the manila envelope.

That was his secret, for the time being.

Right now, he couldn't afford to tell her because if word got back to Sam Reynolds that the police knew about it, then he might disappear if he hadn't already.

Hunter could hint at the possibility though. He could encourage Olivia to think, more than she had been doing.

"How does he afford his Corvette?" Hunter asked. "And that mansion he lives in?"

The questions jolted Olivia and she blinked rapidly.

"You're saying he's corrupt?" Her voice was incredulous.

"From all the evidence so far, there's a strong possibility he is. The content of the blogs hints at high-level collusion involving your company. Power and money are strong persuaders."

"I still don't believe it," she said. "Sam Reynolds would never do such a thing. Never! And if we start acknowledging that flaky conspiracy theories have any truth to them then we're on a dangerous road."

"You might already be on that road," Hunter pointed out. "And what will your stakeholders say if it proves to be true and you have to explain that you were warned about it by the police and that you were asked to cooperate, but you did nothing?"

There was a short silence.

"Okay," she capitulated, anxiety was evident in her voice now. At last, Hunter thought, she had started to consider the consequences. The fallout that could occur, the lawsuits, the negative publicity that would plummet the share price. "Let's assume your theory holds water. What are you theorizing, to start with?"

"That Reynolds may have sold off your company assets. That would most likely be your customer database, the contact details of your gamers and paintball players. And that somebody is deliberately using them in a targeted way to promote enlistment into the armed forces. That's my theory."

"My eight-year-old son plays the action game," she said. "The basic version of it, anyway and I can promise you it's harmless."

Hunter shrugged. "What are the seventeen-year-olds seeing? The eighteen-year-olds? The ones who can quickly swell the numbers of the Army without waiting a decade?"

"That, I don't know." She stared at him defiantly. "And there are many ways that marketers can get hold of kids' details. You're seriously implying our database is involved?"

"Does Sam Reynolds have access to it? Or could he get it?"

She was silent.

He pulled out a chair at the table's head and gestured to it.

She sat down, and he sat next to her.

"Sam," she said, looking down at her clenched hands. "I trust him. He's been my right hand for – for more than five years now. We've been through the entire Carl Commando journey together. I always joke that it's like we're Carl's parents."

"Has he changed at all during that time?" Hunter was leaning forward now, intent on getting the answers he needed. In contrast, Olivia was still clasping her hands together, shoulders hunched, her body language keeping him out, even though his questions were finding gaps.

"Of course, he's changed. We've both changed. People don't stand still!"

Her phone beeped and she glanced down. "I have to check this. My little boy is at home."

She glanced at the message and then looked away from it, making Hunter think it wasn't urgent.

"Any changes in his lifestyle? When did he buy the Corvette he drives and that luxury property he owns?"

Olivia took an angry breath and Hunter braced himself for a furious denial, an insistence that Reynolds had bought all of this with his own money.

But then she shook her head.

"He said he'd had an inheritance. He said something like that. I remember now."

"How long ago?"

"A year? Maybe eighteen months?" She shook her head. "I don't know why I'm even telling you that. It's playing right into your hands, that he got a payment from somewhere. That's what you're implying."

It was a fact, not an implication, Hunter thought as he leaned back in his chair.

"Do you know how much it costs to get people into the Army, the Navy, the Air Force?"

She glanced at him uneasily. "I've never thought about it. It's not a question I've ever been asked. With what I know about marketing, though, I'd guess it's expensive and that it's a difficult job."

"It costs billions," Hunter told her. And it's been extraordinarily unsuccessful, despite all that spending. Numbers are declining. Everyone knows it. It's in all the reports we get, it's no secret. Recruitment drives are on the go all the time and in so many different ways. But you see, I reckon that between them, Reynolds and – well, I won't name names at this stage," Hunter said, even though he could see the arrogant tilt of Rogan's head in his mind. "Reynolds and somebody high up in the Department of Defense have colluded. They put their heads together and they figured out that if Carl Commando was militarized just a little more, if the toy and the game were tweaked, and if the right elements were added, it could create a wave of recruits that were not only keen and ready, but also prequalified in terms of skills."

"Are you saying a game can do that?"

"Not just a game. A multi-pronged strategy involving the game and other forms of specifically targeted marketing, skills development, and maybe a whole lot more aspects that work together. And the point is that you need to check whether your information got leaked to enable this and whether Sam Reynolds got a piece of the pie for having done his part. And it would be a big pie. Coming up with a solution to solve the recruitment problem would be a game changer for the military. Saving on that massive marketing budget would mean mountains of cash to spare for the people who enabled it."

She was looking paler now, her lips pressed together.

"If it did get leaked, this would be a catastrophe. Would he do it?" she said, and Hunter had the feeling her words were more directed at herself than him. "Would he really do such a thing?"

"We need to find him," Hunter said. "Find him, ask him, and get to the truth of it. It's not the possible misuse of the database that's my biggest concern. It's because somehow, as a result of this, murders are happening. Collusion aside, Ms. Montgomery, that's why I'm sitting here now. And maybe you do know where Mr. Reynolds is."

"How would I know that?" Olivia said, sounding genuinely puzzled. "Are you implying I'm lying to you?"

"Does he have a conferencing place he uses outside of the office? A spot he likes to go for private meetings?"

"If he does, I'm unaware of it."

Hunter waited. That had been a reflexive denial. She hadn't thought about her answer. Now, after having blurted that out, she was starting to think.

"You sure?" he prodded.

Thoughtfully, she took out her phone and began scrolling through.

"There was something he said, a while ago. I'm starting to remember a conversation we had. He might have mentioned the place he was coming back from, in passing. Perhaps I can find it."

34
High-Speed Pursuit

"How long ago was it?" Hunter asked Olivia. "Any information will help. I need to get there urgently." Already he was out of his chair and turning toward the door.

"Well, I said I think I know," Olivia looked more unsure now, as if she'd made a promise she wasn't sure she could keep. She'd stopped scrolling and her fingers were now hovering over the screen. "I – I feel like I'm betraying him by telling you."

Now, Hunter understood the reason for her hesitation was that she felt she was giving Sam Reynolds' secrets away.

"Reynolds might be betraying you," Hunter said. "Only when I get face to face with him can I find out what the real story is."

Olivia pressed her hands against her face, her fingers on her temples as if her head was throbbing.

"I can't believe all this is happening. I really cannot believe Sam would have done such a thing. He's too loyal to have sold off our mailing list or misused our gaming software – it's making me feel as if I'm in a bad dream. And to have been involved in murders?" Her voice was incredulous. "Detective Harden, I'd put my reputation on the line to say he isn't."

Hunter wasn't so sure. The evidence was speaking for itself and more compellingly than Olivia Montgomery was doing. What he gleaned from this was that Sam Reynolds had hidden his private activities well. He'd kept them out of sight. The amount of money involved probably had something to do with that. Money talked – and the people receiving it didn't.

"The venue. Please, can you take a look," he said. Conflicted as she was, Olivia was now wasting time. Every second counted.

Olivia frowned, her attention back on her phone again.

"There are reams of conversations between us. And it was a few weeks ago, at least."

The room seemed very quiet as she scrolled, her eyes narrowed, her focus intent.

"Okay," she said, but she sounded uncertain. "I've got something here, but I don't know what it means. Sam referred to it in a kind of shorthand. The Wes."

"The Wes?"

"That's all he said."

"And the context?"

"The entire message goes: 'At the Wes now, wrapping up meeting, can be back in 15.'"

So the Wes, whatever and wherever it was, was a maximum of fifteen minutes away from the Dreamland Creations offices. That narrowed things down.

Hunter thanked her and then got on the phone with Cody as he strode out.

"Okay," he said. "This hotel. I've got a lead from my side."

"That's great," Cody sounded frustrated. "Because I've got a list of hotels, all the way from large to tiny, as long as my arm. Whatever your lead is, it'll help."

"It's the Wes," Hunter said. "That's all I have. It must be shorthand for something, and it's within fifteen minutes of Dreamland Creations – possibly closer."

"That's giving me something." More encouraged now, Cody began clicking his keyboard, fast. "Okay, I'm doing a search with what I have so far. I'll search for those letters and narrow down the names. Then I can plot them geographically."

While Cody compiled his list, Hunter ran down to his car and climbed inside, ready to go.

"West End Heights, West Towers, Westville – those are all too far, though," Cody said.

"It was definitely close by. Fifteen minutes of urban driving. That's not more than a few miles in radius."

"Here's one! The Wessex Arms. Small boutique hotel catering for weddings, meetings, romantic overnight stays. And it's about five miles from Dreamland Creations."

Hunter was about to hang up and rush there, but he held on another minute. Always better to make sure.

"Any others? Can you look again? We don't want to run after one and miss the other."

"Good point. I'll search once more."

Silence as Hunter waited, tapping the wheel."

"I've found one other possibility," Cody said. "The Westfall. Very small hotel that caters for events, functions, and private meetings. It's a little further, but I guess it's still within the fifteen-minute radius if you're driving a Corvette."

"Where are they both?" Hunter asked.

When Cody sent the coordinates, Hunter saw that the Wessex Arms was closer to the police station than the Westfall was. With time of the essence now, he and his partner would need to head out in opposite directions.

"You take the Wessex Arms. I'll go to the Westfall. Hopefully, if he's in a private meeting at his usual spot, one of us will be in time to gatecrash the party. And maybe also recognize that background in Gonzalez's video."

He jumped into his car and roared out of the Dreamland Creations parking lot. The afternoon was sullen and cloudy. More rain was threatening, and the roads were already getting clogged with the start of the rush-hour exodus. Hunter turned on his lights and siren, zigzagging through the rows of traffic, watching the hotel's coordinates inching closer.

In fourteen minutes, he was there. The Westfall was set back from the main road along a side road and looked more like a destination venue than one that attracted passing trade. It was decorated in the Spanish style, with bright white walls, blue window frames, and a red climbing bougainvillea providing a burst of color along the front wall.

In the parking lot, he saw a crimson Corvette parked at an angle, taking up two bays.

Success at last. It looked like Sam Reynolds was here.

There were a few other luxury cars there and he didn't know which one might belong to the man Reynolds was meeting. Was this man Bryan Rogan?

Hunter parked near the entrance and rushed into the hotel.

The lobby was decked out in blue and gold. A huge mosaic provided the backdrop to the reception desk and a fountain trickled in the corner. Hunter hurried up to the desk.

The receptionist looked over her eyeglasses at him, patting down her shiny black ponytail.

"You have a guest here, Mr. Sam Reynolds," Hunter said, showing his police ID. "He's meeting with somebody. I need you to take me to that meeting room, now." He stared around the lobby. Which direction were the conference rooms? If he had an idea, he'd go there himself.

She stared at him nervously.

"I – I can't do that, sir," she said.

Hunter kept his demeanor easy. She would have been trained by her employers to keep guest details confidential, and he needed to convince her to bypass this order.

"It's very important to cooperate with the police in a situation like this," he said calmly. "It's a criminal investigation. People have been murdered."

She flinched at the word, clearly shaken.

If she didn't tell him which direction to go, he would try to find out himself. There was a corridor to his left that looked as if it might lead to meeting rooms. Maybe he should head down there and take a look. But just as he was about to go and see, the receptionist checked her ledger and turned to him again, looking worried now.

"I understand the importance, I really do. The problem is that the meeting's finished." She flipped a page and nodded. "It ended about five minutes ago. It was – well, it was in boardroom number three, but I don't think there's anyone still in there."

Hunter turned away and rushed down the corridor. There were the boardrooms, four of them. Two doors and another two. He looked inside all of them, just in case. All empty. In boardroom three, which had a six-seater table, two of the chairs were pushed back.

He recognized the view behind the table. It was very similar in color and design to the slice of footage they'd seen in that badly taken video. For sure, this was where Gonzalez had worked and filmed Reynolds doing his illicit deal.

He must have just missed Reynolds. He'd still been on the premises when Hunter arrived, just not in the boardroom.

Turning back, Hunter ran through the opulent reception area, burst out of the boutique hotel, and raced toward the parking lot.

The growl of a powerful engine throbbed in his ears. The Corvette was reversing out of its double bay, tires squealing.

"Wait!" Hunter shouted. He rushed forward, waving one arm, holding up his police ID in the other. "Mr. Reynolds, wait!"

But the car shot forward with an ear-splitting growl. He just had time to see the dark-haired man gripping the wheel. And then, it was gone.

Sam Reynolds had clearly seen Hunter. No way had he missed him. He'd chosen to ignore him and had fled.

"You're not getting away."

Chasing down a Corvette might seem like a hopeless task, but it was more likely to succeed than not chasing it at all.

Hunter wrenched his car door open, slid inside, slammed it, and started up. And then he was speeding out of the parking lot, slewing the car to the right the same way the Corvette had gone. Beyond that, he didn't know which way it had turned.

Hunter got on the radio, briefing Cody. "He was here, but he left. I'm chasing him. He headed east. Don't have more yet."

"On it," Cody replied laconically.

Driving as if he'd been trying to outrun the devil himself, Reynolds had vanished from sight. His speed had been enough to give him a critical early lead. It would be all too easy for him to disappear, and now that he knew the police were chasing him, he might decide to do exactly that.

Hunter bore down on the pedal. Where was he going? Could he anticipate and take a shortcut?

To have any hope of catching him, Hunter needed to put himself in Reynolds' shoes and think the same way he would have done when he fled the hotel. He'd have been in a panic, needing distance and to disappear.

He would not have gone in the direction of Dreamland Creations, knowing the police were on him. He'd go the opposite way out of sheer instinct.

That meant right. And he'd want to hide. He'd be looking to take a turn, to get a few steps ahead rather than continue along the traffic-clogged main street where his car would be easily visible.

Would he have turned down this road?

Hunter decided on yes. Reynolds would probably have taken the first turn he saw, hoping to get out of sight. In which case, Hunter was going to speed ahead and take the following road. He was going to travel parallel to his target. That way, with no sign of the police behind him, Reynolds might ease off on the gas after a minute and not keep going at full tilt. No point in attracting more police attention if you'd lost the one chasing you.

Hands clamped on the wheel, using his light, but no siren in case Reynolds was listening out for it, he sped up the next road. It was empty, he was lucky with the traffic, and he hoped that would give him the edge he needed. How far would Reynolds have gone? Glancing at the map, he saw there was a crossroad ahead, and that meant Reynolds might change direction again.

Time to join the road he suspected the Corvette was on and see if his strategy was successful.

Mashing his foot down, he slewed the car to the right.

And with his pulse quickening, he saw he was correct.

Reynolds had slowed down when he thought he'd lost the police. Perhaps he'd been on the phone, making calls, putting together contingency plans.

Hunter veered onto the road ahead of him, siren now blaring, driving directly into his path. With the scream of brakes, the Corvette screeched to a stop.

But then, disaster.

Panicking, Reynolds veered his car hard left. He almost sideswiped Hunter's car as he sped past, the Corvette fishtailing in reaction, and then he swung it around a corner and disappeared from view.

He was on the run now, for all he was worth. The strategy had almost worked but almost was not enough.

Gritting his teeth that defeat had been snatched from the jaws of victory, Hunter hit the gas, twisted the wheel, and slewed the car around in a hard turn, the wheels bumping over the curbside.

He was on the same road now, but far behind. With every second, Reynolds was accelerating faster, and now, having almost been caught, he wasn't going to slow down.

This long road led over a sharp ridge, and then, according to the map, joined up with a network of streets on the other side. Most likely, Reynolds was hoping to lose him in those zigzag streets.

"He's gotten away from me," he radioed Cody. "He's fled onto North Lane, going over the ridge."

"North Lane?" Cody's reply came, loud and surprised, over the airwaves.

"Yes. Any officers on the other side? It's a long, straight road that runs for miles and I won't catch him. We need to trap him up ahead."

But, to his surprise, Cody came back immediately.

"If it's North Road, keep going. Give it everything you've got. I drove that road yesterday. When you're over the ridge, you'll see he's in trouble. I'll get there as soon as I can."

Doubtful, but trusting his partner, Hunter sped up as fast as he could go, wondering what he'd find when he crested the ridge, and whether it would be enough to slow the desperate Reynolds down.

35
Chasing the Unknown Abyss

Hunter's hands were tight on the wheel as he sped along the road, which narrowed as it reached the ridge ahead. He hadn't seen any sign of trouble and wondered if Cody might have misjudged the situation.

The blacktop was clean and smooth, reminding Hunter of a racetrack.

He reached the steep peak of the road. And then, on the other side, he saw an annihilation zone.

Yellow roadwork signs littered the sidewalks. The road was completely dug up and half the blacktop was missing. The remainder of the surface was covered in potholes. It was rough and rutted, and to slow traffic down at the start of the roadwork and prevent the dust from overpowering, the city had added a few temporary speed bumps. They were narrow and sharp.

It was the worst terrain possible for a low-slung sports car.

In front of him, the Corvette's brake lights flashed crimson as Reynolds approached the roadwork sign. Hunter could imagine Reynolds swearing. The car veered hard right to try to get over the first speed bump. Flattening his foot, Hunter closed in. His higher-riding car could cruise over the bumps. He hit the first one practically flying but getting over fast.

Now, Reynolds was panicking, and Hunter heard a harsh, metallic scraping sound as he went too fast over the next one. He was trashing his car, and he still wasn't getting over them fast enough.

Hunter jolted and bounced over the second one, and then pulled level with Reynolds, closing in, forcing him off the road.

"Pull over!" he yelled. "Pull over!"

Reynolds glanced at him but returned his focus to the road.

Determinedly, Hunter edged the car closer. "Pull over!" he insisted. Any closer and he'd scrape up against the Corvette. But Reynolds was in too much of a panic to know or care.

He was staring frantically around, and Hunter thought he would have tried to backtrack if he could. He would have reversed and shot back the way he had come.

But at that moment, a car crested the ridge behind them and bore down on them, lights flashing, siren blaring.

Pulling in front of Reynolds, Hunter breathed a sigh of relief. The cavalry, in the form of Cody, had arrived – and now, Reynolds couldn't run.

He jumped out of his car and ran around to the Corvette's tinted window.

"Out!" he ordered. "You should have stopped when I called you back at the hotel. You're already in trouble, Mr. Reynolds."

But he knew that. As he climbed out, Hunter was shocked by his demeanor. He'd expected defiance, bravado, even resistance.

Instead, Reynolds looked like a ghost.

His skin was sheet white, glazed with a sheen of sweat. His mouth was tight, his face twisted. This wasn't what Hunter had expected. Was it because he'd been caught?

"Come over here. Get in my car," Hunter said. He grasped Reynolds' arm, but the man pulled away in a reflexive action.

"No need for that," he protested weakly.

"There's every need. You already tried to run. Don't try it again."

Hunter didn't let his arm go as he escorted him to the police car. He opened the door and Reynolds got in. Hunter walked around to the driver's side, got in, locked the doors, and then drove the car a little further off the road.

Now, it was time for answers, with Cody's vehicle diverting traffic behind them.

"You were just at the Westfall. Who were you meeting?" he demanded.

Reynolds shook his head. "It was a private meeting."

"This is not a time for evasion. Who were you meeting with?" Turning toward him, Hunter saw again how pale he was, how his gaze was darting in every direction.

"I – I can't say."

"Is it the Secretary of Defense's assistant? Bryan Rogan? Is that the man who's been trying to twist the situation for his benefit?"

"Not him!"

Shocked, Hunter realized that left only one option – the man at the top. He'd thought Charles Harrison to be riding on Rogan's influence. But maybe he'd just positioned things that way. A clever man could have done that intentionally to make people believe it was Rogan doing the work, when he was pulling the strings.

"Higher than that?"

Reynolds' eyes widened and although he didn't speak, Hunter saw the truth in them.

"What have you been colluding about? What are your plans?" Still met by a wall of silence, he pushed on. "There's no point in having misplaced loyalty or protecting your connections. People have died. And we need to know why."

The only sound was Reynolds' rapid breathing. Then he shook his head again, more determinedly this time.

"I can't tell you. I can't say anything about it," he said.

"What's Day Zero? You know about that, don't you?"

Reynolds' face twitched but he didn't reply.

"You need to start talking or I'm going to bring you in and sit you in a police interview room until you talk. I don't care how long that takes. You'll give us answers eventually."

Reynolds stared ahead. A thousand-yard stare, Hunter thought, as he looked at him more closely.

"There's more to this, isn't there? You're not talking – why? You scared?"

Reynolds turned to him, and Hunter was jolted by the look in his eyes. It was the expression a man might have on the way to the gallows.

His voice was hoarse and shaking.

"I never knew that any of this would happen. I don't know what's going on myself. This whole thing has – it's run away with me. All the way. If they find out I'm here with you, I'm a dead man."

A bead of sweat trickled from Reynolds' temple down to his clenching jaw.

Staring at him Hunter felt cold with shock.

He'd thought Reynolds was intimately involved in this; that he was in the loop at the top level. But his words and his abject fear told a different story.

What the hell was going on?

36
Covert Fears

"We're taking you in," Hunter said to Reynolds. "Whatever's going on, however scared you think you are; people have died because of this. They didn't deserve it. And more are going to unless we can stop it. You need to tell me what you know. Now."

He hadn't thought Reynolds could turn any paler, but he managed to. He looked positively gray. Perspiration was now streaming down his cheeks. He stared out of the car window as if worried already that a threat might be closing in.

"Please. They'll know you've found me. They'll see my car out here. Anything – anything right now could be enough." There was supplication in his voice as he turned back to Hunter.

Hunter was finding it difficult to summon up the level of sympathy Reynolds clearly thought he deserved. After all, he'd been complicit in this whole sorry business. If he'd sounded the alarm at the start, done the right thing and said no – maybe this monster wouldn't have become what it was now.

For now, it was going to be a good plan to keep Reynolds and his car away from any watching eyes.

"Detective Lamarr will drive your car to the underground parking lot of your choice and park it there for you. Then he'll bring the keys to the police station, where you'll be."

"Where I'll be. Right. Okay. I get it."

"Where do you want your car to be parked?" Reynolds would be the best judge of where his vehicle would be safe and away from prying eyes.

"You can – you can take it to the mall near my office. What's it called? The Diagonal, I think." He shook his head as if incapable of thinking about it further.

Reynolds had accepted his lot. He slumped in his seat in silence.

Hunter glanced at him once more before getting out. He called Cody over and quickly briefed him on what Reynolds had said.

Cody nodded. "Sooner that car's out of sight, the better, it seems."

Hunter knew that Cody was thinking along the same lines as he was. They had gotten Reynolds – and they needed to protect their witness as fiercely as if they were fighting along enemy lines.

Hunter climbed into the car only after the Corvette had growled its way back along the rutted road with Cody at the wheel, going easy on the gas. Hunter knew he'd take the back road to get to the parking lot that Reynolds had mentioned. He knew the place and he didn't think it was called the Diagonal. He thought it was called the Ellipse. It was Reynolds' error and it showed Reynolds' mindset.

He was barely coherent, in the throes of a deep fear, not thinking straight and not remembering properly. It meant that it was going to be even harder to get information out of him.

Ironic, Hunter thought, joining the main road with a silent Reynolds slumped in the seat, his back hunched, head bowed. The Carl Commando toy was all about soldiers, battles, and war. And now, he was embroiled in a war too and needed to figure out the best possible strategy to win.

*

As Hunter approached the police station, having patiently eased the car through stop-start afternoon traffic for the last few miles of the journey, Reynolds became restless all over again. Squirming upright in his seat, he took a look at the building with horrified eyes.

"Look, you can't take me in here! People will know. They'll see. This is going to get me killed. Are you not listening? Maybe you, too. We need to go somewhere else! Not in here."

"Nobody is going to get you in here," Hunter assured him, thinking again that this witness sure was protesting a lot about a situation of his own making.

"How do you know? They control the police, I'm telling you! They control the police!"

"Not yet," Hunter said grimly, deciding he was going to drill down hard into the exact definition of the word 'they'. "And don't worry. I'm not bringing you through the front entrance. But you are going in."

Parking in the service bay at the side of the building, he turned to Reynolds.

"The sooner you give me answers, the better. If you don't want to spend too long in an interrogation room, remember that."

He checked all around him before getting out of the car.

At this time of day, there was a lot of activity at the police station. Some people were wrapping up for the day, others were heading back inside to complete paperwork after an afternoon out of the office. There was a shift change now and the day cleaners were leaving.

Hunter decided that all this activity was probably advantageous. Easier to hide in a crowd, he believed. With so much movement and people coming and going, it should be easy to get Reynolds where he wanted him.

He climbed out of the car and went around to open Reynolds' door, and held onto him as he climbed out. Reynolds' legs were shaking, his teeth chattering. Fear had him tightly in its clutches, but Hunter knew that being in the grip of dread might not stop a man from making a panicked bolt for freedom.

Without anyone outside noticing, waiting until the narrow strip of blacktop with its yellow signs was clear, Hunter hustled him to the service entrance and got him inside. There were voices and the sound of footsteps coming from down the corridor and Reynolds tensed.

Hunter pushed him ahead, doing this quickly because it had to be done. They went down the corridor, taking a right turn just before the end. That took them to a row of three side offices– that were used for spare interview rooms and overflow workplaces.

Opening the closest one, he shoved Reynolds inside, slamming the door just as the voices approached and passed by, heading for the evidence room.

He hadn't brought him in officially nor had he processed him as a suspect. He hadn't passed through any of the usual channels or been taken into the system, fingerprinted, or officially recognized as being a guest of the LAPD who was here for questioning.

So far, this was strictly informal and off record. Hunter wasn't necessarily happy about this, but he acknowledged that for his suspect's safety and the possibility of getting him to talk, this was the best way. Irregular as it was, it might just be effective.

The room contained a desk with a chair on either side. The window blinds were drawn and after locking the door behind them, Hunter checked that the window latch itself was locked.

Reynolds slumped down into the chair as if his legs had been cut off at the knee. He stared at Hunter with the thousand-yard look that he was becoming used to seeing.

Getting out his phone and notebook to record this interview, Hunter sat in the other chair. There was no water jug in this room but digging in his laptop bag produced a sealed bottle of water which he handed to Reynolds.

Although Hunter thought his mouth must be very dry, Reynolds didn't take the water. He stared at the bottle with that faraway look and Hunter reminded himself to approach this calmly. Reynolds' fear was going to create a wall and he'd have to do his level best to chip a few peepholes through it. Smashing it down wasn't going to work. He knew from experience that pushing hard and threatening would only cause a man in this state to push back.

"So," he said after a while, during which the only sound was Reynolds' unsteady breathing. "Seems like you got yourself into some trouble and it's been getting deeper. Would you agree?"

The barest of nods.

"We now need to figure out how to stop this," he said, but Reynolds was shaking his head already.

"There's no stopping it."

"There will be," Hunter countered.

"Months ago, maybe, but now? I doubt it. It's too late." The wobble in his voice was audible.

"Calm down, Mr. Reynolds," Hunter said. "Panicking helped nobody. You're a COO."

Reynolds' eyes flew wider as if current circumstances had completely divorced him from his own reality and he'd temporarily forgotten that he was, in fact, a high-level exec.

Seeing that had gotten through to him and jolted him out of his fearful state, Hunter continued.

"You're used to making decisions under pressure. Remember who you are and what you're capable of."

There was silence in the room, apart from the clicking noise of Reynolds swallowing.

"If I thought my abilities as a COO would help to solve this unsolvable problem, I would have done something by now," he replied.

But at least now there was a thread of defiance in his tone which wasn't there before. Some spirit was still in Reynolds, some fighting stance was resurging, and Hunter knew they were going to need it.

"You may be correct that your abilities as a COO might not be able to fix this situation." Making sure to keep his movements calm and easy, Hunter leaned back in his chair, arms relaxed, demeanor controlled. "But I still want to know how it started. So why don't you tell me? Knowing the history of this will help us a lot."

Reynolds' face twitched. Hunter waited. All his attention was focused on his suspect. All his instincts were alert, figuring out the best way of getting through to him.

Seeing that Reynolds wasn't quite ready to talk – though he wasn't retreating inside himself the same way he had been doing – Hunter tried a different angle.

"You are going to risk being in some trouble for this. I won't pretend otherwise. But what you decide to say and do now could make a lot of difference to the level of trouble this ends up being. If this is as big as you say, then we are going to be open to making a deal for information. It could even include going into the witness protection program."

Watching his face at those words, he thought that had gotten through.

"You could start again somewhere else under a new name. Maybe even relocate overseas. You don't have to think of this as the end of it all." Hunter paused. "I'm not promising anything. It depends on your level of cooperation. I'm telling you what could happen. What my colleague and I could organize."

If his powers weren't stripped away. A shiver of unease chilled him as he thought about that. What if Reynolds was right? What if it was already somehow too late?

But the information he'd given Reynolds had clearly provided the other man with food for thought.

He stared at Hunter, still not really seeing him. Then he turned and gazed at the wall, the blankness of it matching his own stare.

And then, he took a deep breath. In an uncertain voice he began to speak.

"It was nearly two years ago. And it was – well, it was a complete coincidence to begin with."

He frowned. "Actually, I'm not sure about that. I thought so at the time but as I said the words now, I'm wondering."

Hunter leaned forward, controlling his eagerness. At last, he sensed Reynolds was ready to tell the truth.

"Now I'm looking back, it might have been intentional," Reynolds continued. "They could have planned this all along."

37
Crossroads of Decision

He couldn't do this.

After close to an hour of agonizing, of turning every possibility over in his mind, Daniel knew that he was not going to be able to carry out the orders that the contents of the black bag had conveyed.

Standing up from his bed, his shoulders were painful with tension and his body felt clumsy with stress.

He looked at the weapon and examined it closely, his hands so damp with sweat that they had nearly slipped from his grasp a few times. The silenced firearm was heavy and deadly, and he knew what he was supposed to do with it, but he didn't know if he could.

Letting out a shaking breath, he climbed to his feet. Nausea bubbled inside him – a few times during this past hour, he'd been close to throwing up. Whenever he thought of the implications, a tidal wave of dread surged, and he began to retch.

"It's not right, man. No way is this right."

He spoke the words as strongly as he could, but he didn't feel strong inside, he felt a mess.

The weird thing was that, shamefully, it wasn't the act itself he was the most worried about.

He'd killed often enough in the game, in realistic ways. He'd trained and he'd exercised, he'd done his push-ups and his skips and his runs. He'd played Carl Commando paintball and some of the instructions in that specific type of paintball game had been to shoot to kill.

That, Daniel had excelled at. He'd been able to shoot to kill from any distance permissible in that paintball game.

If the chips were down, he thought he could draw on that muscle memory and dissociate himself enough to do the act. It wasn't the act itself. It was the fact that he feared, deeply, he'd be caught.

And it was all the implications surrounding that.

Daniel knew he had an imagination, more so than the rest of his group of friends and soldiers-to-be. His imagination and the ability to figure out creative options in a situation are the things that often won him the edge. Right now, his imagination was running wild with him, and it was offering up scenario after scenario, all bad.

Captain Dan – destroyed and disgraced, never again the person that Daniel aspired to be. Social ostracization. His friends visited him in jail and asked him how he could have done such a thing. His mother crying her eyes out before giving him a piece of her mind as to how he could have ended up like this. His father with that dull resignation, saying, "I always knew you were gonna be a loser. No hope, I guess."

He moved over to the desk, where he counted the money yet again, his fingers riffling through the sheaves of notes. So much money!

But what good would it do him if he was caught?

It would do him no good. It would be as much use to him as the paper notepad in Luke's small bedroom that his little brother had drawn a picture of money on with his crayons one time, and then – something only Luke could do – gone to the store and tried to spend it.

What a laugh that had been. The cold tension inside him eased off for a moment at that funny recollection of his kid brother. Maybe Daniel wasn't the only one in the family with a good imagination.

But going along with a request like this was too risky, and now he had to consider all the hard choices that he was now trapped between.

Being caught for shooting – actually shooting – somebody, compared to being caught for breaking and entering? Surely he had a chance with the lesser offense. He would have no chance at all with the more serious one. It would be game over.

Yet again, he picked up a damp dishcloth he'd brought from the kitchen and wiped every part of the gun he could find. He'd done that several times over the past fifty minutes. It felt as if his fingerprints, his DNA, were already ingrained in that weapon and that it would be traced back to him in the future, even if he never touched it again. That thought was unleashing a level of paranoia in his mind that he hadn't thought himself capable of.

He picked up the phone with clumsy hands. It would be important to explain himself during this call he was going to have to make. To say why he was making this choice so that they understood because, with dark certainty, he knew that this was not the end of it. They had paid him money and it was not going to be as simple as retracing his steps back down the road to the bench where he'd found this deadly paraphernalia.

Putting down the gun yet again, its barrel still wrapped tightly in the dishcloth, he dialed the number that had called him, just fifty-nine minutes ago.

"Daniel?" The call had barely rung before it was picked up. The suddenness of it surprised him as he'd thought he'd have a few more moments to listen to it ring and to plan what he would say.

"I – I can't do it," His voice was husky. "I'm really sorry. I've – I've looked at everything, you know. Looked at this from all angles."

His hand strayed out again, almost of its own volition, to touch the exposed grip of the gun, and Daniel snatched it back. He'd just wiped the whole damned thing! What was he thinking?

"Anyway, I thought I'd better explain that – that what worries me the most is that I don't have any protection if I'm caught. I mean, I'll go to prison for life. I – I'm afraid of that. I'm not a scared guy, but I'm afraid of that."

He paused. This was proving surprisingly difficult and the silence at the other end of the line was worrying. Was this man even still there? Was he listening?

Feeling as if he was battling up the steepest and most insurmountable of hills, he continued.

"So, what do I need to do? Please tell me. I'll – I'll be able to return everything to its place, including the money or is there somewhere else I should take it?" He paused. "I know there'll be – there'll be some consequences for what I've done, but I'll take those. If I have to – to go to jail for a year or two I'll do it, but it's better than life, right?"

That seemed to be all there was to say.

He was still breathing fast. And this man on the other end had still said nothing. Of course, he was mad at him, that was clear. He was mad and maybe because of that, he wasn't going to say anything at all.

Uncertain how to proceed in this situation, so far removed from anything he'd yet encountered in life, Daniel hesitated. Maybe he should just hang up now. That might be best. He'd been the one to make the call, after all.

And weirdly, he didn't feel any better after having gotten this explanation off his chest.

He'd thought that somehow he'd feel right that he'd feel good inside after having elected to do the wise thing as far as the law was concerned. But there was a nervous mess of guilt lodged inside him that was refusing to budge.

Guilt? How bizarre was that. It was as if he'd let this guy, whoever he was, down, and that he'd somehow compromised his future by doing so.

Feeling thoroughly miserable, Daniel moved his finger to the red button to end this call.

But just as he touched it, the voice spoke.

"There are consequences, Daniel," it said, and his gut twisted again, twisted hard.

He'd expected this.

"Consequences?" he asked.

"If you take this job, you are protected. That has been explained to you already and yet you have failed to understand it." The man paused, and now shame added itself to the mixture of guilt and fear that was roiling around in Daniel's stomach. "Do you really think you are alone? You are part of an elite squad, a chosen battalion that will lead the ranks in the months to come. Others have already performed and succeeded and are on the road to riches and success."

Daniel swallowed. He hadn't known that. Would it have made a difference?

"You're supposedly an intelligent man, so this is your last chance. There are consequences for refusing. Events will be set in motion if you end this call without accepting the job. I will not be able to stop or control them because it is part of the new system."

"What do you mean?" Even though he dreaded the answer, Daniel was surprised that a small part of him – a tiny part – felt relieved by what this man was saying. Because if there was no choice then there was no point in arguing. He'd tried to do the right thing. He'd done what he could, but it hadn't been enough.

"I mean this," the voice continued. "One target will be taken. And you have the choice of who it will be. Either it will be the woman who is our enemy and whom you have been briefed on. Or else… it will be somebody else and I will brief another member of our battalion accordingly. Your choice, Captain Dan." There was a deeply ironic note in the voice. "One of the two will die."

Now, the call was cut off abruptly and a picture flickered onto the screen of Daniel's phone.

It was a photo of his little brother, Luke, climbing off the school bus.

38
Conspiracy of Power Unveiled

With all his attention sharply focused on Sam Reynolds, Hunter waited as the corrupt COO finally spilled the truth about what he had become embroiled in.

The locked office was hushed, but faintly, from down the corridor came the sounds of people leaving the police station for the day, the noise of footsteps, and the chorus of goodbyes. The day was almost over. Hunter knew that the orders for him to quit managing the case, leave the LAPD precinct and relocate – which he now believed came directly from Harrison, not from Rogan – could fall on his head like an ax blade at any time. He hadn't opened any emails from Gibson, just in case, although he'd seen one earlier on his phone.

Information might provide what he needed to stop this.

Reynolds' voice was wobbly but as he spoke, it gained momentum. "It was – it was one of those public-private sector collaborations, one of many I'd been invited to, with a whole bunch of high-ups and dignitaries. They always asked Fortune 500 delegates to be there, and I was usually the one who went. I mean, with the success of Carl Commando – it was like, we were the leader, the one everyone looked up to."

He swallowed hard and Hunter saw to his surprise that Sam Reynolds was trying to hold back tears. The man had gone from being a confident, arrogant, untouchable COO to a crying, shivering wreck.

"I regret that decision. I regret it so bad."

Now, he reached for the water bottle and snapped it open, gulping a mouthful down and almost choking on it.

"What do you regret?" Hunter watched as Reynolds struggled to pull himself together.

"I was seated next to – to an influential individual in the military."

Even now, in a locked room, he wasn't ready to say that name aloud, but that was okay with Hunter. He'd pressure him on that later.

"Anyway, we hit it off, mainly on the topic of how misunderstood the military was, how it plays such an important role in our national security and the career options it offers. I was – you know, it's something I've always felt passionate about and we've always had our critics, right from the get-go. People who felt that we were just promoting violence."

He shook his head, suddenly appreciating the enormity of what he was about to say.

"I don't know if I can carry on with this," he said. He was sweating again.

"Your choice. Carry on now, or we wait and speak again later," Hunter said easily. "Take some time to get your thoughts together, but nobody's leaving this room until I know more."

"I – okay, I spoke to this man, and we had a really good rapport going. It felt, like, quite special to speak to him and he opened up about his challenges. I remember he didn't call them problems. He called them challenges. It was the enlistment that he was trying to fix because, so few people wanted to join the armed forces. He said we could use Carl Commando as a direct recruiting and training tool. All it would take was my collaboration."

Hunter felt cold shivers cascade down his spine.

So, now he had the answer from the source, and this was what it was about.

This was what the entire agenda had been. It was devious and brilliant and spoke of an uncanny ability for timing and manipulation.

The man he now knew to be Harrison had seen a gap that would allow him to solve one of the country's biggest, most expensive, and most enduring problems.

It was a stroke of dark genius that he'd executed with the skill of a military operation.

Rogan was simply the go-to here, the man who was actioning the recruitment instructions. Perhaps he didn't even know everything there was to know. Harrison had a clear talent for using people to fulfill his aims.

Staggering in its scope, Hunter had never believed that the killings were linked to something so vast. Something that had the potential to change the trajectory of so many young lives – and the course of an entire country.

With shock still resonating inside him, he began to probe deeper to get the details and hopefully find out exactly how this master plan had led to multiple murders.

"So, tell me how this played out? Did he suggest meeting up afterward?"

"We met up after the event in the bar. He said – he said that he had a brilliant idea that could present a win-win for us. At that stage, it didn't seem like it was anything but above board. I didn't realize – I didn't know then how it would change," he said. "There we were in this bar, just the two of us. Sitting at this table at the back, drinking a cognac that was more expensive than anything I'd ever ordered. It was weird. It was like a head rush."

His words powerfully portrayed to Hunter exactly what it must have felt like for Reynolds to be taken into the confidence of such a powerful man. Those expensive cognacs had played a part too, he was sure. Deliberately done. Drunk on alcohol and the proximity to power, in that glamorous setting, it was clear how Reynolds had been so effectively influenced. And maybe the money had been mentioned early on.

"What did he say?" Hunter scooted his chair just a little closer.

"He said that I could help him a lot and that my contribution might be a game changer for the whole of America. It was- it was persuasive. I had this feeling that this was so much bigger than just my contribution to an action figure. I felt like I could be a national hero."

"Did he say how it would work?"

"He was – well, cagey about it at first. We set up a further meeting and then another. And it was only at the second one that he set it out. Some of the details, anyway, although he said that this was a national security issue, so confidentiality was key."

Hunter was sure it was. Not so much confidentiality as secrecy.

"Anyway, he said this would require an exchange. That this action figure and this game could be used as a direct marketing tool that would help to channel people into the military. And do more than that. It could equip them with the skills and the mindset they'd need to succeed. They'd be fit, skilled, and ready for action."

Now a trace of color came back into Reynolds' cheeks as he spoke and Hunter realized that this was something he had bought into completely, something he believed.

"You see, the mindset is everything, and he – he told me that the younger age at which it was instilled, the better and that part of the problem today, why the Army is battling for recruits, is that the youngsters are so ill-disciplined. The action figure and the associated activities were a chance for us to help America correct a problem. Of course I bought into it! Who wouldn't do that? It seemed such a brilliant idea."

"You must have given him something in exchange to kick off this project. What did it involve?" Hunter asked.

When Reynolds was silent, Hunter continued.

"I'm guessing it meant you handing over control of a lot of the information, the features, the intellectual property?"

Reynolds tightened his lips.

"I'm going to get into huge trouble for speaking about this," he muttered, backtracking fast.

"As of now, you're a state witness," Hunter reminded him. "We're doing a deal here. That means you cooperate to avoid the full extent of the trouble."

He didn't want to lose momentum. It was essential that Reynolds kept talking now, while he was still outpacing his fears.

Reynolds clenched his hands tightly on the desk. There was visible tension within him but at least he wasn't backing off completely.

"I was told..." He hesitated. "Hell, repeating this is something I never thought I'd have to do, that this was all seamless enough I wouldn't have to."

Hunter nodded as Reynolds continued, voice wobbling again.

"He said I'd have to hand over the mailing list, all of it, for every activity, on an ongoing basis. All customer details. I'd have to agree to certain parameters that would change the look and feel of the toy. I'd have to hand over control of the game's software – they wanted to make changes. He had some people working for him – I'm not sure who. That was difficult to do, and it took some maneuvering on my side. The mailing list was easier, I just added myself and copied it. I know it was so wrong, but it all felt somehow legitimate, that I was doing it for a bigger cause, the good of America."

Now, shaking his head, he muttered, almost to himself, "Jeez, I've just dug my own grave by saying this. I can't believe I've said all this."

Hunter couldn't afford for the flow of words to dry up – not yet.

"What did you get in exchange?" he asked.

"I've said enough, haven't I?" Reynolds' words held a querulous note.

"Full disclosure!" Hunter's raised voice resonated in the small room. "When you cooperate with police in a deal against charges this serious, the terms and conditions are all from our side. Not yours!"

"Money," Reynolds said, with a twist of his mouth that told Hunter some of his defiance was making a comeback. "That's what I got, and I was promised more."

"I need numbers. And how it was done."

"Cash advances upfront. A few of them, very generous. They came to over five million so far. And the agreement was that when the first intake of prequalified recruits were all signed up in a couple of months, I'd get a flat fee of four hundred million dollars," he said. "That's nearly half the Army's annual marketing budget, he said. For my efforts and help."

Hunter was jolted by the magnitude of that amount as Reynolds continued. "He said that would happen and I believed he'd honor his word; that I'd become wealthier than I'd ever imagined."

He had some of the picture now. This was how it had begun. And Hunter could see the insidious way that it had been presented to Reynolds. The double whammy of being the savior of America, combined with the compelling force of good old-fashioned greed must have been impossible to resist.

"The killings. You haven't told me about them yet."

Reynolds was shaking his head. "Look, all I know is that things have gone bad. Suddenly. It was all peachy until it wasn't. I don't know a thing about these killings, I swear it, but I've – I've been threatened. Anonymously. Not by this individual although he's obviously behind it, I can see that. I've had messages telling me not to speak about this to anyone, not ever. My heads on the block if I talk."

"You met with this person today. Were those threats mentioned?"

"They weren't. It was a routine meeting. It was to talk about the progress made in the military sign-ups."

"And what progress had been made?"

Uneasily, Hunter was becoming aware of the scale of this behemoth.

"They have a few hundred thousand already signed up for initial interviews. That's eighteen-year-olds, and it's vastly increased from previous years. I mean, even though I know things aren't right – in the meeting, that still seemed like a good thing, right? Hundreds of thousands getting ready for the next round of intakes? Motivated guys who'll go into a career?"

Anxiousness was in his eyes as he stared directly at Hunter.

Hunter wasn't going to waste time by sharing his perspective on the ethics of indoctrinating young men into the military. Instead, he asked a pertinent question.

"Did this meeting touch on the killings?"

"They weren't mentioned."

"How about the blogs? The exposure of information?"

Reynolds swallowed. "I think – I think there have been leaks, in the past. Leaks from somewhere. A few people are involved in this so I guess that there are ways for word to get out. You can never trust everyone and sometimes not anyone. That's what – what he told me."

"And what did your connection think of those blogs, those activists, even the opposition companies?"

Reynolds took a deep breath.

"He knows they're a big threat. A big danger to his plans, and he did say that he was going to manage the threat. He just sort of mentioned it in passing."

Hunter knew this was key.

"How? Did he mention the murders?" Hunter was going to get him for this, whatever it took.

"No! No, he didn't. He never spoke about them at all." Reynolds paused.

Hunter stared him straight in the eye.

"It's time for the name, Reynolds. Give me the name of this person. We both know who it is and now, I need you to speak it out loud."

Reynolds took a deep breath, and then, he spoke the words that Hunter had been waiting to hear.

"Charles Harrison. The Secretary of Defense. But you're never going to pin these crimes on him. Not in a million years. He's covered all his tracks and there's no way to catch him now."

39
Deadly Directive

"We're going to get him," Hunter emphasized, his words confident as he stared at the quailing Reynolds across the interview room desk. "We are going to pin these crimes on Charles Harrison."

But Reynolds shook his head, his face pinched with tension.

"You'll never do it. He's been too careful every step of the way. I don't know who any of his other connections even are."

"He's done these killings. He must have done."

To his shock, Reynolds shook his head once more.

"I know he couldn't have done them himself. He was out of state this morning on an official visit somewhere with his contingent. He only got back an hour before our meeting."

That was a bombshell.

It smashed Hunter's theory to smithereens.

Would Harrison really have delegated such an important job to somebody else? The only person that Hunter believed could have done this was Rogan – but Rogan would have been part of the contingent, as his second-in-command.

Hunter didn't see him trusting anyone else, especially when there had already been leaks and betrayals within his carefully constructed world.

Hunter knew he had to go further into Harrison's mind in order to get the full picture. Yet again, the secretary of defense had outfoxed them through his actions.

He left the interview room, closing and locking the door behind him.

If he hadn't had a suspect to keep an eye on, Hunter would have gone out onto the streets of LA and walked around the precinct block with the darkness surrounding him, the flash of headlights in the distance and the cool evening air in his lungs.

But he had a suspect to consider and couldn't go far.

"What the hell's he been doing? How has he been doing it? And what is he looking to achieve with it?" Hunter muttered.

All critical questions. Reynolds didn't know the answers. It was an example of how Harrison had kept his activities compartmentalized, the way a good soldier would do. It was a cunning strategy.

Hunter went a few paces down the corridor and into the small adjoining office. There, he sat in a chair, picked up a pen, and jotted some notes by hand on his notepad, summarizing what he knew so far. Too paranoid he might mistakenly leave his notes where another officer could see, Hunter decided on an alias for Harrison.

"H didn't commit these murders. Alibi for at least one."

"Did H organize them or were they committed without his knowledge?"

Hunter considered that question, then shook his head.

"H has to know about them and have been the one to authorize these killings, because of what he said in passing to Reynolds."

Harrison was a hands-on man, who was looking to obliterate all threats to his plans. Hence he was pulling strings to get Hunter redeployed.

But how had he done these killings?

Had he gotten a lethal, trusted assassin to work for him, and if so, who was this person?

Hunter considered the question, tapping his fingers on the desk, letting his thoughts roam – as creatively as they wanted to. Imagining seemingly impossible scenarios might be helpful here – after all, what had been done so far was seemingly impossible.

A man with a thirst for power had found a way to achieve it. He'd set out, in collusion with a hugely influential company, to start brainwashing a generation of boys and young men.

He was in the process of solving one of the most difficult and problematic challenges facing the Department of Defense, and that was the problem of how to get keen, well-qualified recruits to fill the Army numbers.

This had enabled him to pay – or at any rate, part-pay so far – a mind-boggling amount of money to Reynolds. And Harrison was tipped to be the next President as a result of his turnaround of the military enlistment and his influence.

But the murders?

How were they being done?

Hunter thought about that game and the teens who played it, the way that game influenced their thinking, and how this, combined with independent contact from Army recruiters, encouraged them to join up. Not only were they already partially skilled, but they were well prequalified in terms of their mindset.

Harrison had been able to engineer all of this. He'd had an inordinate amount of power and influence over these young minds.

What else had he used it for?

Suddenly, Hunter realized what the answer could be.

He sat upright in his chair, looking up from his notes, his mind racing as he allowed it to roam beyond what a reasonable person might do and into the territory of what a power-obsessed person might be capable of desiring.

And how he would achieve it.

A footfall from outside the office made him jump. There was a tap on the door, and he quickly went to the door, opening it to let Cody in.

"The Corvette's in the basement parking. Keys are here," his partner said, glancing in the direction of the locked interview room. "I'm guessing he's in there. Told you anything?"

Hunter turned to the computer and powered it up.

"He told me what he knows and that it was Harrison behind all this, but what he knows isn't everything. Harrison couldn't have committed the murders himself because he was out of state this morning."

"Would he have trusted anyone else with that? Given that there clearly have been leaks so far, because how else would the information have gotten out there?" Cody asked.

"That's what I'm looking for now," Hunter said. "I have an idea and I want to see if it's correct."

"What does it involve?" Cody asked, raising his eyebrows as Hunter started opening up window after window on his computer.

"It involves looking through all the recent crime reports for California state. And then, if I need to, all the crime reports for other states also. I'm looking for something specific and I want to see if I can find it. If I can, it'll confirm my theory."

"There's not an easier way to get this information?" Cody asked.

"Not that I can think of," Hunter said.

"Can't we put a wire on Reynolds? Send him in again to speak to Harrison?"

Hunter turned to face his partner, making a rueful face. "That was my first idea, but I don't think it's wise. They've just met up today and if Reynolds contacts him again and wants to meet, he might get a heads-up that something's gone bad. The one thing we don't want, now, is for him to suspect we're onto him and start getting even more secretive than he is already."

"Okay. I see we want to avoid that. So this is plan B?"

"It is," Hunter said.

"You might need some help with that," Cody said laconically.

"I'd appreciate it," Hunter said.

He was sure that if he searched hard enough, he could find what he suspected was there. It might not be easy, though, because of the sheer volume of information to look through. But that was no reason to give up on the plan, it was simply a reason to work faster. Especially since time was limited. They couldn't keep Reynolds locked up in a private office overnight and it was already early evening.

And Harrison could be making his countermove at any time.

Hunter's fingers flew over the keyboard. His eyes scanned the information. It must be here somewhere. If it was, it would tie up all the loose ends he'd been wondering about. It would explain his theory.

Where could it be? Let him find it, he prayed.

And then, at almost the same time, he and Cody spoke aloud.

"I've found it!" Hunter said.

"Got something here!"

Hunter looked at Cody's screen and then he stared at his own.

Three crimes and three seemingly identical Mos.'

One from San Francisco, two from New York City.

Three identical murders – two bullets in the head of each victim. All within the past week.

Hunter was sure that there might be a few more to be uncovered if he widened the search or looked for longer.

Quickly, knowing every second counted now, Hunter called up the details.

One victim was a newspaper reporter for a small independent publication that specialized in exposes, the New York State Investigator. That tied in with the other murders and Hunter was sure it was for the same reason – but it was way across the country.

The next one, just two days later, was a freelance computer programmer in the Silicon Valley area, who'd been twenty-eight years old at the time and working on what was described as 'private projects for individual clients.' Thinking of the Carl Commando game and those leaks, Hunter saw the connection.

And the other?

Now, this was disturbing and not what he'd expected to find.

The other San Francisco victim was an eighteen-year-old boy – Cameron Grieg. He was in his final year of school.

*

There was no time to get to San Francisco, although ideally, Hunter would have preferred to sit face-to-face with the family for this interview. But a phone call would have to do.

While Cody went to supervise Sam Reynolds – taking him a bottle of water and a cup of coffee – Hunter shut himself in the office and made the call that he hoped, finally, would unlock the answers.

As he listened to it ring, he saw his fists were clenched and made an effort to relax them.

The phone rang and rang, and he began to fear that the contact number for Cameron's mother, which was the only one he'd been able to get at short notice, would end up ringing unanswered.

And then, at last, a woman picked up.

"Anita Grieg," she said.

Her voice sounded hollow and hopeless and ragged – exactly the way Hunter had expected a bereaved mother whose son had been brutally murdered just a few days ago – to sound.

"Ms. Grieg? It's Detective Harden here, LAPD. I heard about your son's tragic murder. It may be connected to a case I'm dealing with. Can I ask some questions?"

"Connected?" She sounded confused. "Yes, I suppose you can but how would Cameron's – Cameron's murder – be connected with something in LA?" She stumbled over her son's name, causing Hunter's heart to clench in sympathy.

"There's a possibility it may be. Can you tell me the circumstances?"

"He was coming home at night. He'd been out with friends. He was shot just outside the front door." Her voice was tight with barely controlled sobs. "It was so random, so shocking. Nobody knows why. The weapon was silenced."

"Did your son play the Carl Commando game?" Hunter asked her.

A surprised pause followed.

"Yes. Yes, he played that. He was obsessed with that game. He loved it." Sadness resonated in her voice. "It was his dream to join the Navy SEALs one day. That was what he wanted to do. He'd already got an interview organized and everything."

"Had he had any trouble in his life? Anything going wrong?"

Hunter didn't know exactly what questions he needed to ask to get the shape of this monster.

"Nothing!" the mother protested tearfully.

"How about anything unusual? Anything you were not quite sure about?"

"He – well," Her voice tailed off.

Hunter waited, glancing again at those crime stats on the computer screen and then down at his notepad where his jotted notes were scrawled across the page.

After a pause, she continued. "He had something going on in his life that he wasn't telling me, that I could see."

"How could you see?"

"He was spending a lot of time texting on his phone. He was withdrawn, you know," she said.

"Do you have his phone?" Hunter asked.

"No, I don't. I don't know where it is. I think it was taken during the – the shooting," she said.

"Did he drop any hints about this trouble, or did you ask?"

"He'd always been an independent boy, so I didn't push it. I mean, I was sure it was innocent, probably something to do with a girl or something he was battling with at school. He never used to ask me about those things. He'd sometimes share with his younger sister – he adored Maddie but she's thirteen and obviously could not help with the school side of things."

"Would it have been to do with his friends?"

"His friends? Are you saying one of his friends would have killed him?" Incredulity resonated in her voice, as if she'd never have believed his friends capable of such a thing and was astounded by his insinuation.

"Did he have lots of friends he played the Carl Commando game with?" Hunter said.

"Well, yes. Some school friends, some people he knew outside of school and I'm guessing that some would have been strangers to him, that he only knew online. But I mean – you really think one of them would have killed him? Is that within the bounds of possibility?"

"There may be a connection," Hunter said. "Was he spending more time out of the house than usual? Did he travel anywhere?"

There was a pause.

"Now you mention it, yes," she said. "He was away for a night, a couple of days before he died. He said he was with a friend, and it was during the school vacation, so I didn't ask. He often goes to friends overnight. You think I should have asked?"

"No, of course not. Not if you didn't usually," Hunter consoled her. "When he came back, did he seem troubled at all?"

She paused again.

"Nobody asked me this yet. Nobody else seemed to think it was important. But yes, now you're mentioning it, he was troubled. Very. He seemed depressed. I heard him crying in his room that night and I wondered if he'd had a fallout with his friend. He had a nightmare that night, and woke us all up shouting the house down."

Hunter had cold shivers now. He stared down at the pen in his hand, seeing the overhead light reflecting across its silver barrel, as he began to realize why such a bad nightmare might have happened.

"Is that so?" Hunter asked. "Did he often have those dreams?"

"When he was a kid, yes, after his father was killed in a car crash. But not for a long time since then," she admitted. "He seemed very down, very morose the next day, but then, a couple of days later, he was back to normal and so I left it." She let out a deep breath. "I know I sound like a bad mother for not having looked into it, but he was such an independent boy. He hated it when I poked my nose into his business, as he called it. I decided respecting his boundaries was more important. So – that's it. I don't know what else I can tell you. I'll never get him back again, there's no second chance. No time for what ifs."

Her shuddering breath sighed in Hunter's ear.

"You've been very helpful and I'm so sorry for your loss," Hunter said.

He hung up, thinking hard about what he'd learned.

Now, he was starting to see the logistics of these killings, like a darker shadow lurking beneath murky waters.

And they were horrific.

Hunter had to bury his head in his hands for a moment, letting the darkness surround him as he took in the extent of the evil and the manipulation.

If he was right, then what Charles Harrison was doing was using the game for his own purposes. Not just to create a huge pool of prequalified Army candidates that would fulfill his mandate as Secretary of Defense, turn the armed forces around, and set him on a path to the presidency.

He was also choosing from that, a smaller pool of young men, and these, he was grooming and using to be his killers.

If Hunter was right, then Charles Harrison was gathering his own personal assassination squad. They were skilled and indoctrinated in following orders. They would be able to work under remote instruction. They could fetch and carry each other. And if one of them refused a mission – then it was an easy task to dispose of them. Simply deploy another one to do the job.

From what Cameron Grieg's mother had said, Hunter was guessing that he'd been sent on a job – perhaps the Silicon Valley programmer murder. Maybe he'd regretted it afterward, maybe he had threatened that he'd go to the police. Either way, Hunter was guessing, Harrison had used another of his warrior squad to take him out.

It made all the sense in the world, and it was the perfect closed circle.

Leaning his elbows on the desk, Hunter realized something else.

If Harrison was behind this and masterminding the process, then that gave them the window they needed to bring down this evil.

"He's instructing them himself," Hunter muttered. "He has to be doing it himself. No way would he delegate something this important, that could smash his entire strategy if it's found out. But if he's using burner phones and disposing of them regularly, which I'm sure he is – then there's only one way it will work. And that's to catch him in the act."

40
Countdown Chaos

Sitting with Cody in the office next door to where Reynolds was still locked away, Hunter made his plans. With both of them speaking quietly, it felt like a council of war.

Guerilla warfare against a powerful enemy whose reach had extended further than they had thought.

"We need to figure out who he's going to go for next and then, we need to be there. Those killers are receiving instructions from Harrison directly, I'm sure of it. But he's being very careful and very clever."

"So we need a multi-pronged strategy here, then," Cody said. "Firstly, we need to pinpoint Harrison. Get close to him at the right time and know where he's going to be."

"He's got to be somewhere private when he issues the instructions for these murders," Hunter said.

"You don't think we can bring him in anyway and lean on him?" Cody suggested.

It was a tempting prospect, but reluctantly, Hunter decided it wouldn't work.

"So far, with Reynolds' testimony, we can get him for collusion and bribery and a whole lot of minor offenses, but he's powerful and wealthy and those might end up sliding off. And if he has a small army of hackers and killers at his disposal and he's not locked away in prison, we might find our witnesses start disappearing. Fast."

Cody nodded somberly.

But how to work the logistics?

The first part, Hunter hoped he could do. The second part, he wasn't sure of at all, and it would be far more dangerous. He'd need to locate Harrison's next target and get there first.

Hunter's hopes were on the website No to Violence and on Brixton in the IT department, who was busy trying to call up the details of that hacked site.

"Keep an eye on Reynolds for me?" he said. "I need to drive downtown."

It was time to head out for what would be the most important meeting of his career. If it didn't succeed, then this entire strategy was doomed to failure.

*

"What the hell is going on there, Hunter?" Gibson's voice was furious. Standing in his office, which was on the second floor of the neighboring LAPD station, with a view of chimneys and concrete walls out of the small window, he glowered at Hunter. He had his laptop bag over his shoulder and was clearly on his way out.

"You're supposed to be wrapping things up with these cases and handing them over. I know this is contrary to what your agenda is, but these are orders from the top and you need to accept them! I was on my way to you to enforce them. Now you're here. Why?"

"You might as well put that bag down," Hunter said.

Gibson drew in a sharp breath. "What do you mean by that?"

"I mean that we need to have a serious conversation. You're not going to like what I tell you. You're probably not even going to accept it. But it's urgent – critical, in fact. And it's true. If we're both sitting down, then you have a better chance of hearing what I have to say, calmly."

For a moment Hunter thought Gibson was going to explode. He could see the stresses of the day etched in his face, the pressures of having been pushed to follow orders that deep down, Gibson must know were irrational.

"You're walking in here and giving me orders?"

"I'm encouraging us to have a reasonable conversation."

It wasn't going to happen. Gibson was too mad. No way was he going to sit down. The situation had just turned into a powder keg and if it exploded, then Hunter's chances of getting him to see the truth were zero.

Day Zero.

The words rang in his head again. Now he understood what they meant. Day Zero was not just the day that the first wave of Army enlistment swelled the forces and cemented Harrison's political power, thanks to the leverage of Carl Commando.

Day Zero was darker than that. It was the day that Harrison was going to start unleashing the next phase of his quest for power.

What would a psychopathic megalomaniac be capable of, if he had a private force of killers at his disposal? And a massive army behind them, full of young recruits who had already been conditioned to obey orders?

Hunter knew that the scenarios were unimaginable and terrifying. He was a student of literature, but history was a better teacher when it came to acknowledging what humans were capable of doing.

A manipulative person with an end goal in his sights could cut through opposition like a knife through butter, change society, persecute detractors, and hunt down those who sought to stop him. He could plunge the country and the world into a state of war in his quest for dominance.

Some people would believe it could never happen. Some would believe it wasn't happening and would turn a blind eye. The 'ordinary people' would only start to protest when it was way too late.

After all, nobody who ended up living in Nazi Germany had believed that could happen – so fast, so unstoppably.

"There's nothing reasonable about your actions, Harden!" Gibson said, still standing squarely in front of his desk, which had a few neat piles of paperwork on it and a wilted plant in a red pot.

"Here are the facts," Hunter said. He kept calm, kept his voice down. No point in shouting back. That would only spark the conflict between them more intensely. He remembered the words of one of his lecturers back at university, who'd been a follower of martial arts. When your opponent was bringing a nine-out-of-ten to the situation in terms of aggression, you needed to bring a one-out-of-ten yourself to tone things down.

"What are the facts?" Finding nothing to spark his anger off, Gibson's voice was already calmer.

"The facts are that we have a witness in custody right now who is willing to testify that Harrison has bribed him with substantial amounts of money and the promise of hundreds of millions more. We do have some limited footage of a cash handover to back this up."

Now, Gibson gaped at Hunter. "Why? Why would Harrison do that?"

"Long story short, to further his own political ambitions and seize absolute power," Hunter said.

"Show me the proof of this. I need proof and I need details." Gibson put his bag on the floor and folded his arms.

"I'll give you both as soon as you've agreed that we can put resources on this immediately. We need to catch Harrison in the act, and we need to stop him. Both will be a challenge, but to start with, we need to figure out where he is now and have people standing by. And then, we need to figure out what his next target is and have people watching and waiting there."

There were two possibilities. Olivia Montgomery might be one. She'd cooperated with the police and therefore she was a potential stumbling block. Remove her, and Reynolds would be in control of Dreamland Creations, which would suit Harrison perfectly.

The other was that rogue blog, No to Violence, that had recently been hacked to prevent an expose from being published.

Two potential targets and Hunter had no idea which one Harrison would move on first.

"If we are fast and lucky, then we might just stand a chance of stopping Day Zero," he continued to Gibson. "If Day Zero goes ahead, it would mean the unleashing of a level of conflict and instability that the world has not seen for decades. If I've read Harrison right, we could be on an unstoppable path to another world war, with the United States at its epicenter."

Gibson was still looking astonished, his anger now taking a back seat to the blindsiding shock of what he'd been told.

"All I need is for you to agree, now, that we can go ahead with this, urgently," Hunter said.

His boss was thinking more clearly now, he could see it. His logical mind was prevailing over the flare of anger.

"Show me the evidence and if I'm convinced, we can go ahead." Gibson nodded.

"Come with me," Hunter urged.

As he raced down the stairs, ready to rush back to his own LAPD police station, his phone rang again.

Picking up as he scrambled into the car, he found himself speaking to Brixton.

The IT department manager sounded pleased with himself.

"That site, No to Violence," he said. "I've been able to track down the original details and I'm tracing it back. If it goes according to plan, then I should have the site owner's name and address in a few more minutes." He hesitated. "But Hunter, I should tell you – those address details were wiped. That's why it's taken me so long. Whoever hacked that site got in there first – at least a day ago and they already know where the site owner lives."

Gritting his teeth, Hunter sped out onto the road.

No to Violence had been exposed already. Now he knew where Harrison's sights would be set.

With that head start, they might already be too late to stop another killing.

And they would lose their chance to trap Harrison in the act.

41
Conspiracy's Dark Revelation

When Hunter burst into the back office of the LAPD police station, he saw Cody look up from behind a row of three different laptops and one large computer screen.

"Gibson's on his way," Hunter said, rushing over. "What do you have so far?" He hoped that Cody could get a location on Harrison before Gibson arrived.

If anyone could do it, it was Cody, who was as skilled as a sniffer dog when it came to rooting out these details.

"I'm looking for where Harrison could be staying tonight," Cody said. "Trying every angle, without him getting a heads-up about it. I've managed to get his schedule for the week. He's in LA today and tomorrow, for sure. Seems to spend a lot of time here."

"No wonder," Hunter said. LA was one of the epicenters of his Day Zero efforts. And since it was where a lot of the anti-Carl Commando movement originated, it was no wonder that the Secretary of Defense had adjusted his schedule to focus on it. "Any meetings now?"

"No. He's not in a meeting now. And interestingly, I see here that Rogan stood in for him this afternoon. That meeting was with a group of the Army logistics personnel in this area." Cody quirked an eyebrow, reaching for the cup of coffee on his desk and staring into it with an expression of puzzlement when he found it empty.

Hunter took the cup from him, went over to the jug at the back of the office and refilled it. Right now, his partner and friend needed all the fuel he could get to power him.

"Thanks," Cody said, taking it from him and draining half the cup in one gulp.

"So the logistics guy is standing in for the main man?" Hunter cast his mind back to the first meeting he'd had with Rogan, remembering his obnoxious attitude, his sense of entitlement, and his bullying demeanor.

He was the perfect foil for Harrison. He was so utterly dislikeable that nobody thought the man in charge of him could be worse. Only now did Hunter realize that he was the perfect dumb muscle, following orders, but acting as if they were his own idea.

"Unusual for the main man not to attend, since he's in the area and all," Cody said, raising one of his almost nonexistent eyebrows. "But then, I guess, this has been a busy time for Harrison's private activities."

Hunter nodded in agreement. "He's doing this in secret – but where?"

"I've had some of my spies at various big hotels reporting back," Cody said. "And so far, nothing on Harrison. I've found out where Rogan's staying, with a few others from the contingent. They're at the Hilton. But not Harrison."

"Are you sure?" Hunter asked.

"My friend at the front desk swears that he's not with them. He was there, the day before yesterday, for a short meeting. Lots of security and fanfare in place. But he's not staying there. My contact there has discreetly asked around, calling a few of the other major hotels where the government dignitaries usually do stay. And there's no sign of him."

Hunter checked the time. It was after eight p.m. Gibson would be on his way here and then Hunter would have a narrow window of time to persuade him. Not knowing where Harrison was, could be a deciding factor in the success of this operation if he did say yes.

With a shiver, Hunter thought of those soldiers, young men armed with guns – he was wondering where Harrison had obtained the weapons from. Maybe an Army store somewhere was a few weapons short. Brainwashed and no doubt coerced also, they were setting out to do their bidding.

The most dangerous opponent – unknown, faceless, and desperate, with everything to lose. He could well imagine the tactics that had been used to ensure their cooperation. Little crimes first, leading to bigger ones. Threats galore. Money involved, for sure. And a feeling the whole way through that they'd already gone too far, that the person issuing the orders was the only person who could save them from terrible trouble.

"He can't be staying with a friend," Cody said, finishing his coffee yet again. "Surely not, for something like this?"

Hunter had an idea.

"Cody, what if he owns a place here? He might have bought himself a house, knowing that he needed somewhere private to operate from. Being in a house would also give him much more of a chance to come and go without being seen – and also to dispose of those burners he must be using."

A cellphone graveyard, in a deep hole in the backyard – that was the picture Hunter had in his mind.

"I'm going to check that out right now." Cody turned back to his screens.

"Not only in his name," Hunter said. "Look for any directorships he might have, any companies he owns. It might be in another name, just to make it even more obscure."

Cody moved to the largest of his laptops.

"Let's get that search started there," he said. And then, Hunter heard footsteps heading down the corridor, brisk and purposeful.

Gibson had arrived, and now it was make-or-break time.

The police chief looked stressed as well as angry as he marched inside. Behind his wall of laptops, Cody was barely visible from the door and Gibson's gaze focused immediately on Hunter.

"Now, explain to me what's going on, Harden, and fast. It seems to me that you've got the whole police department headed on a collision course with disaster. I need answers, now."

"Short answer," Hunter said, keeping his voice calm and level, "Harrison's corrupt. He's looking to gain absolute power. He's weaponized himself using a small army of killers. Via collusion with a top-level executive at Dreamland Creations, he's managed to create a partnership to enable massive numbers of recruits to be channeled into the Army. This is going to put him in a key position to run for the presidency. And when he does, his agenda is going to cause major-scale destruction."

Gibson stared at him, his gaze like steel.

"These are serious allegations. One might even say treasonous."

"Not if they are correct," Hunter argued back.

"This is from left field. There hasn't been a hint or a murmur of anything building up to this."

"It's been very well managed, in top secrecy. There's been a zero-trust policy in place, meaning that all information has been suppressed and all leaks have been dealt with. At least one of the programmers responsible for making changes to the Carl Commando game was murdered a few days ago – perhaps because he was leaking information. One of the young men I believe was his killer, was then murdered. A New York journalist was killed the same way. Here are these cases. Take a look at the reports. They're identical to the crimes we've been investigating, it's just that nobody has yet joined the dots. And don't forget, we're sitting here with a case involving three seemingly unexplained murders that are clearly hits. This is the only explanation."

Gibson shook his head, frowning deeply as he stared down at the pages Hunter handed him.

"If you are wrong, do you realize what it means for you? And for anyone who supports this theory?"

Hunter shook his head. "I'm not wrong. He's manipulating others to kill. He's doing so extremely effectively. It's creating a closed circle that excludes him and absolves him of guilt. The only way that I can see for us to do it is to get him at the moment when he's issuing instructions. That way he won't have a chance to get rid of whatever burner phone he's using."

Watching Gibson carefully, Hunter had no idea how he was taking this. His face, drawn in harsh lines, gave nothing away other than the deep worry that had already been there to start with.

Gibson was a good man; he was not a corrupt person. That, Hunter believed. But this was a big ask. To accept a theory that could indeed be interpreted as treason if it was proved incorrect?

"We already have a witness, right here in this police station, who has said Harrison bribed him. He's been splashing the cash around, buying supercars and luxury homes. This is not a totally unfounded theory," Hunter said.

"I get that," Gibson said eventually, his voice taut with strain. "I get it. But tell me now, what's your next step? You're asking me to buy into a theory that's quite frankly explosive. It's been very well concealed so far if you're right about it. How do you suggest we prove it true?"

Hunter stepped forward.

"Harrison is currently taking down one of his most outspoken critics who's been trying to expose this information. It's a local blog, small but effective, called No To Violence. He's already hacked the blog and if his pattern of behavior is consistent, his next step will be to use one of his armed human assassins to take down the owner. We're working on finding out who that is and where they are. But to catch Harrison in the act, we need to be there at the time when he's issuing instructions. Otherwise, he'll get rid of the burner phone, and we'll have nothing on him."

"And where's Harrison? How do we know where he'll be?"

At least he was saying 'we'. Maybe that meant he was at least partially on board with the theory. But they didn't yet have any answers there. They didn't know where Harrison lived. With so little direction, it might be that

Gibson regarded this as an unacceptable risk, even if he was partway persuaded by what Hunter had said.

Except then, Cody popped his head up from behind his wall of laptops, causing Gibson to spin around in surprise.

"I've got something," he said. "Hunter, you were right. Harrison owns a property here, a three-bedroomed house on the expensive side of Lakewood, registered in the name of a company that he's a director of. Seeing he isn't in any hotel I've been able to find, and this looks like a pretty comfortable and private piece of real estate, I'm guessing he's there."

Gibson was still frowning.

"I'm halfway convinced. I'm willing to investigate it myself. But I'm not calling any additional personnel. For a car ride to a private house, where you say Harrison is residing, I don't see a need to bring anyone else into this potential minefield. So, it's us two only. We take a drive there, knock on his door and see what there is to find. Low key." He stared at Hunter.

"Us three," Cody said, getting up from behind his desk with a scrape of his chair. "I'm in this with you."

Hunter was too tense to feel any relief at this decision. There was still so much that could go wrong. Harrison could have covered his tracks or else, despite all Hunter's worries, he might not be communicating with his killers tonight. But this agreement was all he was going to get; he was lucky to have it and now there was no turning back.

"Let's get going," he said, heading for the door.

Gibson followed, still with an air of reluctance about him that made it clear he was going along with this despite major doubts and that he was not fully committed to the decision.

But, as they headed out, there was a clatter of feet from the stairwell.

Hunter spun around to see Brixton, his headset still in place and his phone in his hand. He was racing downstairs from the IT department's floor.

"Hunter!" His voice was a whiplash, filled with urgency.

"You found the physical address of the website's owner?" Hunter turned to face him. He must have done, surely? There could be no other reason for him having rushed down here.

But a look at his face told him that something had gone terribly wrong.

"Hunter." Brixton reached out a hand and grasped his shoulders. He sounded as if he was fighting desperately for calmness in getting out what he was going to say. "Hunter, we got the address. I needed to tell you fast. It's –" He took a shaking breath. "No To Violence is registered in the name of Amy Harden. She's the site's founder and owner. And the physical address – it's hers."

42
Dark Choice

Daniel felt as if he was choking.

Crouched in the darkness, in the flower bed behind the house where he hoped he would be unnoticed until it was time to act, he felt as if he could not breathe. This was something he had to do. Somehow, he'd gotten into this so deep he couldn't get out again.

It was this woman – or it was Luke. If he didn't do this, his brother would come to harm.

All his life, Daniel had been his little brother's protector. That had been his role. He'd had a tough time of it himself sometimes – at home and school – and he'd promised that the little guy would have it better, that he'd never have to go to bed hungry because their dad was furious, that he'd never miss the school bus because nobody got him out of bed in time, that he'd never suffer the bullying that Daniel had endured when he was younger before he toughened up and fought back and they moved on to a weaker target.

The fact that his brother was even under threat due to Daniel's actions was unthinkable. Impossible. It went against everything he'd ever worked toward. If Luke was hurt or killed, it would be his fault.

Now, breathing fast, with trauma filling his mind, Daniel knew that there was no choice.

He was working for an agent who was undoubtedly evil, but the problem was that they were also invisible. He had no idea who they were. Maybe he should just accept that he was a slave to them now, who'd have to do whatever jobs came his way, and as long as he succeeded in them, he'd earn money and his brother would be safe. That might be the only solution. There seemed nothing else he could do.

And it all started here.

Now.

He tensed, as the headlights swung around to the front of the house and the car pulled in. She was home now. That meant it was time. He'd need to act fast and decisively. He already had the window latch loosened and it was open enough for him to squeeze in easily. Then he'd be in the living room. That was where the cameras were, but if he killed her, then these people would get to the footage first.

She'd be vulnerable in her home. He could leap through the window, do the job and be out again, without anyone seeing or knowing, thanks to that heavy silencer. Then he had his escape route mapped out. Over the fence to the back of the house, along the path behind the house, across the road, across a park, and he'd be able to get a different bus back home. He'd have the gun with him in a backpack, under a rolled-up sweater but he didn't think anyone would suspect it while he was on a bus.

It was just now – his thoughts were in a maelstrom. His hands were sodden with sweat as were his armpits.

From inside his pocket, he heard his phone buzz and felt a flare of terror. They were checking up on him! Not Luke – please, they must not harm his kid brother.

He grabbed the phone and saw the message.

"Daniel. Is it done?"

"She's just gotten home," he replied. *"10 minutes."*

Hopefully, she'd come into the kitchen at that time, maybe to fix herself a drink?

Swallowing down another wave of nausea, feeling the implications of this act like a massive cloud of darkness that eclipsed his future, he waited. The ski mask felt tight and suffocating on his head.

And then, the front door, which he could just see the edge of, swung open and he took a sharp breath. This was it; this was the time he was going to act. He'd change his life forever; become a person he had never wanted to be…

But don't think about that, he chastised himself. Think about what you're here to do and do it. Don't think beyond that. Just think of it. It's all you need to do.

As the living room light went on, Daniel tried his best to summon up a wave of hatred for this woman. Hatred would help him. He could ride the emotion, let it fill him, remind himself that she was a bad actor, an enemy of the people who were paying him and that she sounded like an evil woman who deserved what she got. Most likely, she was as bad as his dad. Or that teacher in the fourth grade who'd ignored the bullying when he complained about it and then given him a failing mark in English. She was one of those, a bad person.

She was like the worst of the opponents in the game, the ones they'd all learned to hate. It would be just like the game; it wouldn't feel any different. He would leap through the window and do it and then it would be done.

He would pretend he was in the game, he'd shot enough people there, and as the levels progressed, it had become more and more realistic. He could do it there, he could do it here. He'd been paid and he was under orders – just like in Carl Commando.

His gloved hand closed tightly around the gun's grip.

But then, when the person walked into the living room, Daniel bit his lip so hard he tasted blood.

This was not the woman he'd expected to see.

It was a young boy, a couple of years younger than Luke. He had deep red hair and a little smile on his face as if he'd had a happy day. He glanced incuriously through the window, looking at the gap in the curtains that Daniel had carefully made to be able to see inside. He couldn't see Daniel and had no idea he was there.

He knelt and reached for a plug point beside the couch and produced a phone charger.

"Got it, Mom!" he called, looking pleased at his accomplishment.

Then, he headed back to the passage, veering right through an archway that Daniel remembered from last time led into the kitchen, with a small dining room beyond.

A moment later, Daniel heard the slamming of the refrigerator. The little boy and his mom were getting something – juice, milk, maybe food, fixing dinner.

He was utterly paralyzed now.

Her boy, at home with her? He should have realized this from the photo he'd stolen. He should have been prepared for it, but somehow, his mind hadn't put two and two together. He was going to have to go in and shoot this woman with her boy in the house.

A boy like his little brother Luke. A boy who would be without a parent.

Never had Daniel thought that he would suddenly come up against a concrete limit in his own mind, an impenetrable barrier that told him he could not pass.

That was what he was experiencing now. This was something he could not do. No matter the consequences, he was utterly unable to shove the window open and scramble inside, run down the corridor, veer left into the dining room, and put those two bullets into the woman's head.

Not with the boy there.

Maybe he'd never been able to do it at all.

The painful tension in his muscles began to ease. He couldn't think about the future or what this would mean, he was all done with thinking. There was no more room for thought. Only a decision and the decision was no.

He lowered the gun. He bowed his head. Time to walk away. That was as far as he could think – time to walk away.

As he turned, he sensed a commotion coming from behind him and his head jerked up. Then, Daniel stared in consternation at the figure rushing toward him from the darkness of the backyard.

It was a man – dressed identically to him in a close-fitting jacket, a ski mask, and gloves. He looked fit and strong and in his hand, he held an identical-looking gun.

"Hey!" Daniel had barely gotten out that one, cracked word before the man reached him. A fist punched into his shoulder, sending him sprawling back so that his head crashed against the wall and his legs slithered out from under him.

"Fight back!" his brain pleaded. "Fight back!"

He had a grasp of strategy from the game and after one confused instant, realized exactly what was going on. This person who'd been messaging him had doubted his ability, perhaps because he'd said no earlier on. And he'd assigned somebody else as backup, somebody who would now finish the job.

With a lance of horror, Daniel knew that the job now included him, too.

If he was killed now, who'd look after Luke?

With everything to fight for, he raised his arm defensively, knocking the man's gun hand aside, then lashed out with his leg, aiming at his attacker's torso. It felt confusing and strange to be doing this in real life. It was nothing like the paintball or the couple of karate classes he'd done. This was lethal and shockingly violent, and the intent in every fiber of his attacker was clear.

One powerful swipe of his arm, and he blasted Daniel's defense aside. His hand shot out, a closed fist striking him in the solar plexus so that the breath burst from his mouth, and he gasped painfully for air.

Flinging up his left hand to protect himself, Daniel clutched at the gun with his right, because this man wanted it, he was going to try to take it. As best he could, he lashed out with his foot, and this time, he got in a good kick, hard and forceful, landing on the other man's knee. He heard him grunt and felt a surge of triumph. He was going to beat this gunman.

But then the counterpunch landed, so fast he didn't even see it coming, a left hook from the darkness smashed into his jaw. His head snapped back and hit the wall again and this time, pain exploded in his skull.

A halo of light flickered in front of his eyes and his arms no longer obeyed his command to get up and fight.

The world was going gray, it was blurring out. He'd lost this fight.

His last memory was of a strong hand, tugging the gun from his grasp.

43
Fractured Sanctuary

Icy disbelief filled Hunter as Brixton spoke the words.

Amy? His ex-wife's address. How could she be linked to this site?

This must be a terrible mistake, it couldn't be correct, Amy would never have been caught up in this. Frantically, his brain tried to persuade him that the information was wrong, and that this nightmare could surely not include his ex-wife and his son.

But the disbelief was followed by realization, cold and implacable.

Amy's distracted behavior recently, her caginess about what she'd been involved in, all the additional demands on her time with those after-hours calls and meetings – and it aligned with her beliefs about violence. She'd disapproved of the dangers in Hunter's job for a long while now. It was one of the major factors that had driven a wedge in their relationship.

This was what she'd done to fight the problem. Being Amy, she'd decided to address and expose some of the contributing factors toward violence that she'd identified in society.

His ex-wife. His son.

It might already be too late. He'd seen the swiftness with which the other victims had been targeted. But if it was humanly possible, then he was going to try to stop it.

Time felt as if it was moving in slow motion.

He saw Cody's face, filled with shock, turning to him. Gibson, behind him, looking concerned by this bombshell.

"I'm going to get there," he said. "As fast as I can. And you go to Harrison."

He paused. If the worst had happened, then Amy and Matthew should not have lost their lives in vain. The timing was now all important.

"Wait outside until I call you," he said, his shocked brain realizing how this needed to play out. "If I can get evidence – if the killer is still there with a phone – then it's what we need."

Too late. The words stormed Hunter's mind as he sprinted down to his car. His mind recoiled from the fact that his ex-wife and his little boy would have had to pay the ultimate price in this brutal war. Behind him, he heard the pounding footsteps of Cody and Gibson as they raced to their car, each of them now in a different battle against time.

His mind was filled with the frantic thoughts of a father whose world was about to be shattered. Hunter's hands were shaking as he climbed into the car, knowing that he might be heading out to face an unspeakable scene.

Then, in the back of his mind, a verse began repeating itself, the rhythm familiar, the words that depicted the ultimate chaos were allowing his mind to focus. It was the same poem he used to read before exams, before important challenges. The words of William Blake took his mind to a faraway plain that somehow, in the bleak, worst-case scenario depicted, brought him a sense of calmness.

"Turning and turning in the widening gyre,
The falcon cannot hear the falconer.
Things fall apart; the center cannot hold.
Mere anarchy is loosed upon the world,
The blood-dimmed tide is loosed, and everywhere.
The ceremony of innocence is drowned;"

He was surprised by how cool and deliberate his actions were as he activated lights and the siren, and burned rubber accelerating out of the parking lot.

With the rhythm of the words keeping him centered, he headed in the direction of his former home. The poem played itself in the back of his mind, damping down his frantic worry, allowing his mind to take every gap through the evening traffic he could find, cool logic overriding the parent's terror. There was a space to gain ground. He swerved through it, mashing his foot down but keeping the judgment he needed to do it without taking any dangerous risks.

As he drove, he tried to call Amy, tried to warn her, desperately hoping that the call would get to her in time. Her phone rang but she wasn't picking up.

He tried once more, but when the phone went through to voicemail again he left it and focused on getting there fast.

On to the main road, following the route he knew so well even though this felt unlike any time before. Not allowing himself to think about what lay ahead. Not allowing the panic or despair to take hold. Clinging to the words that guided him along the route, as they had guided and calmed him at other crisis points in his life.

"The darkness drops again, but now I know.
That twenty centuries of stony sleep
Were vexed to nightmare by a rocking cradle."

He was on his road now, speeding along to the house near the junction at the end, a house that had been a family home and surely now, surely could not be a bloody crime scene?

"And what rough beast, its hour come round at last,
Slouches towards Bethlehem to be born?"

As the conclusion of the poem played itself in his mind, he was there. The next few seconds found him stamping on the brakes, flinging himself out of the car and racing up the path to the front door.

He didn't have his key with him, a deliberate decision taken after the divorce that he should not walk into this home at will anymore but should rather ring the doorbell or knock like a guest would do. It had been done for reasons of respect and boundaries. Reasons that he was regretting now because they would mean a delay.

But not a long delay. Approaching the door, Hunter didn't slow his speed at all. In fact, he ran faster. He sprinted up to the door, legs pounding, impetus building.

Reaching it, he launched himself off the ground, lashing his booted foot out, trusting that his coordination at this moment would be adequate for the job, thanks to the mental calmness that the mantra of words had provided as he drove.

His sole crashed against the door at the point of the latch, with an impact that shook through him.

And the door burst open, the wood wrenching off the lock.

He stumbled down, recovering fast after the airborne kick but still staggering forward as he crossed the hallway. His momentum allowed him to catch his balance again. Now, he couldn't restrain the stress that thrummed inside him. Was he too late?

A crash and a high, desperate scream from the dining room to his left alerted him where to go. He veered that way, the rug slipping under his feet as he raced there.

He got to the doorway and rushed through.

There was Amy on her feet, a chair knocked over, her arms extended in front of her, hands gripping the arms of a tall, rangy man in a ski mask and a black jacket who had his back to Hunter. He had a silenced pistol in each of his gloved hands. Amy was struggling with all her might, muscles quivering as she held him at bay.

But his strength was winning the day. As Hunter watched, the pistol in his right hand began turning on an inexorable path to her head.

44
Echoes of Dark Victory

"No!" Amy's scream resonated in Hunter's ears.
"No!" Hunter yelled.

He launched himself at the attacker, who twisted around as he approached, letting go of one of Amy's wrists as he fumbled with his gun, now aiming it at Hunter.

He reached the man and grabbed his wrist with only one thought in his mind. Up. He needed to get that hand up because the bullet was going to fire.

It couldn't fire in a downward direction. Hunter could not allow that because as he had flung himself across the room, he'd seen a small form, crouched under the table. His son. Matthew was there in the room with the killer, hiding away from harm – but not for long.

A hard wrench of his own hand against his opponent's steely wrist, and the bang of the silenced weapon resounded in the dining room.

Glass shattered from the light fitting and rained down onto the table.

Now, Hunter grabbed the man's other arm, twisting the wrist viciously, so that one of the weapons clattered down onto the floor.

"Out!" he yelled to Amy. "Take Matt and go! Upstairs. Bathroom."

That was the room in the house with the sturdiest lock on the door. He needed them safe. This was not over yet. This ski-masked man was fighting hard. He wrenched his hand out of Hunter's grasp and made a grab for the gun. Hunter yanked him away, knocking over another chair, which crashed to the ground. It got in the way of his legs as he stumbled over it, his opponent now seeing his chance and dragging him forward so that he almost fell.

But Amy was acting fast. Diving under the table, she grabbed Matthew and ducked away, hugging the wall, a protective hand over her son's head, getting him out to safety.

That intensified the fight in the dining room. Now, the man pushed him back so that he crashed against the table. It rocked and then fell onto its side, the smashed glass from the light fitting scattering across the floor.

"Back off! You're not getting her! You're not getting my boy!" The words were his, gasped out as he struggled, wrenching himself to the side to avoid a flying kick, then stumbling over another chair and this time losing his footing.

Hunter crashed onto one knee, glass slicing into his palm as he tried to break his fall, a red-hot moment of agony. Then there was no time to think about the pain because the shooter was swinging that barrel around toward him again.

Plunging forward, Hunter went on the attack, moving into his assailant, crashing his head into his solar plexus, hoping that this fast, desperate move might unbalance him and deflect his aim. With a hoarse gasp – the first sound he'd uttered – the other man reeled away. Using his impetus, Hunter lunged to his feet, grabbing his leg, and hurling him backward. Now it was his turn to trip over a fallen chair. Legs flailing, the tall attacker went down.

Hunter did not hesitate. He dove over the chair, knowing he had to finish this quick, that he might only get one chance.

One knee on the gunman's wrist. The weapon went skittering away across the floor. In the struggle, his ski mask had slipped halfway off his face, showing his mouth, drawn back in a snarl of rage, his dark eyes fixed on Hunter's. Blank intent, without any mercy, was visible in his stare. His leg chopped out, his knee getting Hunter in the chest and smashing all the breath out of him as he wrenched himself free from Hunter's grasp in a final, desperate move.

The black-clad man scrambled to his feet again. He was going for his gun and Hunter had only one chance left to stop this, one moment to act. And one action that might work.

His hand lashed out as the man moved, grabbing his ankle as he prepared to surge across the floor to his weapon.

Hunter's bleeding hand closed around it. Pain lanced through him as he tugged hard and pulled with all his might.

The man lost his balance, his weight crashing down, his head hitting the floor with an audible thud.

He lay still.

Jumping up, Hunter grabbed the cuffs off his belt, working with feverish haste. He clamped one cuff around his wrist. A moment later and his hands were cuffed behind him. Blood was welling from the cut on his palm and spattering down onto his opponent's face and onto the floor where it made a vivid, scarlet stain. He was gasping for breath. The other man's eyelids were flickering, and Hunter guessed he'd be out for a few more minutes. It gave him time to act.

He had got his adversary subdued but it wasn't over yet. The most critical part was still to come.

Hunter needed his phone.

"Amy!" he shouted, as he tugged the man onto his side, searching for it. "Amy, I'm okay. For now. Stay there. Stay where you are."

"Okay." The voice came back, faint but resolute, from behind the locked door.

He needed to find the attacker's phone.

It was in his inner jacket pocket. He felt it there, rummaged inside and pulled it out.

And stared in dismay. In the melee, the screen had broken; it was smashed to smithereens. The phone was unusable.

Now, the trap they had hoped to set for Harrison could not be sprung. They had needed to catch him in the act. Against someone this wily and this powerful, it was the only way.

Hunter closed his eyes, breathing hard. He'd saved his family, he'd defeated one of Harrison's assassins – but without the immediate proof they needed, it might all be for nothing.

And then, in the darkness and silence that followed his battle, he heard something outside.

From around the back of the house. Faint, but audible.

A muffled groan.

In a moment, the tumblers clicked into place in Hunter's mind, unlocking what had happened. There had been two of these soldiers here; perhaps one was sent as backup? The other was outside.

He rushed out of the dining room, through the front door, and rushed around the side of the house.

There, in the flower bed below the kitchen window, lay another man, huddled on the ground. Also, in black, also wearing a ski mask. He groaned again as Hunter reached him. And as Hunter got there, he heard the buzzing of the phone in the man's jeans pocket.

A message was coming through – and he knew who it was from.

Hunter dug into the man's back pocket and tugged out the phone. He opened it, hands frantic with haste but found he could not us it. It was asking for a fingerprint. Well, that was possible.

Hunter grasped the young man's hand, tugged off his glove, and pressed his finger to the screen. He was not awake enough to protest or struggle, his movements groggy and uncoordinated.

The screen opened, and there was the conversation, stretching back, in little green and white balloons of text. Stark, clear, and incriminating.

The most recent text – one awaiting a reply.

"Have you done it, Daniel? Time's up. Tell me – if you want to see your brother alive again."

Quickly, Hunter got out his own phone and sent a message to the two men he hoped were waiting outside Harrison's house. Hoping this would work, hoping that the jaws of the trap would close.

"I got a phone. Replying now."

Then, using the phone of this young man, Daniel, who would almost – but not quite – become one of the killers, he texted back, feeling a surge of nausea as he keyed in the words that might so easily have been true.

"It's done. I shot her. Now what?"

Gripping the phone hard, standing above the groaning man in the dark, cool night, Hunter waited.

45
Fallen Puppeteer

He was the puppet master, pulling strings in the darkness, pushing forward an agenda that only he understood. Day Zero was close – so close. But these obstacles had been more difficult to overcome than Charles Harrison had expected.

This was an important one – the eradication of the woman running the No To Violence website. Sitting in the upstairs bedroom of his LA property, he monitored his remote soldiers carefully.

He hadn't trusted the one he'd chosen, so he'd sent another in as backup, to do the job if the first one's nerve broke. A wise soldier always had a backup plan and Harrison knew that he was wise, strategic, and thought further than anyone else he knew.

Alone in the well-equipped study, with an oaken desk, a leather director's chair, two armchairs, a red desk lamp and a brandy decanter, he keyed in the messages, checking up on his soldiers. This phone would need to be disposed of straight after this. He had a few more ready. This one would join the others – its Sim removed, its innards destroyed, and then its remains tipped into a conveniently dug hole on this very property.

He'd plant something over it, like he had with the others. Nobody would ever know a burner was buried here.

Of course, Harrison had thought at length about what he'd do if he was discovered now. He knew that unless he was caught in the act, he'd be able to get out of it. Nobody could connect him to the phones. He had his GPS disabled and he didn't use the phones for long enough for law enforcement to be able to set up a tracker on them. He knew which the slowest service provider was, the one that police found most difficult to work with, and that was the one he used.

Number after number, burner after burner, and it wouldn't be long to go until Day Zero launched. With floods of people joining the Army, the propaganda he'd planned would roll out. He would keep a careful track of his naysayers, using either his soldiers or his hackers to eradicate their influence.

People were like sheep that he knew. They found it easier to follow the herd than to stand up for themselves. They wouldn't believe they were being manipulated until it was too late.

And his plans, when he was president – oh, the scope of his ambitions! The little people would never believe what he had in mind. The acquisitions that he and his army would make, the territories they would gain. It would ensure a new world order – yes, there would be war, but he had no doubt that his side would win.

It was all for the good of the country and the world, of course. He envisioned a powerful master state controlled by him that would gradually consume and control more and more land, and more and more power until it became the ultimate force in the world. And he would be the world leader.

His followers – Rogan for instance – knew some of his plans, but not all. They were exactly the type of narrow-minded muscle he needed to achieve his aims. And the remote soldiers and hackers were well manipulated. What an extraordinary success the game had been in that regard. Carl Commando had been the deciding factor in the battle for power.

Smiling to himself in the quiet of the night – the only sound was a car engine in the distance and the clang of something near the road – he took a sip of his cognac, feeling invulnerable and in control.

Next, he planned to murder Olivia Montgomery and put Sam Reynolds in control of Dreamland Creations. By then, things would be shifting and there would already be massive structural changes in society. He didn't think it would create much of a stir, considering Day Zero would already have taken place.

Glancing down at his phone, he frowned. This took a long time. What was the delay?

He sent a message, asking if the job had been done. Now, his mind focused on the immediate present, instead of his future plans, he watched the screen carefully.

A message blinked through Daniel's phone. So the coward had come through for him after all – and now he would be his, forever.

"It's done. I shot her. Now what?"

He began to type a reply.

"Congratulations, soldier. Now you are part of the elite force that will..."

But then, he hesitated. Was that a noise outside?

The next moment, he jumped violently as a crash from the first floor resounded through the house, sending his heart rate into overdrive. That was the front door, dear God, they'd broken in the front door, they were going to catch him in the act. Already he could hear footsteps in the corridor.

Sick horror filled him for a moment before he remembered that he had planned for exactly this possibility. Get the phone out, throw it from the study window. It would land in a deep, watery drain that he'd prepared and left open for exactly that reason, and that would buy him enough time to save his skin.

He moved to the window and wrenched it open.

And a bright flashlight blinded him, shining up into his eyes, and causing him to flinch.

A cheerful voice called up.

"Evening, Harrison! Officer Cody Lamarr here. You been having drainage issues down here? Seems a bit wet! Better not accidentally drop that phone – but if you do, don't worry. I'll catch it!"

Harrison stared down, aghast, phone in hand, trapped in the beam of the flashlight. He realized to his horror that Lamarr, straddling the drainage ditch, had his own phone in his other hand and was filming him – he was on camera in real-time – and this was something he'd never envisioned.

His plans were collapsing around him. What had seemed like a kingdom cast in stone, had proved to be nothing more than a flimsy house of cards.

He twisted away from the window just as the study door burst open and there was Officer Gibson, gun in hand, moving toward him.

"Hands in the air, Harrison." His voice cut the silence as the incriminating phone dropped from Harrison's numb fingers to clatter down on the desk. "You're under arrest!"

Epilogue
Healing Paws

The thunder of tiny paws raced around the living room as Hunter and Matthew sat on the couch, drinks in hand.

A beer for Hunter, a juice for Matthew, and dinner tonight consisted of a big plate of fries on the table in front of them, drizzled with ketchup and truffle mayonnaise.

"You see, Dad," Matthew said, as the new ginger kitten, named Arthur, chased the gray one across the carpet, up the cat tree, and then, in a death-defying duo of leaps, onto the curtains where both kittens hung, attaching themselves like little mobile decorations, swaying gently with claws firmly stuck in. "Two cats are better than one."

"I see that." Putting his beer down, Hunter walked over to the curtain, gently lifting first one, and then the other, of the furry fireballs away from their fabric-shredding foothold and placing them back on the floor. Immediately, the game started up again. This time, Merlin was chasing Arthur.

Watching Matthew chortle in rapture at the kitten games, Hunter basked in the warmth of relief.

After the devastating close call of the break-in two weeks ago, both Amy and Matthew were seeing a psychologist for trauma counseling. Hunter didn't want that terrible incident to cause any deeper scars than necessary. The sessions seemed to have been going well. Matthew was a resilient kid and tough as nails – but Hunter personally thought that the companionship and fun of these two little felines had been a major factor in helping him heal.

In fact, Amy had told him that it had been his phone call that had saved her. Her phone had been charging on the sideboard. She'd gotten up to answer the second call, thinking it must be urgent – and had been near the door when the gunman had burst in, instead of a literal sitting target at the table.

She'd grabbed his arms in terror, Matthew had dived under the table – and just a few moments later, Hunter had arrived.

He knew that an incident like this might make Amy reconsider a lot of things and that was a worry that he couldn't stop, but also couldn't answer now. After this, she'd be justified in wanting to make a change and move away. It might happen and if it did, how could he argue against it?

But for now, she was sitting tight and recovering well.

Hunter was busy with the massive case against Harrison, which involved tracking down and debriefing close to fifty of the young men he'd programmed as hackers and remote soldiers. One by one they were being identified, receiving counseling, and Hunter hoped that most of them would be rehabilitated into society over time. The one who'd attempted to murder Amy, who'd now confessed to three previous shootings, would be facing life in prison.

Daniel had been offered immunity from all charges for turning state witness – the same immunity that Sam

Reynolds, now fired from Dreamland Creations, was getting. Evidence against Charles Harrison, as well as lesser charges against Bryan Rogan, was solid as a result.

Harrison would be going down for this, for life. He was already in a maximum-security cell, bail denied.

Hunter had spent some time with Daniel and had been impressed by him. He might have been led along the wrong path, but he was a tough guy. And when the chips were down, he'd made an incredibly tough choice and defied his programming, a decision that had saved two lives.

"Eek! Do you think they'll reach the top this time?" Matthew stuffed a ketchup-loaded fry into his mouth as Merlin and Arthur both clambered up the curtains again. Hunter got up and once again, removed them, placing them on the cat tree. It struck him as somewhat ironic that they seemed to prefer the curtains, which their little claws were already turning into lace, over the expensive custom-built cat tree.

But shredded curtains were a small price to pay for a healing son. And when the cats were bigger, he could buy new curtains. The ones he had were old, anyway.

"Dad?" Matthew asked.

"Yeah?" Hunter took a fry and dunked it in the mayonnaise.

"My friend said that Carl Commando is being taken off the market. Is that right? It's not a cool toy anymore."

"That is right," Hunter said. "The company's been downscaled and sold to a competitor, and they're rethinking their entire offering, I believe. But yes, Carl Commando's history and a lot of people have been trashing those toys."

Visibly, on social media, throwing them into the trash as the story hit the news and Dreamland Creations' share price plummeted, along with the number of Army sign-ups, an unexpected backlash. Nobody wanted to be part of this debacle now, and whoever the new Secretary of Defense was, he'd have an even tougher recruitment job and be more closely scrutinized.

"So, aren't you glad you didn't get one of those toys?"

Matthew thought about that for a moment. "Yes. I am glad. It seems like all the cool kids are throwing theirs away."

He reached for another fry, snorting as the kittens latched onto the curtains yet again.

Hunter felt a wave of contentment.

Things weren't perfect – he knew that. Amy's future plans might be in doubt, and although his job was secure once again, the issue of corruption in the LAPD was still unresolved. But a dangerous psychopath was behind bars, Day Zero had been averted, and his son was happy.

Just for now, just for today, Hunter decided, life could not be better.

About the Author

Steve Mark Kahan has a remarkable track record of propelling seven startup companies from their early stages to achieving the pinnacle of success – either going public or being acquired, collectively generating a staggering $5 billion in shareholder value. This seasoned entrepreneur is not only a seasoned business leader but also a dynamic communicator, having graced the TEDx stage twice.

As a Wall Street Journal bestselling author, Steven has penned influential works such as *High Velocity Digital Marketing* and *Be a Startup Superstar.* Residing in picturesque Sugar Land, Texas, Steve finds joy in the simple pleasures of life, surrounded by the love of his wife, children, and grandchildren.

Printed in the USA
CPSIA information can be obtained
at www.ICGtesting.com
LVHW030144120524
779803LV00009B/958